I0584159

SURVIVORS

Survivors, Book One

Amy Marsden

A NineStar Press Publication

www.ninestarpress.com

Survivors

© 2021 Amy Marsden
Cover Art © 2021 Natasha Snow

Printed in the USA

ISBN: 978-1-64890-350-2

First Edition, August, 2021

Also available in eBook, ISBN: 978-1-64890-349-6

CONTENT WARNING:
This book contains depictions of death, gore, war, trauma, pandemic, violence, and murder.

It's Jennifer's 24ᵗʰ birthday and she planned to spend it having fun with her friends. Instead, she ends up running for her life through the dark streets of London.

Her world is torn apart by a new disease, the likes of which have never been seen before. The government's decision to conceal its deadly nature exacerbates the panic, and in all the confusion Jennifer is bitten by an infected person.

That's it, right? Her life over.

Wrong.

Immune to the virus's ravaging effects, Jennifer finds herself with a small group of survivors. Together they must fight to stay alive long enough for a cure to be found. Humanity won't be beaten so easily.

But madness looms large, and safety seems forever out of reach.

To Fay, my muse, my firecracker, my wife.

Author's Note

When I started writing this story way back in 2012, I had no idea how relevant some of the contents would be today. 2020 and 2021 have been years of global fear, tragedy, and loss as people struggle for their health and livelihoods, and I hope when this book is released we are past the bleakest days. I hope the world is healing.

I want to acknowledge the bravery and sacrifice of essential workers around the world, from health workers to shop assistants to factory workers and more. You've all done and continue to do such an incredible job.

Stories are powerful. People have been enjoying them since the dawn of language. I hope that even though this story is about a devastating virus, you can also see the humanity shining through. Don't let this pandemic beat you.

Chapter One

JANUARY 11TH

Going to protests had become second nature to Jen. The gatherings were numerous, loud, and full of energy, but so far none of them had achieved anything. The world remained in the dark. Uncertainty pervaded the air like it had a physical weight, heavy and viscous, and Jen had long since grown used to it. She would be more uncomfortable if things were normal.

Fire threw orange light across the street, the shifting shadows dancing over riot gear as the crowd surged forward. Shouts and screams merged into a meaningless cacophony. Smoke hung over everything, obscuring people on the ground nursing broken noses, broken arms, broken legs. The camera spun in a disorientating way. Had the police attacked the news crew? Nothing would surprise her anymore. The roar reached a crescendo—

Jen switched the television off. Insecurity seemed constant, but she wasn't going to let it ruin her twenty-fourth birthday. She'd seen it all before, anyway. The riots were becoming more and more frequent. She turned her attention back to the object in her hands and put all the confusion and dismay out of her mind.

The camera wasn't the best on the market, but Jen loved it regardless, and she hadn't been able to stop thanking her parents after they dropped it off yesterday. Jen liked the weight of it in her hands, ready to freeze everything away from the ravages of time. Her old camera had been damaged from years of use and abuse, and she vowed to take much better care of this one.

A sharp bang broke her concentration, and she jumped up as the door to the apartment burst open. *What the—*

"Jen? Damien?" Rhys's strained voice sounded from the kitchen. *What's going on?* He'd said he couldn't make it tonight.

She entered the kitchen on light feet. If this was a prank for her birthday, she wasn't going to be happy. She hated surprises.

"There you are," Evelyn said. "C'mon, we have to go." They were all there—Rhys, Evelyn, Amanda, and Rachel. Her friends. Instead of greeting her with smiles, hugs, and excitement, they looked scared, their bodies rigid as they stood in the kitchen. Rhys looked winded as he leaned on the kitchen counter, sweat running from his shaved head to his square jaw.

"What are you talking about?" Jen cut her laugh short as Evelyn threw a pleading look her way. This didn't seem like a prank.

"Hey, guys," Damien said as he entered the room, not a hair out of place. Jen had been ready for a good half an hour, but Damien had procrastinated and rushed to get dressed.

"Listen, we don't have much time." Rhys struggled to slow his breathing. Worry trickled down Jen's back. This wasn't like him at all. "I'm not even supposed to be here." He still wore his army uniform. *What are those stains?*

"What's wrong?" Damien asked slowly. Rhys wasn't the type of person to play jokes on people.

Amanda shrugged. "I have no idea either. These two—" she gestured at Rhys and Evelyn as she shrugged out of her jacket and put her phone and purse on the counter "—found us walking up the stairs. Running like the devil was chasing them."

"You all know about the new virus, right?" Rhys looked at them for confirmation, his dark eyes intense.

"Yeah, of course we do," Jen said. People talked of little else. That and the less exciting news about a food recall and less on the shelves. "It'll be okay. They'll find a cure soon." Conspiracies had sprouted up saying everyone who got the disease died, or the government had created it to stop overpopulation or some such nonsense. Fearmongering.

What worried Jen was how long they were taking to find a cure. With millions of people infected society had ground to a halt. Jen's university had closed its doors last November, and she didn't know when it would reopen. Restaurants and cafés had followed suit. It was a nightmare. Criminals became bolder too, with crime on the rise.

Quite a lot of the protests were about demanding to know what was going on. The majority of them devolved into riots these days, but the government kept assuring everyone they were doing all they could. Some people didn't even believe the virus was dangerous.

"It's much worse than the media is portraying—"

Rachel cut him off. "What do you mean '*worse?*'"

"The world's governments have been censoring the media. They've covered up the extent of the damage because they didn't want to frighten everyone. I wouldn't be surprised to find they've been silencing whistle-blowers and destroying evidence. It's spread all over the world—they couldn't keep that quiet—but they have lied about how dangerous and out of control it is."

He looked at them with wide eyes. "You get the disease through bodily fluids like blood or saliva getting into your system, like if someone with the virus bites you. It's yet another thing the media didn't mention. The urge to bite drives those who have been infected. It's *always* fatal. Once you get it, that's it.

"Our government has tried to manage it, but it's not working. I know because the government brought the army in to try to keep it contained. We've failed." He took a deep breath. "Little over an hour ago, two of the quarantine zones close to London were breached. It was chaos. Infected people have escaped."

"But it will be okay, right?" Damien asked, his brow furrowed. "It can't be that bad. You'll round them back up, and everything will be all right." He didn't sound convinced by his own words.

"That was the plan, but—I don't think you understand the severity of this," Rhys said. "You're my friends. You're the only family I've got. I left my post to warn you, it's *that* serious. You need to pack some things and get to the barracks as soon as possible. Knightsbridge is our best bet. The streets were fine coming here, but they won't be for much longer. We need to leave before it gets out of control and people start panicking. This virus isn't like anything we've seen before." Horror haunted his eyes. The trickle of worry down Jen's back threatened to become a flood.

Rachel let out a high-pitched laugh. "This isn't funny, Rhys."

"This isn't a joke." He stared at them all. "*Please.* Pack some things and come with me to Knightsbridge."

The words were barely out of his mouth when a loud explosion shook the building. Jen grabbed her camera to keep it from falling off the table. She slung the strap over her head, adjusting the camera to hang at her side.

Amanda cursed. "What was that?"

Rhys ran to the cracked window, the night outside appearing fractured. Jen heard screaming as she followed him. A car had exploded down on the street and—*oh God, is that someone on fire*? Jen tasted bile in her throat. People ran through the street, shouting, panicking. A woman dived on somebody. *Are they biting them*? Jen leaned closer to the glass, trying to get a glimpse of the mayhem outside. The woman pinned someone down, her teeth deep in their arm. The poor person screamed in pain. Jen took several deep breaths and swallowed nausea down.

"No, no, no," Rhys muttered to himself. He turned away from the window, hunched like an agitated animal. "Okay, listen. This is moving much faster than I anticipated. There's no time to pack anything. We have to go. *Now.*" He ran back to the front door, easing it open and peering out. Everyone stood still as statues. This couldn't be happening. Everything was fine a minute ago. What was going on?

"Okay, c'mon. There's no one around." Rhys waved everyone forward.

Jen grabbed some shoes—she didn't want to go out into the cold January night without anything on her feet. Rhys edged out into the corridor, and everyone crowded after him. Damien closed the door and locked it as he pulled his trainers on.

They travelled from the second floor to the ground floor without seeing anyone else. The screams were louder here, the smell of burning stronger.

Rhys motioned for everyone to crouch down before they reached the main entrance. "My car is across the street. On my mark, we all run to it. No hesitating, okay? Jump in and we'll be at Knightsbridge in no time."

Jen turned her camera on and took a photograph of everyone's silhouettes against the flames. Black against orange, shadows against light. She made a quick decision to document everything. People deserved to know the truth of things. She switched the camera off to save the battery.

"Rhys, there are dead bodies out there," Rachel said in a small voice, her arms wrapped around herself as the fire flickered over her ashen face.

Jen risked a glance around Rachel. She'd never seen a dead body before, and a morbid fascination took hold of her. One lay face down in the middle of the road, and the other was the burned body of the person she'd seen earlier. She saw no sign of the person who had been bitten, nor of their attacker. Jen forced herself to take a big, calming breath.

Rhys turned and looked at each of them. He tried to put on a brave face, but Jen saw the fear break through the cracks in his mask. "Yes, people are dead. Yes, more people will die. But I promise you, I will get you all to the barracks. You'll be safe there."

Jen glanced at her friends. They were all frightened, but they seemed to believe him. Damien nodded as he listened. *I hope you can keep that promise, Rhys,* she thought. *I really, really do.* She couldn't see much from their vantage point, but what she had seen so far had been awful. Had she seen a person *on fire*? The car still burned, throwing shadows in every direction. Could she feel the heat, or was it her imagination?

"Okay, *move.*" Rhys turned and bolted for the door, leaving everyone scrambling in his wake.

Jen burst out onto the street, the heat of the fire hitting her like a slap to the face. She narrowed her eyes against it and kept running, glad she'd picked up her flat ankle boots. Sudden panic squeezed her lungs. What if she tripped and fell? What if the crazy woman lurked somewhere in the darkness and grabbed her?

A scream broke through the air. Jen twisted around, searching for the source of the violent sound. The crazy woman *was* there, a little way up the street. She lurched to her feet—she'd been kneeling over someone—and started sprinting toward them. Terror chased adrenaline into Jen, spurring her faster. She would make it, she would make it, she—

Slipped. One minute she ran straight for the car, the next she lost her footing as if in slow motion. Her left arm took the brunt of the impact, scraping against the concrete. *Should have been looking where you were going!* Groaning, she pushed herself up. She'd landed in thick, warm liquid. *Oh no, oh God.* Her whole left leg and most of her back were covered in blood. She could smell it. The burning car had masked the vile metallic odour, but it clung to her like a second skin. The stench wound down her throat and stabbed its way into her lungs. She couldn't shove the nausea away this time. Jen retched as Evelyn and Damien appeared at her side, hauling her up and pulling her along between them.

She fell into the car. Rachel dragged her further in as Evelyn followed, Damien squeezing after her and slamming the door shut. The crazy woman smashed into the side of the car, splintering the glass. Someone screamed. Rhys pressed the accelerator to the floor and the tyres screeched as they drove away. The woman tumbled to the ground behind them, fading from sight as the night swallowed her.

Jen couldn't stop shaking. Her heart pounded against her chest as the blood cooled against her skin and soaked through her clothing. Her night had turned into an horrendous nightmare she couldn't wake up from.

"Shit, Jen, I nearly had a heart attack when I saw you fall," Evelyn breathed heavily, her long dark hair sticking to her neck as her skin took on a waxy pallor.

"Yeah, me too," Jen responded. Was that her voice? So weak? She breathed in deeply, trying to regain some semblance of equilibrium.

"Are you okay? You fell hard," Damien asked.

"Yeah. I don't feel any pain right now." Adrenaline was a wonderful thing.

"Were any of you bitten?" Rhys asked, his voice taking on a sharp edge.

"N-no," Rachel answered. Her brown eyes were open too wide, her breathing too shallow.

"No, I wasn't bitten." Evelyn sat up a little straighter.

Damien and Amanda both answered *no*.

"Jen?" Rhys looked at her in the rear-view mirror. "What about you? Did the infected woman bite you?"

Jen shook her head. "No, she was too far back. We made it to the car before she got close to any of us."

Rhys held her eyes a moment longer before nodding. "We should make it to Knightsbridge soon."

Silence fell. Jen pushed her thoughts out of her mind and focused on her breathing. *In and out*. Rhys turned off Monmouth Street. *In and out*. They picked up speed. *In and out*. Were her parents okay? Her breath hitched. No. She would remain calm. *In and out*. She would find out soon. *In and out*. She should have grabbed her phone when they left. *Idiot*. The coppery stench of blood filled the car. She clenched her fists. She would not give in to panic. She would *not*.

Rhys cursed, bringing the car to a halt. A van had overturned in the middle of the road with no way past. People milled about, confused and scared. Jen's heart jumped into her throat as a group broke away from the crowd and started running toward them. Rhys cursed again and reversed a little way up the road before he turned down another one. Their pursuers grew small in the rear-view window. What had they been hoping to achieve?

People were desperate, and anxiety did *not* mix well with fear.

Chapter Two

The night sky glowed a deep orange to the south, like a twisted sunset as mad as the world around them. Jen shivered. She wanted to get to safety as soon as humanly possible. *Let's hope it's Knightsbridge.*

"What about our families, Rhys? My brothers? I left my phone in the kitchen," Amanda said, her voice trembling.

"Let's focus on us right now," he answered. "We can ask about everyone else when we're safe."

They made it to Charing Cross and through the Admiralty Arch without any trouble and accelerated down the Mall. The road stretched off into darkness, the only light shining from their headlights. When had the electricity shut off? The trees lining the street rose out of the blackness as if to grab them and prevent them from passing. Buckingham Palace loomed ahead, dark and silent.

They'd driven about three quarters down the Mall when something sailed out of the gloom and smashed into the front window. Rachel screamed as Rhys pulled hard on the steering wheel, sending the car into a tailspin. They came to an abrupt halt facing the way they'd come, and Jen's knuckles were white from gripping Evelyn. The acrid smell of burnt rubber made her cough, and shouting erupted from all around. A brick hit the window where Damien sat, causing the already weakened glass to shatter. Arms reached in and seized him, trying to pull him out through the window. Jen shouted, helplessness stealing under her skin. A cricket bat crashed into the driver's window, and another brick struck the back of the car. The ubiquitous attackers ripped open the car doors and reached in to pull them out.

Jen managed to kick her assailant in the face before someone hauled her out onto the hard ground. The man cursed as his lip started bleeding, but he didn't give her a second glance as he dived into the car and slammed the door.

The others weren't so fortunate. Rhys rolled on the ground, trying to pin one of the attackers down. Another one of them had Rachel by her hair and tugged her away from the car. Jen moved forward with the intention of helping her friend, but Rachel brought her leg back and kicked him between the legs. It wasn't forceful—the angle was off—but he still let go of her and fell back with a pained whine. Rachel stood over him with a shocked expression. In all the time Jen had known her, she'd never argued with anyone, never mind had a physical altercation. She couldn't imagine what Rachel was thinking. *If* she was thinking at all.

When Jen reached her and started to drag her away, the man on the ground stirred as if to rise. They didn't wait around. She and Rachel ran to the edge of the road where Evelyn tended to Damien's head.

"Are you all right?" A cut split his lip, and he had a nasty cut above his right eye, which covered half his face in blood. Jen tried to wipe some of it away, but she ended up smearing it all over and making it worse.

Amanda and Rhys stumbled over to them, the former supporting the latter. Rhys' struggled to put weight on his left foot, and blood dripped down his chin from his nose. Amanda had a cut on her left cheek. Concern sparked in Jen's chest. A squeal of tyres broke the oppressive night, and she turned to see their car disappear into the darkness. A stifling fear threatened to overwhelm her at the thought of walking through London. Looters and mobs likely roamed the streets, taking advantage of the mayhem. Their assailants had attacked a *moving vehicle.*

If this infection is as bad as Rhys says, she thought with horror, *who knows what's going to happen*? Unbidden, the image of the crazy woman rose in Jen's mind. Mobs and looters were the least of their problems if they came across infected people.

"Come on, we're gonna walk from here," Evelyn said decisively. "We are *not* going to wait around to get beat up or worse. And I'm definitely not going to get infected with that *horrible* disease. Let's go." She pulled Damien to his feet and set off down the Mall, her strides strong and forceful.

"It might be for the best, anyway," Rhys added as everyone followed Evelyn. "The car makes us a target, and a lot of the roads might be blocked." He held a knife. *Where did he get it from? Does he have blood on his hands?*

She looked around and saw the man he'd been grappling with, lying on his back in the middle of the road, not moving. Rhys had killed him. He'd killed another man. Part of her knew it was self-defence; another part had gone numb with shock. *He's in the army. He's been deployed in wars before. This won't be the first time he's killed someone.* She was naïve not to have thought about it before.

The others didn't seem to have noticed. Or, if they had, they didn't seem to care. She looked at Amanda, who *must* have seen something. She appeared to be in a state of shock, but even as Jen watched, she shook herself, took a deep breath, and walked with a firmer step. Jen decided to follow her example. There was no point dwelling on what had happened. *Self-defence,* she told herself, then deliberately stopped thinking about it.

"It's going to be chaos here, so we need to stick close together," Evelyn said as Jen tuned into the conversation.

"Yeah," Damien said. "It's a shame we couldn't get the cricket bat those bastards had." He tried to project an air of confidence, and it worked, despite his bloodied face. Or perhaps because of it. He rubbed Jen's arm. "How are you holding up?"

"Okay, I guess. As good as can be expected." She gave him a shaky smile, hoping to appear as confident as he did. His obvious concern told her it hadn't worked.

He leaned in close and whispered, "I'm terrified as well." He winked and took the lead, his head swivelling left and right as he tried to spot any danger.

Evelyn fell in beside her and gave her hand a quick squeeze. "Best birthday ever, huh?"

Jen gave a humourless laugh. "Oh, definitely. I always wanted to see the collapse of London."

They fell silent—any attempts at levity too forced. Instead, they made their way toward Buckingham Palace as quickly as they could. Tension choked the cold air like a rubber band stretched too far, moments away from snapping. The fountain and palace materialised out of the night, towering over the empty road. An eeriness clogged the air. Jen switched her camera on, lined up the shot, and took a picture.

A tortured wail sounded through the air, and as one they broke into a run. Jen worried about Rhys's injured leg, but she needn't have bothered—they didn't get far before three people burst out of the park on their right. The group stumbled to a halt. Jen saw dark stains up their arms in the dim moonlight, and a metallic smell drifted through the air like a cloud of noxious gas. But their wild eyes struck Jen the most. No sanity remained in them.

Before her instinct to run kicked in, Jen took a picture. The flash seemed to startle them for a moment, the two men taking a step back as the woman raised her arm over her eyes. For a few seconds, everyone stood still. The atmosphere was hushed, as if the world itself held its breath. One of the men shattered the silence with an animalistic howl, and all three surged forward.

Someone yelled, but Jen couldn't focus enough to figure out who. Fear rushed through her, lending her much needed strength. A glance over her shoulder showed an infected man right behind her, almost within touching distance. A jolt of terror urged her on. She knew her newfound speed wouldn't last, however. Her muscles already ached. Why didn't she run more? *Shit, shit, shit.* They were going to catch her. An image of the crazy woman attacking someone earlier flashed through her mind. Oh, God, she was going to die. *She was going to die.*

The desperate thought cut through the fog clouding her mind like a ray of burning sunlight, and she let herself slow. She couldn't outrun them, so she did the only thing she could think of that might give her a chance. Skidding to a halt, she half-turned and braced herself. *Oh God,* she thought as the man rammed into her shoulder, throwing her off-balance. She managed to remain upright, at least. The man crashed into the ground, his momentum carrying him forward a few paces. His teeth scraped her arm on his way down—the same one she had damaged when she'd slipped in blood. Pain flared, but she ignored it. She could *not* afford to get distracted.

Rhys had the same thought as her, and the man close to catching him was caught off guard. He succeeded in grabbing Rhys, however, and they tumbled to the ground in a heap of thrashing limbs and pained grunts.

Mere seconds passed. The man Jen knocked down had already stood up again. She steadied herself once more, intent on fighting for her life. She wasn't going to roll over and die. She *wasn't*. As she psyched herself up, the man lurched for Rachel instead. Jen called out a warning, fear making her voice shrill, but the man was already on her. Rachel screamed as he bit down into her neck like a rabid animal, and blood spurted. Jen froze with horror as Rachel and the man both collapsed to the ground.

Someone grabbed her and started tugging her away. She recoiled, trying to shake their grip, but it was only Damien. He shouted something, but Jen couldn't hear anything. A faint ringing resounded through her ears.

Rachel, oh God, Rachel. She had to help her. She had to do *something*. The infected man rammed her head against the ground, and her friend went limp. Jen had never seen someone die before, but she instinctively knew what she had witnessed. But Rachel couldn't be dead. No. She *couldn't*. She was going to become a vet, open her own animal shelter. She'd boasted she would end animal cruelty as they'd laughed over coffee. Rachel, who always had a kind word to say about everyone, who had taught her how to ride a horse, who had introduced her to Damien.

The man stumbled back to his feet and turned toward them.

Damien shook her and sound rushed back, crashing around her in violent waves. Shouting, growling, crying. Shock poisoned the air.

"*Go.*" Damien pushed her toward Evelyn and Amanda. "*Run.* I'll lead them away. I can sprint faster than they can." He winked at her, his blue eyes unusually bright in the dark. Then the night consumed him as he rushed back down the road, yelling at the infected to follow. The man and the woman—Jen started when she saw her; she'd forgotten there was a woman—ran after him. The other man lay face down with the knife sticking out of his throat.

An uneasy silence descended as the sounds of pursuit faded away. The night became still once more, darkness smothering everything. Jen breathed heavily, her mind shying away from what happened. Numbness spread through her limbs. Rachel wasn't moving. Amanda took a step toward her prone body, but Rhys pulled her back before she could take another. Evelyn wiped away a stream of tears. Jen wasn't crying. Why wasn't she crying? She should be crying. She raised her hands to her face to check for tears. They were shaking. She clenched them into fists and let them drop back to her sides, defeated.

Damien. Oh God, she hoped he would be all right. He had always been a fast runner. She would see him again at Knightsbridge. She took a step forward, as if to go after him. *Stupid. He's long gone.*

"Come on," Rhys said softly, as if afraid to break the quiet. Tears glittered in his eyes. "We need to move."

They got closer to the Wellington Arch, standing tall and solid in the middle of a large crowd of people. They shouted at each other and ran about, frantic, desperate. Some of them even wore pyjamas.

She exchanged a silent look with her friends as they approached. A mother and her two small children shied away from them, turning and scrambling in the opposite direction. Jen supposed they must look awful—she had blood down most of her left side, and Rhys's nose and hands were bloodied. Evelyn and Amanda had fared better, but they still looked sweaty and terrified.

What had dragged so many people from their homes? She'd witnessed terror and death, yes, but surely there wasn't city-wide chaos. What about the rest of the country? How had the government covered this up? With the prevalence of social media, it shouldn't have been possible. Were other countries coping better? Jen hoped the whole world hadn't gone up in flames.

Evelyn grabbed a tall man as he walked by. "Do you know what's happening? Why are people gathering here?"

The man visibly shook, and his messy hair and puffy eyes gave him a wild look. "The army is going to pick us all up." He spoke quickly, adding to his feral appearance. "Yes, they'll be here soon." He moved away, muttering 'soon' to himself over and over.

"Do you know anything about this?" Amanda asked, turning to Rhys. Her hair stuck up like she'd just gotten out of bed, and her large eyes stood out against her grey face.

"No." He shook his head. "The plan was to move through the city, to try contain it somehow. A curfew was to be imposed, which obviously didn't happen. Everything went crazy too quickly. Maybe the army is telling people to gather here so they can be evacuated. But people would be exposed..." He trailed off, frowning.

"Can we trust him?" Jen asked, gesturing after the tall man. She didn't want to wait for a non-existent rescue.

Rhys looked troubled. "If they are coming, we should stay here. But if they're not," he sighed. "I didn't tell you the extent of the outbreak before—I didn't want to alarm you. When the quarantines were breached, roughly over two hundred thousand infected got out. And that's only from two zones. Large zones, yeah, but still. There are more throughout the country."

Over two hundred thousand? Holy shit. Jen didn't know how to process such a large number of infected people moving around unimpeded.

Evelyn nodded, determination superseding the strain on her face. "So, we shouldn't wait here for the army that may or may not come, not with so many infected people running through the city and infecting more people. Right, well, we move on to Knightsbridge ourselves." When had she become so decisive?

Everyone agreed, and they pushed their way through the crowd. Jen's arm began to sting as the adrenaline wore off. She poked at it for a second and stilled as panic surged along her nerves. The infected man had bitten her, hadn't he? What had Rhys said? *The virus is transmitted by a bite. Shit, am I infected?* Jen frantically checked her arm for any bite marks, dread pooling in the pit of her stomach. She couldn't find anything. Her skin was torn to shreds. Maybe he hadn't bitten her. Maybe she was worried about nothing, and it was the shock of him colliding with her. Maybe—

A loud blast rocked the street as flames sprouted up behind the buildings in front of them. Jen ducked as the ground shook beneath her feet. Another blast erupted, closer this time. The crowd shoved Jen as they scrambled to get away. She looked around in the chaos, making sure to keep a tight grip of Evelyn's hand. Rhys and Amanda were still there, being jostled as well. About seven or eight people came screaming out of Hyde Park. Infected. A *tank* rolled down the road, and she watched as it opened fire, cutting them down.

Sound seemed to pause as people realised what happened, then cheers erupted from all sides. Jen was still too numb to feel much of anything, but the sight of the tank made her breathe a little easier. The army had come to pick them up after all. It rolled past them up to the Arch and kept on rolling up the road to where Jen and her friends had faced nightmares. The night consumed it, leaving behind a silent crowd struggling to control its fear.

One woman screamed and ran after the tank. It was as if a dam had broken open—people flooded after her, yelling for it to come back, crying for it not to leave.

Jen pulled her friends away. "Let's go." They needed to get off the streets before they got trampled. As they moved away, the crowd's pleads morphed into screams, and people rushed back around them. Another explosion beat at Jen's ears, and flames raced up several trees, turning them into a wall of fire.

Jen saw a large group of twenty or thirty people running through the frightened crowd, grabbing and biting them. For what seemed like the hundredth time that night, fear and adrenaline poured through Jen as she pushed her friends back.

"*Infected,*" she screamed, her voice lost among the roaring mass of people. She managed to seize Amanda and Evelyn by the wrists as someone ran into them. Jen crashed to the ground with a soft *oomph* as the wind fled her lungs. She was pushed back down twice before she regained her feet. Lost, afraid, and struggling to regain her breath, she spun in a circle searching for Evelyn, Rhys, Amanda, *anyone.* She didn't see them. *Where are they? Where did they go?* All around her people ran, screamed, panicked. Fear clogged her airways, threatening to drown her.

She turned in another wild circle, hoping to spot one of them, and jumped back as a man stumbled and fell in front of her. He sobbed as he reached out blindly. Jen shuffled away from his grasping hands and noticed a bleeding bite mark on his right forearm.

She turned away and staggered from him, running with the crowd. She risked a glance over her shoulder at him only to immediately collide with someone. This time, Jen stayed on her feet, but the other person wasn't as lucky.

"Evelyn," Jen gasped, reaching down to help her friend back up.

"Jen." Evelyn sounded winded. "I don't know where the others are. I'm so glad I saw you—" She cut off as a woman jumped out of the crowd, screaming and scratching at them. For the second time in as many minutes, Jen found herself on cold, hard mud. She landed awkwardly on her left arm. *Again.* The whole limb was a mass of torn, painful flesh. Brushing her dark hair out of her eyes, it took her a moment to realise Evelyn was pinned beneath their attacker.

No! Before she could think her actions through, she threw herself at the infected woman. She received an elbow to the face for her trouble but succeeded in getting her away from Evelyn. Jen was somehow able to trap the woman face down in the dirt, but she struggled and squirmed like a cat determined not to be picked up. Jen pinned her for as long as she could, but the woman *twisted,* and Jen was the one trapped beneath snapping jaws. The woman was wild and *so strong*. She grabbed Jen's arm—the left one, of fucking course—and dug her nails in. Jen screamed as agony radiated through every nerve fibre. Pain blazed around her elbow. She shoved her good arm into the woman's neck, frantically trying to keep her teeth away.

A foot slammed into the woman's head, knocking her away. Hands reached down and dragged Jen up. She took one look into Evelyn's terrified eyes and started running. Clutching Evelyn's hand with her good one, they sprinted through the streets, not looking where they were going. They had to get *away*. Away from the screaming and crying. Away from the horror and death.

The commotion faded as they rushed through empty streets. The light from the blaze dimmed until they dashed through darkness, afraid to slow even for a moment lest an infected person catch up with them.

Eventually, Evelyn pulled on Jen's arm, forcing her to stop. Jen looked around for one panic-fuelled moment, not understanding why they weren't moving. There were trees in front of her, like the ones back at the Arch. Had they gone in a circle? No, these trees weren't on fire. As she tried to get her bearings, Evelyn sat on the ground, pulling her legs up and resting her head on her knees.

"Are you all right?" Jen wheezed, clutching a stitch in her side. She really needed to run more. Her friend didn't reply. "Evelyn?"

"You should go to Knightsbridge without me," she muttered, curling tighter around herself.

"What?" Jen asked, incredulous. "Why would I do that?"

Evelyn didn't speak. She held out her right hand. Jen leaned down for a closer look, not daring to breathe. An angry bite mark glowered from below her little finger. Jen saw it even in the moonlight, inflamed and bleeding.

She straightened sharply, releasing the breath she'd been holding. *No. Not her. Not Evelyn.* Jen pushed aside all her fears and doubts, burying them deep. She reached down and dragged her best friend up into a hug. She poured all her love into the hug, trying to show Evelyn she was there for her no matter what. Evelyn held onto her as if she would fall otherwise, crying into her shoulder. She clutched her friend as tightly as she could, supporting her as she fell apart.

After an indeterminable amount of time—Jen couldn't have said if seconds had passed or minutes—Evelyn pulled back, wiping away tears. She gave Jen a small smile which died as soon as it was born. "I'm not going anywhere without you, Evelyn. Don't even think about telling me to leave. We'll go to the barracks together. We'll find Rhys and Amanda and Damien there. They'll find a cure, and you'll be back to normal in no time." She tried *so hard* to sound reassuring.

Evelyn dipped her head, regaining some of her composure. She still looked terrified, but she pushed herself up straight again. *She's such an amazing woman.*

"Where are we?" Evelyn asked, her breath hitching in her throat.

"I don't know. Come on, let's get our bearings and go from there."

Chapter Three

They made it to Knightsbridge without running into further horrors. They'd had to hide and wait for looters to pass a couple of times, but otherwise, it had been a rather uneventful walk, especially compared to the beginning of the night.

Crouched across the street from the solid, uncompromising buildings of the Household Cavalry, Jen shivered in the night air. They had been sitting behind a low wall for a good ten minutes, listening to distant explosions and gunshots. Jen wished she grabbed a coat when she left the apartment. She hadn't registered the temperature before, but she only wore a thin t-shirt, and it was *freezing*.

"Should we go up to the gate and ask them to let us in?" Evelyn gestured to the two nervous soldiers guarding the entrance.

Gone was her earlier decisiveness and confidence, replaced by a scared young woman. Jen watched as Evelyn flexed her hand again, the bite mark a bleeding beacon. Jen decided she would be the strong one. Evelyn had been there for her more times than she could remember—when she dropped her stuffed lion in a puddle when they first met as children, when she failed her driving test, when she broke up with Robin. Jen was *not* going to let Evelyn down when she needed her the most.

"Yeah, I don't see another way in. It will be all right. Follow me," Jen said, trying to project an air of certainty. She stood up and marched across the road.

As soon as she rose from her crouched position, the guards levelled their guns at her through the bars of the gate. Perturbed, but determined not to let it show, Jen strode up to them with Evelyn trailing behind. She was surprised the soldiers hadn't noticed them earlier. She and Evelyn had been far from stealthy. She supposed the wall had blocked their line of sight. *I guess they don't want to be exposed out in the middle of the street. Better to be tucked safely behind that solid wall*, she thought bitterly. *They should be out here, helping people.*

"Stop right there," one of the men hissed, his suspicious eyes squinting at them from a narrow face.

Jen put her hands up. "Hi," she said, her nerves making her smile falter. Not the best way to start the conversation, but exhaustion limited her capacity to care. The man glared at her. "We were told to come here by our friend, Lance Corporal Rhys Coyne. He said we would be safe here."

"I've never heard of Lance Corporal Rhys Coyne," the narrow-faced man spat. "Why don't you piss off back the way you came, eh?" He stabbed at them with his gun, still glaring as if they were the cause of all the trouble.

"Johnson," the other soldier said, his thick eyebrows lowering as he scowled at his companion. "We've got plenty of room. Besides, it's our duty to protect the people."

"They could be infected." Johnson rounded on the nice guard, and some of the anxiety swirling though Jen eased. "You want to let them in?"

"We'll check them inside." The nicer of the two guards lowered his gun and produced a key for the gate. Unlocking it, he ushered them into the grounds, quickly closing and securing it as soon as they passed through.

Jen felt the apprehension rolling off Evelyn in waves. She squeezed her hand and smiled. They would be all right. They'd made it.

"Stand separately," Johnson barked. "Arms up, legs apart." He leered at them. *Leered*, at a time like this.

Jen threw him a disgusted look before doing as he asked. The nice guard started checking her for bite marks while Evelyn got the arsehole.

"What happened here?" he asked, pointing at her torn arm.

She didn't think mentioning her collision with the infected man would be a good idea—hell, she couldn't remember if he'd bitten her. The night had started to blur together. She shrugged. "I slipped and scraped it all when I fell."

The man looked at her, and Jen couldn't decide whether he believed her explanation or not. His soft brown eyes narrowed with something in the middle of doubt and trust. After what seemed like an eternity, he nodded and stepped back.

"She's clean."

"Yeah? This one isn't," Johnson backed up and glared down his gun at Evelyn. "Her hand."

The nice guard noticed the bite mark and raised his gun, his gaze hardening. Tears streaked down Evelyn's face.

"*No.*" Jen jumped in front of her and raised her hands in a placating gesture. "Please—"

The supposed nice guard seized her and dragged her out of the way. She struggled, but he was much stronger than her. Johnson forced Evelyn to her knees and levelled his weapon at her once more. She turned to look at Jen, her dark eyes terrified. Jen doubled her effort against the guard and managed to kick him in the shin, but he held fast regardless. *God damn it.* She *had* to get to Evelyn.

"*Please.* You can't do this. You have to help her! There's got to be—"

A single gunshot. Deafening silence.

Jen fell lifeless in the guard's arms, her mind shocked blank. Blood crawled across the ground. She watched as it edged closer to her, inch by inch, a dark stain spreading outward. Jen heard her own blood pounding in her ears as someone pulled her away. Evelyn. They were pulling her away from Evelyn. *No.* She struggled, knowing it was futile. They killed her. Oh God, she was dead. Gone. Just like that. She'd told her they would be okay; they would be safe. She was *dead.*

Johnson called for help to remove the body. *Monster. Fucking monster.* She had to get to him. She had to make him *pay.* She thrashed about, trying to break the other soldier's grip. He grunted with effort before letting her go, and she fell hard. She didn't register the pain as she crashed into the ground, jarring her knees and wrists as she landed inches shy of the pool of blood. Evelyn's blood. It burned her hands even though she hadn't touched it.

Distracted, she didn't see the troop of soldiers jog over until two of them hauled her up and half-carried, half-dragged her away. "*No*," she yelled. "Let me go. Let me *go*."

"Shut up," one of them spat, a grey-haired man who looked as if he hadn't smiled in years. They lead her into the building, and Jen didn't bother paying attention to where they took her. Lethargy spread through her body, turning her limbs into dead weights.

By the time they stopped in front of a plain wooden door, only a woman remained by her side. Jen hadn't even noticed when the man left. Grief dulled everything, like a darkness obscuring her senses.

"Here," she said, not unkindly. "There are showers one floor above so you can clean yourself up, and there's some spare clothes on the bed. We have a lot of rooms prepared for civilians, and I think this one has clothes your size. If you need anything, knock on the door at the end of this hall and to the left. A group of us will be in there for the night." She opened the door and gently pushed Jen in. "Try to get some sleep, if you can." She closed the door behind her, and Jen tried not to think about how much it sounded like a cage locking, separating her from Evelyn and her friends forever.

She looked around the tiny room. A single camp bed and a table with a lamp took up most of the cramped space. Ignoring the shower for now, Jen sank down onto the bed and stared at the wall, the weariness in her bones sapping her energy, her drive. Overwhelmed by the events of the past couple of hours, she curled into a ball and finally cried.

*

Blue eyes winking. Brown eyes pleading.

Jen lurched awake and almost fell off her narrow bed. For one panic-filled moment, she didn't know where she was, her eyes darting around the cramped, unfamiliar space. Memories filtered in slowly, unrelenting in their horror and pain, battering at her like winds in a terrifying storm.

As she moved to sit up, something jabbed into her side. Her camera. It was remarkably undamaged given everything it had been through. She set it on the table with gentle movements, trying not to get any more blood on it.

Blood. It had congealed over her body. Overwhelmed by a desperate need to get clean, Jen grabbed the clothes she had knocked to the floor during her fitful sleep and jogged upstairs to the showers. She stripped and jumped in, scrubbing all the sweat and blood and grime away. She scoured her skin, leaving it red and raw and relishing the stinging pain. She felt more human afterward.

The pile of clothes consisted of plain black combat trousers and a grey t-shirt with 'ARMY' stamped across it in large black letters. The trousers fit well, though the t-shirt hung off her frame. She left her dirty clothes in a heap in the corner, unable to touch them.

Jen opened the door and padded out in black boots a size too big, but she hardly noticed it due to the thick socks on her feet.

She wondered what time it was as she made her way back to her room. Everyone had arrived at the apartment at about seven in the evening, and everything afterward couldn't have taken longer than an hour, two at most. Fatigue spiked through her muscles. It felt like she hadn't slept at all. With burning eyes and the beginnings of a headache, Jen shut the door and sat on the edge of the bed.

She couldn't fight the pain growing inside like thorns. She couldn't face thoughts of her friends. Rachel and Evelyn... She didn't know what had happened to Rhys, Amanda or Damien. Would she ever see them again? Her mind shied away from their likely fate.

She needed a distraction. Jen picked up her camera and rubbed off some of the dried blood. It didn't seem new anymore. It contained images of nightmares in place of celebration. She switched it on reluctantly, her hand moving of its own accord.

The first picture was of herself. Her parents had taken it the day before when they'd gifted her the camera. She didn't recognise herself. The woman in the photograph had bright blue eyes shining with happiness and dark hair free of tangles and blood. Jen stared at the carefree young woman on the screen, an overwhelming sadness at the loss of who she used to be sweeping up her throat. She had to switch the camera off.

Tears began to fall.

Chapter Four

Jen jerked awake for a second time. She lay still for a moment, unsure of what had awoken her. Not bad dreams—they'd been vague, already slipping from her memory. Tiredness still spiralled though her body, so she should be still sleeping. She tried to keep her mind still, but the darkness kept encroaching on her, so Jen decided to explore instead of sitting in this box of a room with her grief-soaked thoughts.

She found the mess hall easily, but she didn't linger. Thoughts of food twisted her stomach, and the kitchen was cold anyway. Next, she found what appeared to be a lounge area containing a TV, pool table, and several sofas and chairs.

Dropping down onto the surprisingly comfortable sofa, Jen picked up the TV remote and switched the news on. The scene on the screen was of a city gone mad—aerial shots of burning buildings, of infected attacking others, of more people lying dead in the streets. It all left a sour taste in her mouth. Some images even showed mobs breaking into shops and making off with different items. People were always quick to capitalise on chaos.

She switched it off, not wanting to look at the confusion and destruction running rampant and unchecked. Instead, she curled up at the end of the sofa, fighting not to give in to the despair crowding the edges of her mind. And *God*, she was losing. Would she ever see her parents again? Damien, Amanda, and Rhys hadn't turned up yet and, in all likelihood, never would. She'd watched as two people she loved were murdered in front of her. A wave of despondency loomed over her, and she lay still, struggling to stay afloat in a sea of uncertainty.

She had no idea how long she sat there, fighting a losing battle with emptiness. The sound of an embarrassed cough startled her out of her thoughts. Twisting around, she saw a pale-skinned boy shuffle from one foot to the other and look at her with hesitation. He was about her height, skinny, and dressed in similar clothing. He awkwardly ran a hand through his short blond hair. Jennifer thought he looked to be about fifteen, maybe sixteen at a push, but she'd never been good at guessing people's ages.

"Hi," he said. His hand twitched like he meant to wave at her, but he aborted the move before it fully began. "Erm, sorry if I disturbed you. I'm Daniel, by the way. Erm, Dan."

He half smiled, but it faded fast. His big blue eyes looked sad and haunted. God, he was just a kid. What had he gone through out there?

"I'm Jennifer," she said, deciding to go by her full name. Jen was happy, with all her friends and family. That wasn't her anymore. She wanted nothing more than to go back to her room and sleep, but she would stay and talk to this boy if it helped ease the sadness in his eyes. "Why don't you sit down?" She smiled at him, hoping it didn't look as fake as it felt.

"Thanks," he said, sitting down next to her. When he smiled this time, it looked more relaxed. "So, erm, are you here with anyone?"

Her face must have fallen because he started babbling. "I—I'm sorry. I didn't mean, erm, sorry, I thought maybe, erm—"

"It's okay, Dan, really," Jennifer said softly. She gave him a small smile to show he wasn't at fault for anything. "There were others, but I'm the only one who made it here."

He looked stricken. "I'm sorry, I shouldn't have said anything."

"Don't worry about it. You didn't know."

He nodded and stared down at his feet. The silence stretched, growing awkward. Jennifer didn't know what to say, so she settled for fiddling with a bit of thread on the arm of the sofa. She had never been one of those people who could strike up a conversation with anyone, but she wasn't shy either. Why couldn't she find anything to talk about? *Maybe because I've never been in this situation before. What do you say when the world is ending?* She shook herself. *Dramatic much?* Her world had ended yes, and no doubt many others, but the rest still spun on. She had to believe that.

Sighing, she reached over and nudged Dan. "Have you had anything to eat yet?" She paused. She didn't know the time. Looking around, she spotted a clock on the far wall showing eleven in the morning.

"Erm, yeah, I had something before I came here," Dan said. "Uh, not much, though. I'm not really hungry."

"Yeah, me neither." Jennifer didn't want to lapse into another uncomfortable silence, so she rose and gestured for Dan to do the same. "How good are you at pool?"

He looked at the table, and the melancholy in his eyes faded somewhat. "I'm good. I'm the best out of all my friends."

Jennifer raised an eyebrow at him. "Modest, huh?"

He shrugged and strode to the pool table. "I'm good at it," he repeated. "If you're, erm, good at something, why fake false modesty? That's what Mum, uh," he faltered, but ploughed ahead anyway, clearly set on finishing his sentence. "What Mum used to say. I'll win." He didn't seem confident, but Jennifer got the sense it wasn't his nature anyway.

"Oh, really? We'll see about that."

Jennifer was glad she'd suggested pool. Dan came out of his shell, shaking off his awkwardness as he beat her. And beat her he did. She lost the game so quickly her face burned with embarrassment. She wasn't amazing at pool, but she had always thought she could hold her own. Apparently not.

"Best of three," she challenged, hoping to keep him smiling and make him forget about the shitty world for a little while longer.

"Are you sure? I mean, I would be ashamed if I'd played like that." He smirked at her, which made her want to play again. She wasn't competitive—that had always been Damien and Evelyn, and Amanda to a lesser extent—but she wanted to see if she could give him a run for his money. Some of the darkness receded as she set up the table.

She lost again. Spectacularly. She may have even played worse the second time. She couldn't bring herself to be bothered, however, as Dan grinned from ear to ear.

"You're terrible at this," he laughed. "I didn't think it was possible for someone to be this bad at pool."

"Yeah, okay, you won, but I'm not *terrible*." She tried to appear annoyed, but Dan's smile tugged her own into existence. She couldn't stop herself from laughing along with him. It felt good. Cathartic. She relaxed for the first time in what seemed like forever.

"I hate to break up your little party, but where can I find the mess hall?" The deep, Scottish-accented voice belonged to a broad-shouldered man with short brown hair and bright green eyes. He stood tall and straight, a strange energy thrumming through him, like he was moments away from bursting into action. Blood and dirt spattered his full combat uniform, which, coupled with his frowning face, resulted in an intimidating first impression. Jennifer didn't want to think about where he'd acquired those stains.

Dan clammed up, leaving Jennifer to do all the talking. "Back down the hall and to the left, erm, sir. Can you give us any new information?"

The man grunted, turned on his heel, and walked away without responding.

"Well, nice to meet you too," Jennifer told empty space. She needed to keep the mood light lest she fall back into the darkness that hovered so close. She turned back to Dan to ask him what he wanted to do next, but her question died on her lips when she saw his face. He looked scared and fragile, his eyes too wide in his face. Seeing a reminder of the chaos outside made her want to curl up in a corner, and Dan probably felt something similar.

"Hey," Jennifer said, pulling Dan back to the sofa. He looked to her for reassurance, and everything Jennifer wanted to say fled her mind, leaving her struggling to find the right words. What could she say to make him feel better?

Dan sighed and leaned forward on his knees, staring down at his clasped hands while she still floundered. "I understand. You don't know what to say because there is nothing to say." Tears slipped down his face and he brushed them aside. "I, erm, I saw, uh—" he stopped and gathered himself before letting everything out in a rush of words and tears. "Me and my mum were picking my little sister up from her friend's house. She shouldn't have gone around in the first place. They came running down the street, I don't know how many. We didn't know what was happening at first. One of them attacked her friend's dad, and everything went crazy. My mum grabbed me and Abby, and we all started running back to the car. We didn't make it." His voice broke, and he started crying in earnest. "My mum, she erm, she fought two of them, screaming for me and Abby to get away. Abby couldn't stop crying. She kept yelling for Mum to come with us. I had to drag her away. We didn't get far before, before—" Dan sucked in a deep breath. "Before they got Abby too." He stopped talking, gasping out great sobs of air.

A lump formed in her throat as she watched his anguish.

"I, erm, I kept running. I couldn't—I couldn't stop. I ran into some soldiers. I literally ran into one of them. They almost shot me. Thought I was one of *them*. They brought me here early this morning." He lapsed into silence, struggling to control his breathing.

For several seconds, his sobs were the only sound in the room. Jennifer couldn't bear it, so she asked the first thing that came to her. "What about your dad?"

"He, erm, he left us ten years ago. I was only four. Abby was two. I don't remember him." He wiped his eyes and nose and shook himself. "I didn't realise how badly I needed to tell someone. I didn't think I would be able to talk about it, with everything still raw, you know?"

"I know." Jennifer breathed in deeply. *A story for a story.* Dan interrupted her before she could speak, however.

"You don't have to say anything. I, erm, understand if it hurts too much."

God, he could only be fourteen, and he had been through hell, yet he tried to be mindful of her feelings. His compassion brought tears to her eyes.

"It's okay. I think I need to tell someone as well." She told him everything, from the crashed birthday party, to losing Rachel and Evelyn, to the others not turning up. She wasn't able to stop the words from pouring out of her once she opened the floodgates. She didn't think it possible, but a weight had been lifted after she let everything out. They sat together comfortably afterward. They had both faced nightmares and survived, and no more words needed to be exchanged on the subject.

A loud explosion rocked them both back to reality. The morning had been far from quiet—the faint pattering of gunfire sounded like rain to Jennifer's ears—but this was the first blast she'd heard since the night before. She rushed to one of the windows, wanting to see where it came from. Black smoke rose above the skyline, blotting out the pale blue sky.

"Did that seem close to you?" Dan asked, wringing his hands together as he peered over her shoulder.

"It looks like it might be coming from one of the embassies," Jennifer replied. "They're all around there, right?"

"Erm, I think so." Another blast erupted slightly to the left of the first. Dan flinched away from the window, looking like he might throw up.

"Are you okay?" Jennifer asked, concerned.

"No, not really," Dan muttered. "They're, uh, they're killing people out there."

"*No,*" Jennifer said vehemently. "They're killing the infected people, so they can't attack and infect the rest of us. They're doing what they can to protect everyone." Jennifer hoped she wasn't lying to him. *God, what if there are innocent people out there, caught in the crossfire?*

"They're protecting people by blowing the city up?" Dan's voice took on a hysterical edge. "That's not right, Jennifer. It's murder. They're dropping bombs all over the place!"

But they weren't. There had only been two explosions in close proximity to each other. Dan was scared. *Of course, he is. I am too.*

"Look, I understand you're fright—"

"Yeah, I am," he cut her off, his voice breaking. He ran a hand through his hair, causing it to stick up in places. "What's going on out there?"

"Panicking is *not* going to help us," Jennifer said, shoving aside her own fear. "You want to know what's happening? Well, so do I. We'll find someone who can tell us, and we'll ask them, *calmly,* what's going on. Okay?" He still breathed heavily. "*Dan,* okay?"

He stared at her for a moment, panic carved into his face, before some of the fear receded from his eyes. He gestured for her to lead the way.

Jennifer realised she had no idea where to go when they stepped out of the lounge. She didn't know where everybody was. *Wait, the room at the end of the hall. Maybe someone in there can help.* Still, she hesitated. They were probably busy and wouldn't welcome the intrusion. Maybe they should go back to their rooms and wait for someone to get them. She didn't want to interrupt anything important. The desire to curl up in her bed rose once more. But *no,* she wouldn't give in to the despair. They would find out what was going on. With a renewed sense of purpose, Jennifer led the way up the stairs.

She knocked on the door and waited. Dan fidgeted beside her. She raised her fist to knock again when the door swung open, revealing the soldier who had brought Jennifer to her room the night before. She looked as if she hadn't slept at all—dark circles stained her tired eyes. *She's probably exhausted. She's going to be pissed we're dragging her away from her work.*

Instead of telling them to go away, however, the woman offered a small smile, which shone through her fatigue and made her look more awake. "Do you need something?"

"Yeah, sorry to interrupt, but we were wondering if you could tell us what's going on?" Jennifer asked, hoping the soldier wouldn't slam the door in their faces. "We saw a couple of explosions before, and, well, we're curious, I guess." She shrugged, unsure of what else to say.

The woman sighed. "You want the truth?" She closed her eyes for a second, and when she opened them again, they were filled with barely constrained fear. "London has fallen—we're starting to evacuate everyone to safe zones we have set up. It will be your turn in a few hours. The whole country is panicking. Quarantine zones all over have been breached."

Words refused to come to her. London was a massive city. How could the capital fall in a single night? It beggared belief. "All of London?"

The soldier rubbed her face. "All of London, yes. We received word quarantine zones across the world have been breached before reports stopped coming in from most countries. It was bound to happen—we were all stretched too far, especially as the governments wanted it to be kept a secret." She shook her head. "I need to get back now. Wait in your rooms until it's your turn to be evacuated. I'm sorry." She shut the door after an apologetic grimace, leaving Jennifer and Dan standing in a shocked silence.

Dan shuffled back until he pressed against the wall. Jennifer clenched and unclenched her fists. *This can't be happening, it can't, it can't.* She repeated the thought over and over, her mind rebelling against what the soldier said. She should have been waking up with a hangover from her party, her friends crashed out in the living room. Not... *this.* Dan muttered something under his breath and his face screwed up as if he were in physical pain. Jennifer jumped when he twisted and punched the wall, letting out a wordless yell. She reached out and pulled him away before the soldiers could come and shut him up.

Once they were back in her room, she let him go. He sank down to the floor and wrapped his arms around his knees, staring blankly at the wall. She sat on the bed, fighting to stop the crushing numbness weighing down on her. The world had gone to shit in a single day. *How is it even possible?* The cover-up must have been beyond comprehension given the number of infected breaking free.

Shying away from thinking about any of it, she curled into a ball, squeezed her eyes shut and willed herself to think of happier times.

*

Shadows draped across the room when Jennifer woke up. Dan's snoring broke the silence from where he lay sprawled across the floor. He looked peaceful, despite everything. She left him to sleep a while longer and moved to gaze out the window. The burning sun had set the sky on fire as it sank below the horizon, orange bleeding to blue bleeding to black. The darkening sky was clear of clouds, and Jennifer saw a handful of stars shining through the dusk. It was difficult to imagine all the death outside when the evening was so beautiful.

The sky had bled completely black when she heard Dan stir behind her. She didn't move—she wanted the serene moment to last a little longer. The stars shined down, safe up high, illuminating the destruction below. There had been more bombings, and she had somehow managed to sleep through them. She couldn't see any fires from her vantage point, but she knew they would be raging throughout the city.

Jennifer turned away from the window with a sigh. Her arm still hurt, and her head felt like someone had taken a hammer to it. *And* exhaustion still clung to her even though she had slept for a few hours. She couldn't feel more like shit if she tried.

Dan blinked bleary eyes at her as he pushed himself to his feet. "Erm, hi." He frowned in the darkness. "I thought we were going to be evacuated?"

"She said it would be a few hours, so there's still time." Jennifer switched the light on, causing Dan to squint in the sudden brightness. "Sorry," she smiled. He looked adorable, like a little confused puppy. With a small shake of her head, she walked back to the table and picked up her camera. "Do you mind if I take your picture?" The urge to get one of him as soon as possible, in case she couldn't in the future, tingled through her fingers.

He looked at her as if she had grown a second head. "You, uh, you want to take my picture?"

"Yeah, I told myself I would document everything. You're a part of that now. If you don't mind?"

"Erm, sure."

He looked a little uncomfortable standing there, not moving or smiling. His wide-eyed gaze and sad mouth reminded her of photographs of children from war zones, their childhoods snatched away from under their feet. Traumatised and unable to understand why their world had fallen apart, they looked lost, their stares often vacant and uncomprehending. Sadness burst in her chest for Dan, his eyes witness to horrors no one should have to see.

She handed him the camera. "Here, you can look through it if you want." She sat back down on the bed and examined her torn-up arm. It wasn't bleeding anymore, and most of the damage was superficial, except the part above her elbow, which appeared somewhat redder and more swollen than the surrounding skin—although it was difficult to tell with all the damage. Curious, she prodded it and winced at the brief flare of pain. The skin was hot to the touch.

Dan's voice broke through her inspection. "These are the friends you lost?" he asked quietly. She nodded, not trusting herself to speak. She still couldn't fully wrap her head around everything.

Someone knocked on the door and entered before Jennifer or Dan could move to open it. A dark-skinned man with a shaved head and a neatly trimmed goatee walked in, his comforting smile betrayed by the tightness around his eyes. "It's time to leave," he said in a soft voice. "Grab your personal belongings, but please, only bring things you can carry." He gestured for them to follow him.

"Do you need to get anything from your room?" Jennifer asked Dan.

"No, I don't have anything," he replied as he switched her camera off and handed it back to her. Jennifer's heart broke for him.

The soldier walked with a firm step, leading them down through the building and out into a large yard different from the small one Jennifer and Evelyn had arrived at. A large triangular structure sat atop a solid wall and thick doors were barred against the outside. Jennifer shuddered thinking about what lay beyond them. She turned her gaze away and instead studied the yard where a depressingly small number of civilians waited. Jennifer counted only four. A group of six soldiers surrounded them, all well-armed, including the man who had brought Jennifer and Dan from her room and the green-eyed man they had seen earlier.

"Okay, listen up," the man's Scottish brogue sounded like the crack of a whip, and everyone gave him their full attention. "We are going to leave the compound and make our way over to the park, where a helicopter is going to pick us up. We are going to move in an orderly fashion, no pushing and shoving, no running ahead or lagging behind. Have I made myself clear?" His sharp voice left no room for argument.

Everyone voiced their understanding, their breaths turning to mist in front of them. Jennifer wished they had provided a jacket as well as the t-shirt and trousers. They stood waiting for only a couple of minutes—although it felt longer in the freezing air—before Jennifer heard a faint hum. The helicopter. She spotted it flying low over the park and watched until it dipped below the treeline.

The Scottish man signalled to his fellow soldiers. "Move out!" He levelled his weapon as two soldiers opened the heavy doors of the gate, revealing an empty street. The soldiers quickly moved out onto the road and motioned everyone forward. Someone cursed as they stumbled out from behind the safety and comfort of the tall walls. Jennifer shivered, the feeling of being exposed coating her like an extra layer of clothing despite being surrounded by trained soldiers who would not hesitate to fire upon any threat. The cold air stung her lungs as she hurried across the road, Dan an ever-present shadow at her side, panting as he rushed along with the group.

Unbidden, thoughts arose of the last time she dashed from a building to a vehicle. Fear rose before she could stop it, causing her to falter. Before, she hadn't known what was going on, hadn't understood the extent of the danger and damage to come. Now, she knew all too well what would happen if they were caught unaware. She wouldn't fall again.

A screech came from the left, and Jennifer whipped her head around, the familiar surge of adrenaline stabbing through her veins. The group flinched away as one, and everyone started pushing forward faster. Two of the soldiers opened fire, killing four infected people as they ran toward them across the grass.

"I said move in an orderly fashion," the Scottish man growled. "What part of my instructions did you not understand?"

People calmed down when they saw the danger had been dealt with. Jennifer had to cover her face as she got closer to the helicopter—the blades whipped the cold air into a frenzy, stinging her eyes and pulling her hair in every direction.

Five soldiers crouched in a circle around the helicopter as the Scottish man ushered everyone on board, handing out headsets as people climbed into the cabin. There were three seats along the back wall and six in the middle of the cabin—arranged three back to back. Jennifer was the last to climb in, and she sat next to Dan in the middle seat facing the open door, fumbling to put her headset on. The soldier who had collected them from her room jumped up after her, sliding the door shut and blocking the view of the night-filled park. He sat down closest to the left side pilot seat, which remained empty. Jennifer twisted around to see the pilot but couldn't get a good look at them. They were busy fiddling with the numerous switches and dials. *Holy shit, how can anyone fly one of these things?* The cockpit was *filled* with controls.

The Scottish soldier hopped into the second pilot seat. Jennifer saw the other soldiers disappear back across the road as they rose higher and higher, away from the threat of infected on the ground. She leaned back into her seat and smiled at Dan, who grinned back. His smile was shaky, but it was there. They were being evacuated to a safe, secure place. *I damn well hope it's safe.* Maybe she could start putting her life back together. Try to find her parents. For the first time since this nightmare began, Jennifer felt able to truly relax.

They were going to be all right.

Chapter Five

Sergeant James Mollino eased back into the pilot seat, slammed the door shut, and exchanged his ordinary helmet for a Westland Lynx one. He didn't have any idea how to fly a Lynx, but he at least looked like he knew what he was doing. Besides, helicopter helmets were so much better looking than normal ones.

"Did you get it?"

He had known the pilot, Sergeant Wright, for less than a day, yet she already had him running errands for her. When she dropped him and some fellow soldiers off earlier, she all but ordered him to bring her some chocolate. *Chocolate.* In the middle of all this shite. Pulling the chocolate bar out from his pocket, he tossed it into her lap, and it disappeared so fast he blinked and missed it.

"Oh, yeah. That's the stuff. Thanks." Wright's midnight eyes lit up as she flashed a wide smile his way, a brief glimpse of white amidst beautifully dark skin. When he had first seen her, he had—incorrectly—assumed she would be shy and quiet due to her small, feminine stature. He knew he'd made an error as soon as she opened her mouth. She was a force of nature, battering him down in a burst of noise and activity that left him reeling. He was pretty sure she could beat him up if she wanted to, even though he was taller and outweighed her.

"Why did you want one, anyway?" he asked, baffled at her insistence.

"I had a sudden craving for chocolaty goodness. Killing things really brings out my sweet tooth."

James grunted. *What a weird reason.* Well, he wasn't one to judge. As long as she did her job, she could eat all the chocolate she wanted.

He turned and looked out over the ruined city, once bustling with activity and innovation, now burning with madness as chaos choked the streets. He had been granted a week's leave and had decided to visit some old friends down in London. James had been in England's capital for less than five days when madness flooded the streets. He had ensured his friends' safety before he made his way to the nearest barracks and thrown himself in headfirst. He was a soldier, and he had a job to do. There was no point whining about it.

The new reports he received not half an hour ago were worrying, however. Quarantine zones all over the world were falling apart, chaos in a lot of major cities across the globe. News of the devastation in London seemed to have panicked the rest of the world, and the government's censorship no longer protected the people. Instead, their ignorance fuelled the fire. The information should have been shared with the public right from the beginning in James's opinion.

"Not the talkative type? I respect that." Wright flashed her bright smile at him again. She was far too happy for the situation they were in. It required sombreness, not cheerfulness.

"Why don't you focus on getting us to Thorney Island," James snapped, tired and irritable from being deployed through most of last night and the day.

"Well, aren't you a little ball of sunshine," she huffed. "I'm only trying to pass the time."

He grunted again, and thankfully the conversation stopped. They flew in silence, clearing London within minutes. The light from all the fires dwindled until they were swallowed by the darkness, the Lynx slicing through the cold air with nothing but stars above and blackness below.

James wanted to close his eyes and catch a few precious minutes of sleep, but he forced himself to check on the civilians instead. He twisted in his seat to give the ones he could see a once over. *They're probably all scared shitless. They'll need to toughen up.* A young couple at the back clutched each other tightly. A skinny kid stared down at his hands, but James didn't think he saw them. A brunette woman fiddled with a camera, of all things, before wincing and prodding at her arm, which looked quite torn up. A jolt of alarm spiked through James at the sight of it. Could she have been bitten?

Scowling, he turned back around. Just his fucking luck. Trapped mid-air with someone possibly infected with a virus that turned them into a murderously violent psycho.

"What's up, Sunshine?" Wright asked.

"There's a woman in the cabin with a torn-up arm. Could be hiding a bite," James said, ignoring the ridiculous nickname. He managed to keep his unease out of his voice. If she had been bitten, it would have been yesterday, as he'd been told all the civilians had arrived the night before. The virus had a short incubation time, only a day or two, so she could become symptomatic during the flight.

"But we picked them up at Knightsbridge. They would have all been screened before they were allowed in."

"Aye, but I don't like it. They could have missed one."

Wright's lips formed a thin line, and he knew a frown marred her forehead under her helmet. "I don't want an infected person on my helicopter."

Fortunately, the headsets they gave the civilians didn't have the built-in communication system, making them glorified earmuffs. The last thing he wanted was people panicking, especially in such a confined space. He twisted again—careful not to knock the cyclic stick—and nudged Trueman, who looked to have fallen asleep. If only James could as well. The man came alert immediately, his dark eyes searching for a threat as he sat up and rolled his shoulders back.

"Sir?"

"Check the woman sitting next to you for any bites, specifically her left arm," James ordered.

He nodded once, his pointed chin stabbing in a quick downward motion, and turned to the woman. She looked up when Trueman tapped her on the shoulder, surprise filling her bright eyes. Said surprise faded as Trueman pointed at her arm, and a guarded look stole over her face. *She better not be infected.* She held out her arm with clear reluctance and winced as Trueman began inspecting it. It *did* look painful. Maybe her hesitation was because of the pain, and not due to a fear of getting caught.

Trueman examined her arm thoroughly before smiling at her and turning and shaking his head at James. "I can't see any teeth marks, so I don't think she's been bitten." He hesitated. "But she's really done a number on her arm, and it's starting to look inflamed and infected."

James did *not* like the sound of that.

"*Infected* infected, or normal infected?" Wright cut in, sounding annoyed.

The woman watched them with narrowed eyes, as did the scrawny kid next to her. James held her gaze as Trueman answered Wright. "I can't really tell. Does one infection look different from another? I thought only a bite or somehow ingesting contaminated blood gets you infected, and as I said, I can't find any teeth marks. It might be an ordinary infection from scraping her arm."

Tearing his eyes away from the woman's piercing gaze, James exchanged a concerned look with Wright.

"What do you think?" he asked her.

She took her time answering. "We're landing shortly. As soon as we do, and I mean *as soon as,* we isolate her and question her. If it turns out to be a normal, run-of-the-mill infection, fine. We'll throw some antibiotics her way and welcome her with open arms. If not, we put her down." James agreed. Standing orders were to shoot infected people on sight. Somewhat more at ease now they had a plan, he settled back into his seat, hoping to relax until they reached their destination.

Not a minute later, Trueman poked him in the arm. "Sir? The lady wants your attention."

He hadn't had a second of peace and quiet since this whole thing started, so he didn't know why he expected some now. Sighing, he twisted around again and raised an eyebrow at her.

"*I haven't been bitten,*" she mouthed, shaking her head and pointing at her arm. She seemed frightened, her skin pale and sweaty. Did she think he was going to throw her out of the helicopter or something? Or was her pasty skin a sign of something more sinister? Flu-like symptoms were the early signs, after all. He nodded at her to ease any fears she might have harboured, and turned to stare out the window again, ignoring her. They would interrogate everything when they landed. Any questions would have to wait.

He wondered how things were in Scotland. *I should be there with the rest of the Black Watch*. He cursed himself for taking a holiday. A *holiday*. He knew Scotland had seventeen quarantine zones spread throughout the country, but he had never been involved with Operation Rabid Dog, which had been scientists more than anyone else. Most of the military had been as much in the dark as the civilians. He'd never been given guard duty at any of the zones, nor had he wanted anything to do with it. Diseases freaked him out, and he hated being around hospitals and sick people. It reminded him too much of his father's last few months.

He stiffened in his seat as he caught sight of fire blazing in the distance. The flames curled into the dark sky, dancing gleefully as they consumed and destroyed. Thick black smoke blotted out the bright stars overhead. Dread sank like a stone in James's stomach, making him feel sick.

"Please tell me that's not Thorney Island."

Wright didn't say anything, which was confirmation enough.

"*Fuck.*" His emotions briefly got the better of him before he gathered them firmly in hand. Were the other safe zones like this? He twisted around to see if any of the civilians had noticed anything amiss, but they looked the same as when he had last checked on them. He turned to Wright. "I think we should assess the situation from the air before deciding anything."

"I agree," she replied tersely, "but we'll have to land soon. I'm running low on fuel."

"What?" Shock erupted up his spine. *We're running out of fuel? How did that happen?*

"Look, I have been flying around all day. I was told I would be able to refuel here," Wright said through gritted teeth. "It's an island, right? How could it have fallen?"

"Maybe there's some fuel left," Trueman said, a thread of optimism weaving around the words. James eyed the flames. The size of the fire and the ferocity at which it burned suggested all the fuel had ignited. Trueman was grasping at straws. Still, if there was even the slightest possibility any fuel remained unignited, they had to try, right?

Wright shook her head, obviously having come to the same conclusion as James. "I'll do a low circuit of the island so we can get a good look at what's going on. I was used for troop transport, so the weapons were removed to make room for people. We'll have to land and engage any targets present ourselves. Once they've been eliminated, we can see if we can salvage anything. How does that sound?"

Risky, James thought, but they didn't have many options to choose from. "All right, when we land, Trueman and I will scout the barracks, you keep the helicopter running and stay with the civilians. At the first sign of trouble you take off immediately. We have to keep them safe."

"Okay," Wright agreed. She tried the radio, attempting to contact anyone who might be listening, but jumbled chatter greeted their ears. Her lips pressed into a thin line as a look of anxiousness passed over her face, like a storm cloud dense with rain.

Even though he had only known her for a short period of time, James hadn't thought he would ever see her as anything less than calm and collected. Watching her eyes tighten was disconcerting as she tried the radio again, and again.

"You can't have thought anybody would reply," James said, watching the fire flare as it consumed another building.

She didn't look at him. "It's not just here. I can't get any kind of coherent response from *anywhere*. It's full of incomprehensible chatter. I don't understand. Has this crisis spread so far so fast the military has fallen apart?"

James's hands flexed on his weapon as alarm coursed through his bloodstream. It couldn't have. But then, the extent of the cover-up was massive. James thought the amount of infected had been well into the millions, climbing past the billion mark around the world.

James shoved his worries down and focused on the island. He couldn't afford to be distracted if there were infected on the ground. He hoped the other safe zones hadn't been overrun. A mixture of anticipation and nauseating anxiety rose within him like the roaring fire down below. He always felt the same way before a mission, had done ever since he'd been deployed for the first time at nineteen. The emotions were familiar to him. Comforting.

He checked his weapons and equipment first, then his body armour. He kept his L85 in perfect working order, as well as his secondary firearm, a semi-automatic pistol. He checked them both anyway. He always did. His heart hammered in his chest as he attached his blade to the weapon. He might be able to stab some infected people with the bayonet instead of using up bullets. As they approached the burning buildings, sweat prickled the back of his neck at the thought that he might never leave Thorney Island. *I hope I do. It would be a shite place to die.*

Flying low revealed a disturbing amount of dead bodies. Most were scattered around the island, but a large group were congregated around what looked like a warehouse. *This is the home of the 12 Regiment Royal Artillery. That must be where they keep their infantry vehicles.* It had yet to be reached by the flames, so James and Trueman would begin there.

Wright brought the Lynx down as close to the building as she could. The civilians were getting restless—they could see the fire, and they had noticed James and Trueman readying their weapons. Well, they would have to continue worrying. James had neither the time nor the inclination to hold their hands.

He jumped out of the cockpit, landing lightly on his feet. The freezing air bit into his skin after the stuffy confines of the helicopter, and his breath turned to mist in front of him as he moved up to the building, Trueman a shadow on his left.

The bodies grew more concentrated here, piled up against the massive doors. They looked to have been trying to claw their way in. To safety, or to attack those already inside? James leaned down to examine a body more closely. A sigh escaped as he saw blood-shot eyes staring from a twisted face, the man's teeth bared in a snarl. A human bite mark, all black and swollen, had gouged his shoulder. Dried blood formed a thick crust around the wound and the sweet smell of rot clogged up the air. The man had been put out of his misery with three shots to his chest and abdomen. James frowned. Those shots had been fired from behind. *Not the warehouse then. What happened here?*

Straightening up, he signalled Trueman forward to the doors. The man moved into position silently and waited for further orders. He seemed like a good soldier, from the little James had seen of him. A courteous man, his politeness bordering on old-fashioned. James edged up next to him and flexed his hands on the grip and barrel of his weapon, his heartbeat loud in his ears. Sucking in a deep breath, he nodded once, and Trueman pulled hard on the huge sliding door. It moved reluctantly, as if something pushed back against it. Once it was open enough for James to fit through, he darted in, levelling his weapon and crouching low.

All the lights were on, illuminating the entire interior. James blinked at the brightness, narrowing his eyes against the glare. *There goes my night vision.* He couldn't see any immediate threat. Silence filled the large space. Glancing down, he discovered what blocked the door. A body was jammed up against it, sitting in a pool of dried blood.

The woman had a sharpshooter rifle cradled in her lap and a semi-automatic pistol—identical to the one James had—lay next to her, which she had used to shoot herself in the head. She had to be, what, nineteen? Twenty? James felt a stab of regret for her, dead so young. He spotted a small bite on her wrist. She mustn't have wanted to live with the infection, like a rabid animal. Brave woman.

He motioned Trueman to move along the left side of the building while he moved up the right. James noted the numerous Alvis Stormers, all lined up along the left wall. He'd never seen so many at once before. Trueman meticulously checked around each one. There were several Land Rovers and two Stormers on James's side, all of which were unoccupied. The whole warehouse was devoid of life. James wiped a droplet of sweat away from his jaw. He frowned. Had it been this hot when they entered?

Trueman finished his side and walked over to James, shaking his head. James glared around the open space. *How did this happen? And so quickly? It's only been a day since the quarantines started to break. What kind of virus is this?* He had no answers.

The two soldiers moved to flank the single door at the end of the garage, directly opposite the massive sliding ones. It *was* getting hotter. They would have to hurry if they wanted to recover anything.

Trueman grabbed the handle and let go straight away, wincing as he flexed his hand. The smell of smoke reached James and he hesitated, frowning. The last thing he wanted was to get caught in a fire, especially one so out of control. But they needed fuel and supplies. After a quick internal debate with himself, James gave the order to open the door.

He immediately wished he hadn't. Thick smoke billowed straight into his face, making his throat raw and tears sting his eyes. The rush of oxygen fuelled the flames higher, and James and Trueman shied away from the heat.

Glowering, he signalled Trueman to fall back to the main entrance. They were too late. James knew their chances of salvaging anything had been slim to none, but it galled nonetheless. He didn't know what they were going to do. They were about to lose their best chance of survival. How well would they manage on foot?

They made their way back outside as smoke filled the large building. Breathing in a lungful of fresh air—as fresh as it could be with dead bodies surrounding them—it took James a moment to realise the helicopter hovered in the air instead of on the ground.

The Lynx's spotlight illuminated a small group of soldiers as they waved up at it. James lay down amongst the bodies, Trueman doing the same. The group didn't seem to have noticed them, which was fine with James. *These must have been who gunned down the infected.*

"Do we engage?" Trueman asked.

He counted ten men, all armed. He didn't fancy those odds, even with the element of surprise. Besides, they were all on the same side, right? More soldiers meant a better chance of fighting back. *What if they're infected?* Doubt seeped in, not unlike the cold stealing under his skin, and he paused. *Why are they out here instead of in the building with the woman?* Looking down his scope, James saw anger and desperation stamped across their faces. Never a good combination.

One of the wilder-looking men lifted his weapon and opened fire on the helicopter. Shock shot through James—was the man an idiot? He'd blown any chance the group might have had for help. James had to give credit the Wright—the pilot reacted quickly, pulling the aircraft further up in the air and angling it so any bullets ricocheted away.

James's mind had been made up for him. His orders were to protect the civilians against any threat. He felt dirty firing upon other members of the same army, but they were endangering everyone on board the helicopter. "Engage," he said, picking a target and squeezing the trigger.

James and Trueman neutralised four of the men before they realised they were under fire. When the penny dropped, the remaining six dived for cover behind their recently deceased friends. They were on a flat, open area; there was no other protection. James ducked his head down behind one of the dead infected as a wave of bullets burst open the bodies in front of him, blood spraying out. The smell was *awful*, and James held his breath as he returned fire, desperately searching for an opening. *Six on two. We need any kind of advantage we can get.*

Lying as flat as he could as another spray of bullets tore up the bodies around them, James glanced back to the warehouse. He didn't know how to operate a Stormer, but if they could get back in, they could take a Land Rover and escape that way. But black smoke churned through the doors, and James clenched his jaw as that option swirled into the night sky with the smoke.

"Sergeant," Trueman shouted, looking up.

James followed his gaze, fearing the worst, and frowned as the helicopter turned in mid-air. What were they doing?

The possibly infected woman sat on the floor of the helicopter, trying to aim an L85. She was doing a piss poor job of it. She looked as if she'd never handled a weapon in her life. *To be fair, she probably hasn't.* The kid tried to help, but he looked to be more of a hindrance than anything.

She couldn't aim, and it looked as if the kick-back from the weapon would do her serious damage, but none of it mattered when she opened fire on the rogue soldiers. She didn't hit any of them, but it was the distraction James needed.

The group scrambled to find better cover, leaving James and Trueman able to fire upon them unimpeded. As the last of the gunfire faded into ringing silence, James lay still, ready to fire again at the slightest hint of movement.

There wasn't any.

After several tense moments, he stood up. Slowly, carefully. Still nothing. Heart racing in his chest, he signalled Trueman to cover him as he edged forward.

He saw even before he reached the bodies the threat had been eliminated. Nine of them were dead, and the tenth lay dying, drowning in his own blood from a bullet to the throat. They wouldn't find out what had happened here from these men. Sighing, James waved Wright down, and she dropped the Lynx to the ground in one smooth motion.

He was upset it had ended like this. He didn't want to kill his fellow soldiers. He shouldn't have had to. What had they been thinking? Irrational anger boiled inside, followed by a wave of sadness that drowned the fury, leaving him deflated. There was no point in hating them. It was over. They had clearly been desperate past the point of rational thinking.

When he got back to the helicopter, James reached up and yanked the weapon out of the woman's hands before jumping back into the cockpit. He didn't want her to accidently shoot him with it. She glared at him as he did so, and he glared right back. She hadn't expected to keep it, had she? He put it next to his own, careful not to knock the cyclic stick as he removed his knife from the L85. He didn't want to accidently stab himself, either.

"You look like shit, Sunshine." Wright grinned at him as they lifted into the air once more.

A jolt like electricity fired through James, and he looked down at himself, frantically searching for blood. There were some dried stains from earlier in the day he hadn't had time to scrub clean, but at least it was blood from people who weren't infected. The last thing James wanted was to be covered in contaminated blood. He had a sudden and overwhelming urge to shower. He had laid down amongst those dead infected, after all. What if he had picked up the virus?

Wright must have seen his look of disgust because she started laughing at him. She wouldn't be laughing if she had been the one getting shot at whilst lying amongst dead bodies. *Actually,* he thought, remembering her earlier cheerfulness in the face of all the horror, *she would probably be cackling with glee.* Scowling, he sunk low into his seat, trying not to think about contracting horrible diseases.

Wright quietened, and they flew in silence for one blissful minute. James's heart rate and breathing returned to normal, but his hands still shook, as they always did after a firefight. He'd never let anyone see before, and he wasn't about to start now. Gripping his fists together, he held them down in his lap and stared as nonchalantly as he could out of the window, glad to get a few seconds of peace as he calmed himself down.

"So, are you not going to ask where we're going?" Wright asked, arching a perfectly plucked eyebrow and shattering said peace.

James frowned. Of course, he was going to ask. And about the woman firing at the soldiers. *Give me a chance to get my bearings,* he thought with a mental sigh. "Where are we going?"

"Glad you asked. While you and Trueman were off gallivanting around burning buildings, I came up with a brilliant solution to our little fuel problem." She looked proud of herself. "Not far from here is the Goodwood airfield, which I think is used for flying lessons. I'm a genius for remembering it. There's bound to be fuel there, and it's within range." She smiled her big smile at him. "Please, there's no need to applaud."

James rolled his eyes at her. He supposed it was worth a shot. It sounded like their only chance to keep the Lynx. "We have enough fuel to get us there, but that's it?"

"Yep."

"So, if it's like here, we've lost the helicopter? We can't fly anywhere else?"

"It sounds bad when you say it like that, but yes, that's the gist of it." Wright sighed and became serious for a moment. "We're out of fuel anyway. If we go to Goodwood, at least we have a chance of finding some more."

"All right, I agree. Goodwood it is." Wright nodded and opened her mouth to speak, but James jumped in first. "And I want to ask about potentially infected back there firing what I assume is your weapon?"

Wright didn't have the grace to look even slightly embarrassed. "Yeah, well, you two were in trouble, and while I can do most things, flying and firing my weapon at the same time isn't one of them. I think she did a fine job." Wright shrugged.

"You gave a civilian an L85 and told her to fire upon soldiers. I doubt she's ever even held a handgun, let alone fired a—"

"Oh, get off your high horse, Mollino," Wright cut in. "You were pinned down and I was in no position to help, so I did the next best thing. In case you haven't noticed, the whole fucking world is coming apart at the seams. Nobody is going to care about a random civilian shooting at crazy soldiers. I highly doubt anyone will ever find out, anyway. I still haven't been able to break through all the random noise blocking the radio."

James didn't know what to say, so he stayed silent. It wasn't that he was ungrateful, because he *was* glad she distracted the soldiers. It was... he didn't know. She wasn't a soldier, and she shouldn't have to be responsible for anyone's life. That was his, Wright's, and Trueman's job.

"Look, I'm very grateful she did what she did. I didn't mean to come across as a bastard," James apologised. "I guess it's because she's not trained for this, and something could have gone wrong. She shouldn't have to be the one to protect us."

"None of us are really trained for anything like this, Mollino," Wright replied, understanding shining in her big dark eyes as she glanced at him. "I suspect difficult times are ahead, and they'll all need to toughen up."

She echoed his earlier thoughts back to him. Mulling over her words, James realised she was right. He couldn't shelter them from everything. Nodding to himself, he settled down into his seat and told himself if they couldn't get in touch with anyone soon, if they didn't find a safe place somewhere, he would try to train them in basic survival skills and hand-to-hand combat. He could at least give them a fighting chance in this mad new world.

Chapter Six

Jennifer wanted everything to be all right with a desperation so strong she almost buckled under its weight. They would fly to safety and she would be able to pick herself back up and put herself back together. But no. That would be too easy.

Wherever they had been going had gone up in flames, her hopes burned to ash along with it. The ever-present emptiness loomed close by, assaulting her relentlessly after seeing safety burn. It stole her laughter and left only tears in its wake. She pushed it back with a firm hand, refusing to let it take anymore of her. The thought of Evelyn and her friends and family was like a knife in her chest, but it gave her the energy to resist. She would be strong for them.

She couldn't believe what she had done. She'd *fired a gun*. Nausea churned in her gut at the thought of it. Had she hit someone? Was she a murderer? She pressed a hand to her stomach, attempting to calm her nerves. She winced as she moved her arm—it burned like nothing she'd felt before. Her head pounded as well, and her whole body ached. She wanted to curl up somewhere and sleep for about ten years.

Sweat drenched the soldier with the goatee. What happened down on the ground? Jennifer didn't think she wanted to know. She still shook from shooting the gun. Clenching her hands into fists, she breathed in a deep lungful of air.

Dan had his eyes closed next to her. Tension warped his face, making him look older than his fourteen years. Jennifer nudged him and offered a thumbs up. *I wish we could hear each other.* He attempted a smile, but it looked more like a grimace. She understood. Was anywhere safe anymore?

Dropping her hands into her lap and clutching her camera, Jennifer got comfortable in her seat again—she didn't know how long she was going to be there. She caught the eye of the soldier sitting next to her. He wiped the sweat from his long face. Raising his eyebrows in a question, he mouthed, *'Are you okay?'* Her grip tightened on her camera. Did they think she had virus? *Did* she have it? She couldn't remember if the man had bitten her or not, but she didn't feel well. The banging in her head showed no sign of abating, and nausea twisted her stomach around itself in such a way she had to take deep breaths so she didn't vomit everywhere. Still, she didn't want them to suspect anything was amiss, so she fixed a fake smile on her face and nodded. She hoped he bought it. He gave no indication of what he thought, folding his arms as he closed his eyes and leaned his head back.

She let out a shaky breath as she sank further into her seat, trying to make herself small. Evelyn had been bitten, and they hadn't even tried to help her. She could still hear the gunshot ringing through the cold air, still see her friend drop to the hard ground. Were they going to shoot her as well? Her stomach roiled—she *really* felt like she was going to throw up.

She sat for a while, numb, not thinking about anything as the queasiness battered her. If she could open her chest and reach inside, would she still find a beating heart? She felt so tired. Worn down. She hadn't known it was possible to feel so hollow.

It wasn't until the helicopter banked that she became aware of her surroundings once more. Twisting to look out the cockpit window, she saw a little airport lit up against the dark, a row of small planes lined up next to each other on the frosted grass. *There must still be electricity here.* The helicopter flew around the buildings once before landing. The soldiers prepared their weapons, and Jennifer drew in a large breath. Why were they at an airport? Did they need to change helicopters?

The pilot powered down the engine. *What's going on?* The rotatory blades kept spinning, refusing to still for a few moments. The pilot motioned for everyone to remove the bulky headsets so they could hear her address them.

"Listen up, people. The helicopter is out of fuel, so we need to get some more. Sergeant Mollino and Corporal Trueman will be busy covering us, so I'll need three volunteers to get the fuel hose." She pinned them all with an intense stare. "Anyone?"

Jennifer looked around. Nobody moved. Dan looked to her to see what she would do. An Indian couple at the back looked terrified, clutching at each other's hands. A long-nosed man with curly brown hair stared down at his feet, refusing to meet anybody's eyes.

A beautiful woman rose to her feet, her blonde hair tumbling down around a face flushed with determination. She looked like she'd returned from a trip to the hairdresser's. *How is that even possible?* Jennifer's own hair was no doubt a mess. The woman raised her chin, steel in her eyes. "I'll help," she said in a quiet but firm voice.

The pilot nodded at her. "Anyone else? I'm going to start picking if no one offers."

Dan looked from Jennifer to the blonde woman and back again, before he stood up as well. "I, erm, I'll help."

Jennifer gave a quiet sigh. She couldn't let him go out there alone. What if there were infected people? She stood up on shaky legs, but as she opened her mouth to speak, the pilot scowled at her. "Are you infected?" she asked bluntly, her obsidian eyes flashing. Jennifer started to worry about getting shot again—if looks could kill she would be six feet under.

"No, I'm not," she said. Her instincts screamed at her not to show any kind of doubt—it would mean the end of her life if she did. Everyone stared at her with fear and distrust plastered all over their faces. "I'm *not,*" she said again, daring them to disagree.

The pilot chuckled. "You've got fire in you, I'll give you that. But if I find out you're lying, I will not hesitate to kill you myself." Jennifer's mouth went dry as she nodded her understanding. The pilot's sudden smile did not reach her eyes. "I'm glad we understand one another. I'll check you over properly later. Right now, we need to get fuel."

"Okay, Wright. We have to move. We have company," the Scottish man—Sergeant Mollino, Jennifer supposed—

said. She followed his gaze and saw two people moving toward the helicopter.

The pilot—Wright—cursed. "I didn't see anyone from the air. They must have been in the buildings, sheltering from the cold."

"Go get the fuel now." Sergeant Mollino jumped out of the helicopter and started firing. As soon as he opened the door, a blast of icy air rushed in, prompting a shiver out of Jennifer. Corporal Trueman followed him, heaving open the sliding door and moving to cover the other side of the helicopter.

"Everyone who volunteered, follow me. Those who didn't, stay in the Lynx. It's the safest place to be right now." The pilot hopped gracefully out of the cockpit. Jennifer's breaths came in short gasps as terror clogged up veins. *Why did I volunteer?* Sergeant Mollino killed the two infected people and scanned the area for more. *How is he so relaxed?* Jennifer felt moments away from fainting.

She jumped out, landing on hard mud, and jogged over to where Wright waited, Dan and the blonde woman close on her heels. Jennifer was surprised at how slight the pilot was—Jennifer's five foot six easily overshadowed her. The woman's attitude made her seem much larger than her small stature.

"Okay, there's the fuel." Sergeant Wright pointed at a large white truck ahead of them. "I need one of you to unhook the fuel hose and the other two to drag it back to the Lynx. Can you do that?" They all nodded, their heads bobbing in tandem. "Good, let's go."

They set off at a run. Jennifer cursed as she jostled her camera. She should have left it in the cabin. *Oh God, what was I thinking?*

They made it to the truck in no time, and Jennifer jumped up and grabbed the massive nozzle, fumbling as she removed the restraints. A loud burst of gunfire startled her, and she dropped the hose in shock.

"Keep going," Wright shouted as she gunned down another infected person. Jennifer scrambled to pull more of the hose out as Dan and the blonde woman seized the nozzle and hauled it over to the helicopter.

The deafening sound of gunfire rang all around as infected people ran out of the buildings. They yelled wordlessly, suspicion and anger etched onto their faces. Some of them even attacked each other. Did the disease make people distrust everyone?

Jennifer's breath stuttered in her airways as the pilot edged back to the helicopter, leaving her to feed the hose out alone. Wright hesitated as Jennifer shot her a horrified look. "I'm the only one who can attach the hose. Don't worry, I'll keep an eye on you."

Jennifer wasn't comforted at all.

*

James thought Wright's words were a little harsh, but he didn't disagree with what she said. If the woman *was* lying to them about being infected, she would need to be killed in order to ensure the safety of the rest of the group. He hoped she wasn't. It would be demoralising for everyone to see an unarmed person executed so coldly.

He hadn't seen anybody from the air, but he kept watch for any movement regardless. Better to be safe than sorry. He gave the buildings another once over—they couldn't afford to miss anything. *What was that?* Turning his head to his left, James saw two people push away from the side of a building. They looked infected. Paranoia engraved itself into their postures, their movements, their expressions.

"Okay, Wright. We have to move, we have company."

Wright swore. "I didn't see anyone from the air. They must have been in the buildings, sheltering from the cold." *She's probably annoyed she can't see through walls,* James thought.

"Go get the fuel now," he said as he jumped down onto the frozen ground. Levelling his weapon and taking his time to aim, he neutralised both threats before they got too close. *I have shite luck, so there's probably more where they came from.* His heart hammered in his chest as adrenaline surged anew through him, strengthening his muscles and heightening his senses. He didn't let his fear show as he scanned around the left side of the helicopter. Trueman would be covering the right. The civilian's needed to see the soldiers calm and in control. It wouldn't do to panic them. His back itched with sweat despite the cold, and he glimpsed the three volunteers as they passed him on their way to Wright. The brunette glanced his way, her face pale with fear. Still, she was brave to help. They all were.

James glared about the airfield as he strained to pick up any sound. He couldn't even hear any wildlife. Maybe those two were the only infected people here. Maybe they could refuel and be back in the air before any more shite came flying their way. James held back a snort at his wishful thinking.

Shots to his left. Wright. Glancing over, he saw her eliminate two infected and yell at the civilians to keep working. He considered going over to help but disregarded the thought before it fully formed. Wright was more than capable of handling herself. Besides, he had his own problems to deal with. Five infected people barrelled out through a door ahead of him, screaming '*Leave me alone!*' and '*I'll kill you before you kill me!*' and other things James wasn't able to make out. *This virus really rips sanity to shreds.* They were all confused, paranoid, and violent. The urge to bite was said to be overwhelming. He hoped he never experienced it.

He opened fire on them, cutting them down as they ran straight at him. James didn't know what he felt as they fell, blood spraying around them. Pity? Sympathy? He shouldn't feel sorry for them—they were trying to infect or kill him after all. But they were just sick people who had no real control over themselves anymore. Clenching his jaw, he pushed the thought aside as more burst through another door.

*

One of them ran straight at Jennifer. Panic held her in a vice like grip, keeping her rooted to the spot. *Oh God, oh shit.* What could she do? She didn't have any kind of weapon. The man drew closer with every second she stood there staring at him like an idiot. The other night materialised in her mind, her friends running for their lives, Rachel standing in the middle of the road as she was attacked and killed. She didn't want that to happen to her. Jennifer's earlier resolve to go out fighting sharply reasserted itself, and she clenched her fists as the man growled at her.

He reached out to grab her. *Oh God, what am I doing?* With a scream, she swung her fist in a wide arc, somehow connecting with his cheek. Pain shot through her hand and she knew she'd broken some fingers, but it was more than worth it as the man staggered back, knocked off balance by her desperate attack.

He straightened, a nasty cut bleeding where she'd hit him. A blast of fierce pride burst through her upon seeing it, and she had no control over the wide grin splitting her face. She steadied herself against the truck, lifted her leg back, and kicked him between the legs with as much force as she could muster. He fell hard to the ground.

Her breaths came in sharp gasps as she regained her senses. Holy shit, she'd never felt so *alive*. Laughter bubbled up, and she did nothing to hold it back. A distant part of her knew it bordered on hysterical, but she didn't care. She was *alive*. She'd gone up against death and won.

The cold air burned her lungs as she gulped it down. She jumped down from her perch on the truck as thunderous gunfire erupted next to her, killing an infected woman she hadn't noticed. Jennifer fell back onto frosty grass, letting out a small gasp. Thick blood and bits of bone and flesh slid down the side of the truck, painting a ghastly picture. Wright lowered her weapon, raising an eyebrow at her as a smirk played about her mouth.

"You okay down there in the mud?"

Jennifer could only nod. She'd forgotten about all the other dangers around, so caught up in her little victory. *Idiot!* Her stomach rebelled and she retched, the nausea swelling to a crescendo she couldn't stop. She hadn't had anything to eat in about a day, so bile was the sole thing to make an appearance.

Wright's face twisted. "Gross." She hopped up onto the truck and fiddled with some switches. A whirring sound reached Jennifer's ears and fuel started flowing through the hose.

The man Jennifer knocked down stirred, but Wright shot him before he was able to get up again. Warm blood splattered Jennifer's torso as she struggled to her feet, and her stomach clenched again. God, it felt like someone had carved onto her torso. Wright shoved her toward the helicopter, and she stumbled, almost losing her footing. The damn pilot was stronger than she looked. "Get on board. I'll finish up here. And clean the infected blood off you."

Jennifer didn't need to be told twice. She broke out into a run, making sure she didn't trip and fall. As she let herself believe she would to make it, a short man came barrelling out of nowhere and tackled her to the ground. Not thinking, she shoved her left hand into the man's face, aiming for his eyes while her broken right hand pushed against his chin, desperately trying to keep his mouth closed.

He howled and grabbed both of her wrists, yanking her hands away from him. He was *so* much stronger than her. "You won't get me, bitch. You won't get me," he snarled as he pinned her down.

Jennifer strained against his hold, but he wasn't budging as he shifted more of his weight onto her. Fear flooded through her as he leaned down to bite her, saliva dripping onto her cheek. *I'm going to die. I'm going to die.* She didn't know what to do. He was going to bite her. Infect her. Kill her. Fury rose up, igniting her nerves and twisting her face. She would *not* die. Bracing herself against the pain, Jennifer head butted him as hard as she could. She felt his nose break, and blood spurted out into her face. Oh God, into her *mouth*.

Shoving him off her as he clutched at his ruined nose, Jennifer scrambled away on all fours. She spit out blood and wiped it off her face with a ferociousness she'd never known. *Oh God. Fuck!* Had she swallowed some? Her throat burned with the memory of bile.

Gunfire still rang out all around as she pushed herself up onto unsteady feet. She backed away from the short man and almost tripped over the fuel hose in her haste. She followed it up to the helicopter, never taking her eyes off the man as he heaved himself to his feet and lurched after her. Jennifer reached the cabin but made no move to climb up.

"*Jennifer.*" Dan's voice. It sounded far away.

Hands reached down to help her, but she pulled away from them. She couldn't go up yet; she had to keep the short man away.

She didn't know what she was thinking. She didn't know how she would keep him away. He was stocky, muscular. He outweighed her. But she had to try. She couldn't let him get to the cabin. Her hand, shoulder, and head ached. Fire raced along her arm. She couldn't win a fight against him. Her thoughts became sluggish, like she had to pull them through tar to make sense of them. Sweat dripped into her eyes, making them sting as she blinked them clear. What was she doing? The man came ever closer. Almost within touching distance. He was going to bite her. Infect her. Kill her.

A loud bang sounded, and the short man's head exploded, showering the helicopter in blood and brain. Jennifer flinched as some of the warm liquid sprayed onto her.

"Get up! Go!" The deep voice had an accent, but Jennifer couldn't say what. She looked around in confusion. Who was shouting? She didn't like shouting. Jennifer cringed away as rough hands grasped her and hauled her to the helicopter. She started to struggle—she had to get *away*.

"Hey! Why are you fighting me? We need to go."

Jennifer knew he was lying. He wanted to hurt her. She redoubled her efforts to escape his grip. She was almost free. A little more... *almost*... a sharp pain lanced through her head, then nothing.

Chapter Seven

James emptied his third magazine. There were *so many* infected. Where were they all coming from? There must have been a breached quarantine zone nearby, and they were being drawn by the helicopter and gunfire. It was the only explanation he could think of.

James didn't have time to reload as a woman launched herself at him, clawing and screaming, spittle flying everywhere. He grabbed his knife and brought it up in the nick of time, sinking it into her neck. Warmth flowed over his hand as he wrenched the knife out and shoved the dead body away. He didn't have time to worry about the contaminated blood as another woman jumped at him. James swung his left arm up to block her whilst shoving the knife into her stomach. She fell back as a man grabbed his uniform, jerking James around to face him. James kicked one of the man's legs out from under him and stabbed him in the throat as he crashed to one knee.

There was a brief lull, allowing James to slam another magazine home. Gritting his teeth, he lifted the weapon and fired into the horde of infected. There were too many. With every one he felled, two clambered over the body, yelling and screaming, their eyes wide with madness.

He glanced over his shoulder to check on the fuel situation. The hose was attached. *Good*. A fleeting glimpse was all he could manage as two men almost knocked him to the ground. *Pay attention*. They were within his reach. His L85 dangled down his side as he elbowed one of them in the face and kicked the other in the shin. He jumped away and brought his weapon up, shooting them both before they could recover.

They needed to leave, *now*, whether they had enough fuel or not. James fired some more into the howling wall before turning and running back to the helicopter. The brunette woman stood face to face with a stocky infected man. *What is she thinking?* Blood was smeared across her face and body. *Fuck! If she wasn't infected before, she probably is now*. She had a glazed look in her eyes, almost as if she herself didn't know what she was doing.

James shot the man before he could bite the woman, and the spray of blood further added to her gruesome look. "Get up! Go!" James grabbed her arm and shoved her toward the cabin. She started to struggle. "Hey! Why are you fighting me? We need to go!" She struggled harder. What was wrong with her? Had the stress caused her to snap? *We don't have time for this*. He hit her hard in the head with the butt of his weapon and caught her before she dropped like a stone to the cold ground.

With the help of the scrawny kid and a blonde woman with blue eyes even more striking than the brunette's, he managed to haul the woman's unconscious body up onto the cabin floor. Jumping up so he sat next to her head close to the cockpit, James emptied the remainder of his clip, felling six infected. His ammunition had dropped dangerously low.

Wright appeared in the pilot seat, her hands a blur as she switched everything back on. "Fuel hose is disengaged. Let's hope the tank is full enough," she said.

Trueman came running around the back of the Lynx, four infected hot on his heels. The second he shot past the cabin, James opened fire with his pistol, cutting them down with little effort as they ran into the bullets. Trueman dived into the cockpit alongside Wright, and the rotary blades started moving. *This is taking too long.* James shot another two infected before he gave up. He stood and rammed the door shut as three people slammed into the helicopter, the thuds resounding around the cabin.

"Can't you go any faster?" he shouted at Wright.

She ignored him, continuing to press buttons and flick switches.

James clenched his jaw as two more crashes reverberated through the helicopter. The civilians were terrified. Tears flowed freely down a curly-haired man's cheeks and panic reflected in a couple's eyes.

James's breathing came in harsh gasps as the Lynx finally lifted off the ground. Looking out of the cockpit window, he saw about a hundred infected people running around and attacking each other. *Fucking hell.* He couldn't believe they'd been down amidst such madness. He closed his eyes and leaned back against the door, trying and failing to get his breathing under control. He needed to show the civilians everything was all right. Put on a brave face. Why couldn't he slow his racing heart?

He felt a soft tap on his arm. Opening his eyes, James saw the skinny kid looking up at him. A crushing weight heaved itself onto his shoulders—*time to take charge again*. Time to be strong for them. He took a deep breath and wet his dry lips before giving the boy his full attention.

The kid pointed at the unconscious brunette and at the three empty seats. *He wants to put her on the seats instead of the floor.* James nodded. He lifted her by her shoulders as the kid lifted her legs. Once she was settled, the boy bobbed his head in thanks and put a headset on both himself and the woman before he sank down to the floor. The kid proceeded to close his eyes and shut himself away from everyone.

James decided to take a leaf out of the boy's book and sat on the floor as well, leaning back against the door. His heart rate finally slowed to a normal pace, as did his breathing.

He balled his hands into fists. He had almost died. There had been so many—James had been fighting for his life. It wasn't a new notion to him. He had been in the army for fifteen years after all, having joined as soon as he turned eighteen. But this had been different. Before, he had fought against people who had their own weapons and orders. People who were in control of their faculties.

Down there, chaos reigned. James had been trying to push back against a screaming horde that wanted nothing more than to tear him apart. The sight of them running and yelling at him, murder in their faces, had left him feeling cold and numb, like he'd never feel life's heat again. The smell of their blood clung to him like a foul aftershave. He could almost taste it, the sticky warmth cooling against his skin. It coated his right hand, the drying blood acting like a glue between his fingers to the point he had trouble opening it. James rubbed his hand against his leg in a futile attempt to wipe it clean, but all he achieved was a bloody handprint on his trousers. He pulled out his water container and washed as best he could with what he had. He would have to hope it was enough. The desire to scrub himself raw arose once more, stronger this time.

James looked around the cabin, trying to distract himself from the cold burrowing deep in his bones. The kid still had his eyes closed, drawing in deep breaths before shakily releasing them. James hoped he was okay. The young couple at the back were still holding each other's hands, the woman resting her head on the man's shoulder. James met his deep brown eyes, strain drawing lines around them. The man nodded at him. James's spirits lifted somewhat. He had protected the civilians. They were all still alive and healthy. His eyes fell on the brunette he'd knocked out. *At least I think they're all healthy.*

Blood spattered her face like a horrific mask. Even though she remained unconscious, a frown marred her face, and her breathing was a wee bit erratic. James's brow furrowed as he continued observing her. She looked worse for wear, all battered and bruised. He was pretty sure two of her fingers were broken, the surrounding skin and knuckles darkened by bruises. Her hair clung to her neck with sweat. Her eyes were closed, and he wondered if they still held the dazed look he'd seen before he'd introduced her to the butt of his weapon. Coming to a decision, James stood up and moved over to check her arm. He trusted Trueman's judgement, but he needed to see it for himself.

Kneeling next to her and moving the camera—which sported its fair share of blood and scratches as well—James lifted her arm up, careful not to wake her. The skin was torn from mid forearm to mid upper arm, with the elbow looking the worst. James thought she must have fallen on it and scraped it against the ground at some point. He couldn't spot any teeth marks amongst all the scrapes and redness.

But there, below her elbow, several marks looked inflamed. James leaned even closer as unease flashed up his spine. Were they teeth marks? He couldn't tell. He pressed a couple of fingers to the skin. *Hot to the touch. Definitely infected.* He withdrew his hand when her face twisted into a grimace and she pulled her arm away a little. He didn't want to wake her up by prodding at it.

He pressed a hand to her forehead. *Burning up. Shite. What are the symptoms again?* She had a fever, which was one. He couldn't ask her if she felt tired or if she had lost her appetite. Sweat dampened her hair, but she didn't seem to be producing excess saliva. She had appeared confused before he'd knocked her out. James assumed she had panicked, but maybe his assessment had been hasty. Confusion, paranoia and aggression were all symptoms of the latter stages of the disease, which deteriorated into insanity. He leaned back and took in her blood-spattered face and body. Even if she didn't already have the virus, it was likely she would get it, encased in so much infected blood. They would need to clean her up or risk the rest of the group.

With a sigh, he sat back against the door. "Wright, you were with the brunette woman getting the fuel. Did you notice any signs she could be infected?"

Wright hummed over the comms. "Well, she did throw up. It was disgusting."

I forgot about nausea and vomiting being symptoms. Get it together, James. "I think she's infected," he said.

"What?" Wright's bark was loud in his ear.

"She has a fever, she's sweating, and you said she was sick. Before we took off, she was acting confused, like she didn't know where she was. They're all classic symptoms, right?" James wanted to be sure she had the infection before he had to shoot her. His throat felt like a desert.

"I didn't find any bite marks on her arm," Trueman said, twisting in his seat to look at the woman.

"No, I didn't either. But you were right. A part of her arm certainly looks infected." James paused, an idea forming in his mind. "What if she wasn't bitten, exactly, but she did come into contact with an infected person's mouth? What if she, say, elbowed someone in the face, and their teeth grazed her arm? It would blend in well with all the other cuts and scratches."

"It's possible," Wright said. "Shit. We're going to have to kill her. After she helped us with the fuel and everything." She sounded more angry than upset.

Trueman studied the brunette. "I can't see any excess saliva. You said she was confused?" He looked to James for confirmation, who nodded. "I thought increased saliva production came before any mental symptoms?"

James frowned. From what he could remember of the lecture he'd had on the virus, that sounded right. Moving back over to her, he looked at her arm again. It was red and swollen, but he couldn't see any black. The initial bite wound always started to undergo necrosis, usually around the time the person started drooling from all the spit they were producing. "The wound's not going black yet either."

"So, she's not slobbering all over the place and there's no necrosis? What does that mean?" Wright sounded as confused as James felt. All infected people presented with the same symptoms in the same order. The only variation from person to person was the timing. James gritted his teeth. He didn't know enough about diseases and biology to understand what these differences meant.

"Can we be sure she's infected with *the* virus?" Trueman asked, giving up his study of the woman and facing forward again. "Could it be something else?"

James heard Wright sigh. "We need a doctor. Or someone who knows the virus inside out."

"Any luck with the radio?" James hoped she'd made contact with somebody. Maybe they could find a scientist somewhere.

"Actually, yes," she replied, her entire countenance brightening.

Relief tore through him, leaving him shocked by its intensity. He realised then how much he relied on the military, on its solid structure and unyielding nature. The military was his anchor. He had felt adrift when they weren't able to get a coherent response out of all the noise.

"The message was broadcast when we were down at the airfield." Wright's voice carried clearly over the comms, and James sat up straighter, hoping she had an answer to all their problems. "It said, and I'm paraphrasing here, it said one hundred and six out of one hundred and eleven quarantine zones have been breached across the British Isles. All military personnel are to begin evacuating civilians to either the safe zones we've set up, naval vessels at sea, or mainland Europe. I'm thinking France, as not only is it the closest, but I don't trust the safe zones. Any one of them could have infected people slip through the net and devastate it. Look at Thorney Island, and that was supposed to be a small zone. So, we fly to France, re-group, find out what's going on in the UK and the rest of the world, and go from there."

Flying to France? James did *not* like the idea of leaving the UK.

Wright must have sensed his reluctance. "It's not like we're abandoning our countries." James started—could she read his mind? "Like I said, we'll regroup, come back over here in force and with a much more cohesive plan, as the original one was shit, and kill all of the infected. We'll be done in time for tea." James could hear the grin in her voice.

He frowned at the back of her head. Regrouping and getting more information sounded appealing, but leaving the UK?

"Why France?" Leaving tasted too much like defeat.

"Were you even listening to what I just said?" Wright sounded exasperated. "Besides, orders are orders."

Well, James couldn't argue with that. He continued to frown at both Wright and Trueman even though they couldn't see him. "Fine," he muttered. "But just so you know, I don't like it."

"France it is, then," Wright said, making no change to the Lynx's direction. Which meant they were already flying there. James's frown deepened into a scowl as he tried to get comfortable on the hard cabin floor. Who knew how long it would take to get to France?

Chapter Eight

Victoria didn't dare take her eyes off the unconscious woman. Ever since the pilot demanded to know if she had the virus, Victoria had been wary. She had seen first-hand what the awful virus did to people. It had taken her fiancé from her. It had taken her sister. Victoria had grieved for them, even after what happened. The gaping wound they'd left had hardened into scar tissue, and she'd long since realised time would never heal it completely. Now, Victoria was mostly angry. Angry at a bloody virus, at the government for covering it up, at scientists for not yet finding a cure. Angry at the people sick with it, and the people who lied about being infected.

The liars most of all.

So, she kept watch as Sergeant Mollino examined the woman, moving a camera out of the way as he picked up her arm. She would not be caught off guard again. Not like before. If this woman lied about being infected, Victoria didn't want to think about what could happen.

The sergeant started talking to the other two soldiers, but Victoria didn't know what they were saying. Did the soldiers think the rest of them would panic if they understood everything? The assumption annoyed her—they didn't know what she had been through. She could handle it. She had already hit rock bottom. The only way left was up.

The soldiers stopped talking, and the expression on Sergeant Mollino's face said he wasn't happy about whatever they discussed. He sat back against the door and pulled out a knife, scowling as he attempted to clean it. He didn't seem concerned about the unconscious woman. *Maybe she's not infected.* Victoria mentally rolled her eyes. *Yeah right. I'm going to keep a close eye on her until I find out the truth.*

Studying the blood-stained woman, Victoria leaned back a little, keeping as far away from her as she could. A pang of sorrow shot through her. Splattered with so much infected blood, the woman would most certainly get the disease if she didn't already have it, and the soldiers would have to kill her. She wondered why they hadn't already. It was a risk being in such close proximity to her.

The woman's pale face scrunched up in an expression of pain, her small nose wrinkling as her lips peeled back over her teeth. Victoria felt ill simply looking at her. *Poor woman.* She noted her torn arm and bruised hands and thought of how lucky she was to have pulled through unscathed. Physically, at least.

Deciding the woman was no immediate threat passed out across the seats, Victoria moved to sit down herself. Stretching her legs out in front of her, she slowly released the tension from her muscles, not realising how wound up she had been. She hadn't slept most of the night before and dragging a massive hose over to the helicopter when infected people were on top of them had been both stressful and demanding, physically and mentally, and Victoria felt drained.

Rubbing the back of her neck and missing the way Mike used to do it, she became aware of eyes on her. Their owner blinked when she looked up, like he hadn't expected her to notice. He offered up a shaky smile, causing his stubbled face to scrunch up. Victoria didn't return the smile. The curly-haired man had been a whining fool back at Knightsbridge, and she didn't have time for those types of people.

She turned away from him and studied the interior of the helicopter instead, desperate to keep her mind from falling back to the last few months. Everything about the cabin was uninspired, from the dull grey walls to the dull grey seats to the dull grey floor. The cockpit was much more interesting. There were so many different dials and switches and screens, Victoria felt a new respect for the pilot. She'd never thought about learning to fly. She couldn't afford flying lessons on an English teacher's salary, especially with a mortgage to pay. It would be a good skill to learn, however. Maybe she would be able get lessons when everything settled down.

There was nothing to do. She didn't have anything to distract her from her swirling thoughts, so she turned her mind to the future instead, reluctant to fall into the past's clutches. Irritation spiked at the thought of the soldiers not telling them anything. *Yeah, they're helping us, but they're also keeping secrets. We should know where we're going, at least.* A small jolt of alarm burst through her, freezing her muscles and stilling her breath. *What if they don't know themselves? What if we're flying blind, hoping we'll end up somewhere that's halfway decent?*

No. She had to think positively. They had a plan. They knew what they were doing.

She couldn't sit still any longer. Standing up, Victoria returned to her self-appointed vigil of the unconscious woman, trying not to remember the last time she'd been this close to someone who had been infected. *Damn it, Katherine, why did you do it? I was your bloody sister.* Katherine had been a headstrong woman, always going after what she wanted. It killed her in the end.

The woman shifted. Victoria's heart picked up pace in her chest, so much so it felt moments away from breaking out of its bony cage. The woman didn't wake up. She moved to a more comfortable position. *Moron.* Victoria felt a little foolish for getting so worked up. What was she even going to do when the woman did wake up? Punch her unconscious again? Her sister's face flashed in her mind's eye, sneering and snarling. She wouldn't be caught off guard, not anymore.

Her skin prickled. Lifting her gaze from the brunette woman, she met the eyes of Sergeant Mollino. A remarkable green, visible even in the dim cabin. He pointed at the unconscious woman and gave Victoria a thumbs up. Did that mean she wasn't infected, or the soldier didn't want to her to worry? She didn't know. And it looked like Victoria wasn't about to find out anytime soon. She didn't know how long they were going to be flying. Victoria looked around, hoping something would catch her eye. Corporal Trueman seemed to be dozing when Victoria glanced at the cockpit again.

A sudden beeping sounded throughout the helicopter. The quiet noise seemed deafening in the small space, and the pilot moved with an urgency that betrayed the seriousness of the alarm. Victoria's stomach dropped.

She saw Sergeant Mollino's face pinch as he spoke to the pilot, and again annoyance mingled with her worry at not knowing anything. The helicopter banked, and a swooping sensation filled her stomach as they lowered to the ground. *What's going on?*

Once they landed, the pilot powered down the helicopter like she had back at the little airport, and a rush of adrenaline washed away Victoria's lingering exhaustion. Was this going to be the same as before? Running and fighting for their lives as infected people bore down on them? Victoria wouldn't go down without a fight. She had won before, and she would win again.

Sergeant Mollino and Corporal Trueman jumped out, moving in tandem like a well-oiled machine. Sergeant Wright motioned for them to remove their headsets.

"Bad news, people," the pilot sighed. "We're out of fuel. In all the chaos of Goodwood airfield, we mustn't have put enough in. Either that or a stray bullet hit the tank somewhere. Fuck me, what a waste of time."

A pressure built up behind Victoria's eyes. They were stranded who knew where, and that bloody awful virus turned people into monsters. She had to take a deep breath lest she start screaming.

"Everybody out," Sergeant Wright said as she leaned over and prodded the unconscious woman awake.

She jerked upright, looking around wildly until she got her bearings. Victoria's fight or flight response kicked in. She was ready to defend herself if the woman started attacking them. Instead, she sighed and followed the boy out of the helicopter. *I guess she's not showing signs yet.* Victoria would be watchful.

She hopped down and followed everyone to a group of trees.

A road and buildings stretched beyond the helicopter. A town? Victoria looked around and saw they were gathered in a field of yellow grass and hard mud, surrounded by bare forests on the left and right. The field cut the forest in two, leading away from the town like a rural yellow brick road. The tall trees were solid and reassuring, the air still, almost peaceful. Despite all the crap they had been through, calm soaked through her bones and cleared her swirling thoughts.

She saw Sergeant Mollino and the pilot silhouetted against the dark shadow of the helicopter. They were deep in discussion, and they both seemed on edge. She didn't blame them. She hadn't stepped back from the edge in a long time. Was the brunette woman taking a picture of them? This wasn't a damned art show.

Sergeant Mollino turned back to everyone. "Okay, this is the situation," he said in a serious tone. Victoria felt a grimness settle around the group. Everyone looked so tired and solemn. "We've lost our best asset—" *at least he's not sugar-coating it* "—but we can't dwell on that. We have to keep going. There's an air base we were flying to, so we're going to walk the rest of the way. It's not far from here."

"What if there are infected people at this air base?" the Indian woman asked. "What if we don't even make it there?" she added, frowning as she looked to the soldiers for answers.

The two sergeants shared a look, the pilot shrugging. "Look, I'm going to be straight with you all. We don't know what the fuck is happening, and we need to find out as much as we can. We're going to go to the base to gather information. We'll protect you."

"Where are we?"

The weak voice belonged to the brunette woman. Victoria watched her with narrowed eyes—she was pale and sweaty, but her eyes shone with lucidity. Victoria remembered another set of bright eyes, except they had been filled with nothing but madness. Shaking the image from her mind, she focused on the soldier's answer.

"We're in Northern France," Sergeant Mollino said, shooting a glare at Sergeant Wright, one she either ignored or didn't notice. Shock stabbed into Victoria. *France? What are we doing in France?* She didn't get a chance to ask though, as Sergeant Mollino turned to the brunette woman, eyeing her the same way Victoria had. "How are you feeling?"

Everyone stared at her. They hadn't forgotten the pilot's interrogation at the small airport. Victoria saw the same questions running through their minds—*is she infected? Is she dangerous?* The need to know tore through Victoria as well. The woman didn't miss all the wary looks everyone threw her way, but instead of wilting under their mistrustful gazes, she stood a little straighter and glared right back at everyone. Victoria admired that, even if she was infected.

"Honestly? I don't know."

The other civilians shied back from her as one, as if they expected her to go wild at any moment and kill them all. *Bloody idiots.* The kid's look of betrayal made Victoria wonder about their story.

"I feel terrible. My arm is killing me. My head feels like it's going to explode. I feel sick, tired. I remember getting very confused and scared, but that's passed now." She threw Sergeant Mollino a look filled with hurt, of all things. *As if he had any other option other than knocking her out.* "I don't know what the symptoms are. *God*, I only found out how horrible this disease is yesterday."

"They're all symptoms," Sergeant Wright said, tightening her grip on her gun.

"I don't think you're infected." Corporal Trueman's quiet voice broke through the building tension.

Victoria looked at him, confused. A small frown occupied his forehead above a sharp gaze fixed on the brunette.

"What the fuck is that supposed to mean?" Sergeant Wright snapped. "She has all of the symptoms—"

"Not all of them," the corporal cut the sergeant off, causing her to glare at him. "No excess saliva production or necrosis, remember?" The sergeant still glared, but doubt cast a shadow across her face. Corporal Trueman turned his intense eyes back to the brunette woman. "I think you're immune."

His declaration was met with stony silence and incredulous looks. The woman herself had a faint crease in between her brow, looking hopeful yet disbelieving. Victoria didn't know what to think. She didn't have a clue about how viruses and immunity worked. That had been Mike's forte, but she knew this disease was brutal. Devastating. Could people be immune to it? Mike had hoped a small percentage of people would have a natural immunity, but as him and his team—and others around the world—researched it, no one displayed any kind of immunity, and he'd become more and more disheartened.

"We need a doctor," Sergeant Wright said, frowning at the woman. "Someone who understands diseases and biology." She turned to the rest of the group, as if hoping one of them would jump up professing intimate medical knowledge. Everyone looked exhausted.

"We need to go," Sergeant Mollino scanned the area around them, a pinched look on his face. "We've been here too long."

The other two soldiers nodded and gestured for everybody to move as they pulled torches from one of the many compartments in their uniforms.

They barely made it a few steps as gunfire burst from behind them, deafening in its unexpected roar. Victoria let out a rather undignified squeak as the soldiers spun to return fire. She stumbled to one knee, wincing as her ankle jarred. *Just my bloody luck.*

"Into the trees! Get behind cover," Sergeant Wright yelled, shoving the Indian couple ahead of her.

Victoria gasped as a strong hand tightened around her upper arm, pulling her to her feet. "Here, help her," Sergeant Mollino shouted. He pushed her in the direction of the brunette woman, who looked startled as Victoria fell over to her and grabbed her arm for support.

With the woman holding her up around the waist and Victoria leaning on her shoulders, they managed to somehow make it to the treeline without falling flat on their faces. *Or getting shot, which would be worse.* Gunfire rang through the air, sharp and loud, causing Victoria to duck her head as they stumbled blindly amongst the trees. Night closed in around them. She couldn't even see the moon. They rounded a large tree, and the woman tried to ease Victoria to the damp ground, but she almost ended up falling on top of her. In the end, Victoria sank the short distance without help. *She must be exhausted from her battle with the virus. If she does indeed have it.*

"Sorry," the woman panted, kneeling next to her and spying around the tree. She jerked back as bits of bark were blown free, raining down on them like little wooden knives.

"Do we need to move?" Victoria asked, digging her palms into her thighs. She didn't relish the thought of walking again anytime soon, especially in a near pitch-black forest. Her ankle *ached*.

The woman peered around the tree again, flinching at a fierce exchange of bullets. "No. I think our soldiers have stopped them from getting any closer." She jumped at another loud burst of gunfire. "For now, at least."

Victoria nodded, stretching out her ankle. Even though it was a struggle to see anything in the heavy darkness, she could tell when the woman looked at her with concern. "I'll be fine," Victoria said before she could ask. "It's only a sprain." Bloody hell, she *despised* being so weak.

The woman looked like she wanted to say something more but thought better of it. Instead, she looked around them, her eyes darting from one tree to the next. Squinting at her, Victoria was struck by how young she looked. She'd assumed the woman was closer to her own age of thirty, but she couldn't be older than twenty-five at most. The tension in the woman's body eased when she found the skinny kid, a pale blur in the night, crouched close by behind a tree of his own.

"Is he your brother?" Victoria pointed at the boy. They didn't look alike, which didn't mean anything.

Victoria had seen plenty of siblings who looked as unrelated as a chicken and a dog.

The woman seemed confused for a moment. "What? No, I met him at Knightsbridge." She shrugged. "I guess, I dunno, I guess I feel kind of responsible for him. He's only fourteen."

Victoria searched for something else to say. With adrenaline flooding her veins, the pain in her ankle had lessened, but she still needed something to distract her from the fire fight raging around them.

The woman beat her to it. "I'm Jennifer. That's Dan." She gestured over to the boy.

"Victoria."

"It's nice to meet you, Victoria. Even if the circumstances are horrible."

She snorted. "They do leave a lot to be desired."

They both ducked down as another spray of bullets tore up their tree. "*God*, I can't believe this is my life now," Jennifer muttered. She squeezed her eyes shut as a loud explosion ripped through the cold night.

"What was that?" Victoria's stomach did a somersault.

Had the enemy brought bigger weapons? She felt so *useless* with her *bloody* ankle. What if they had to make a quick getaway? Victoria didn't want to die. She had for a while, after Mike and Katherine. Those weeks had been the worst of her life, losing everything and not being able to do a damn thing about it. They were awful times to look back on, but she forced herself to remember the crushing darkness, remember she had been through the worst life had to offer and came back out the other side. Those days shaped her into the person she was. If she could pull through that she could pull through this. She *would* pull through this.

"I think it was a grenade," Jennifer whispered. She looked terrified, fear shining out of her eyes so similar to Katherine's.

"Hey, it's going to be all right. We've made it this far. We're going to make it out of here," Victoria said.

It was an awful pep talk, but Jennifer nodded nonetheless, putting on a brave face. Her eyes were still shadowed—*who knew what she's been through? She has the virus for crying out loud*—but at least Victoria had been able to reassure her somewhat.

"Are you sure you're okay?" Jennifer asked, gesturing at her ankle.

"Yeah," Victoria nodded, putting more confidence into her voice than she felt. "Like I said, just a sprain. I'll put some ice on it and I'll be back to running for my life in no time." She smiled, but she saw Jennifer wasn't buying her flippant attitude. "What about you? How are you feeling?"

Jennifer breathed out a soft laugh. "Like shit." She brought her right hand up, showing Victoria the split skin around her knuckles. Her middle and ring finger were crowded with bruises. "I broke these two punching someone, and that's not even the worst of the pain." She winced as she tried to clench her fist and ended up dropping her hand back to her side. "But if you meant the infection, it's okay. I'm not going to bite you or anything."

Victoria nodded. It *was* good to know Jennifer wasn't becoming paranoid and insane.

Neither of them spoke after that. Victoria let the violent sounds of gunfire wash over her as their soldiers traded bullets with the mysterious people who'd attacked them. She wondered why they had. Did they think they were infected? Or did they want to take their supplies? They didn't have much of anything.

The sound of gunfire ceased, leaving a ringing silence quivering through the air. Victoria exchanged a fright-filled look with Jennifer who leaned out from behind the tree again.

"I can't see any movement," she said, leaning out further.

Victoria snatched her arm and pulled her back behind the wide tree. "Are you mad?" she hissed. "You'll end up getting shot. We don't know what's happening, and we should stay here until we know it's safe."

Jennifer winced, and Victoria realised she held Jennifer's left arm, the one with the cuts and scrapes. *Was this where she was bitten?* She dropped the arm as if it was venomous and wiped her hand on her trouser leg. Jennifer saw the action and raised an eyebrow at her, causing Victoria to shrug sheepishly.

"It's okay to come out now," Sergeant Mollino shouted, his booming voice carrying into the trees.

Jennifer helped Victoria up, and together they shuffled out of the forest and over to the soldiers. Everyone looked scared, but Victoria couldn't see anyone sporting a bullet wound. Her sprain seemed to be the most serious injury. *Of course, it bloody is,* she thought with no small amount of bitterness.

"We got them all," Sergeant Mollino said, standing tall and projecting an air of assurance. Warmth radiated from Victoria's chest as she watched him and the other two soldiers, sure for the first time they were in safe hands.

"Miss? May I?"

Victoria blinked at Corporal Trueman, who'd moved close, his hands pointing at her ankle. "Go ahead," she said, bracing herself for more pain as she lowered herself to the ground. Again, Jennifer wasn't much help. "And my name's Victoria."

The corporal rolled her combat trouser leg up and eased her boot off. Victoria sucked in a sharp breath as pain knotted in her foot. The corporal sent her an apologetic look.

His hands were gentle as he inspected the injury. It started to swell as a dark red bruise wrapped itself around her ankle and heel. "Can you wiggle your toes for me?" Victoria did as he asked. He hummed as he examined it for a little longer. "This is badly sprained. You won't be able to walk on it for a while."

Panic's breath was cold on the back of her neck, but she refused to acknowledge it. They wouldn't leave her here. Would they? *No, no, they won't. We'll go to the town and find some ice and I'll be fine.* Victoria clung to the thought like insecurity did to teenagers.

"Our original plan still stands," Sergeant Mollino said as Corporal Trueman helped her get her sock and boot back on. "We go to the air base and see if we can find any information about the state of the world, the UK in particular." He looked at her and Jennifer. "Are you two okay to continue as you are?"

"Yeah, yeah. It's no problem," Jennifer replied. She looked like she was about to keel over, but she smiled at

Victoria. She returned the smile—Jennifer was willing to keep going even though she was in pain and exhausted, and Victoria respected that.

"Are you sure she's safe?" the Indian man asked, shooting Jennifer a sceptical look.

"She hasn't gone mad and attacked us yet, has she?" Victoria said before anyone could open their mouths, feeling oddly protective of a woman she'd met mere minutes ago. *Her eyes do look so like Katherine's.* The man looked taken aback, but Jennifer smiled at her again, thanking her without words.

"Okay, people, enough chatting. It's time to move," Sergeant Wright said as she walked past them, her torch bobbing as she headed down the wide corridor of grass and frozen mud. The weak light from the thin ribbon of moon was enough to illuminate the tall trees of the forests flanking each side, their bare branches catching and twisting above them and filling the night with a faint creaking.

The curly-haired man fell in behind the pilot, almost tripping her up. She shot him a glare and he shied back, stuttering an apology. Victoria smirked. It served the idiot right for being such a, well, idiot.

Jennifer noticed her sneer. "You don't like him?"

"No," Victoria replied as they hobbled after Sergeant Wright.

The young couple walked behind the curly-haired man, grasping each other's hands with such force it was a wonder they didn't cause each other permanent damage. The boy—Dan—fell in next to Jennifer, watching his feet as he walked. Sergeant Mollino and Corporal Trueman brought up the rear behind them.

"He arrived at Knightsbridge around the same time I did, and he did nothing but complain and talk about himself." Victoria snorted. "As if the rest of us hadn't been through the same hell, as if we hadn't lost people too." Her voice faltered as thoughts of Mike and Katherine forced their way into her mind yet again, unexpected and unwelcome. She couldn't think of them. She needed to focus on surviving and finding something for her foot.

Victoria took a deep breath in and ignored the curious look Jennifer directed at her. But instead of the pity she half-expected to see, understanding shone in its place. *Of course, she's lost someone. Haven't we all?* "He was selfish, only thinking about himself," she muttered.

Jennifer nodded and didn't press. They walked a few steps in silence, and Victoria listened as Jennifer's breathing became more laboured. She carried more than half of Victoria's weight, on top of her own injuries and tiredness to boot. Guilt made Victoria's stomach churn, but before she could suggest asking someone else to help her, Dan moved around to Victoria's other side and awkwardly gestured at her.

"Erm, would you like me to, uh, help?" he asked, his eyes darting from Victoria to Jennifer and back again.

"Please," Jennifer breathed out as she hitched Victoria's arm further across her shoulders.

"Sure. I think that's a good idea," Victoria said, throwing an arm around the back of Dan's neck. She put more of her weight on him, conscious of Jennifer's struggle.

Walking was easier with two people helping her, and they were able to move faster. The pilot hadn't set a gruelling pace to begin with, no doubt aware Victoria wouldn't be able to keep up, to which she was immensely grateful. She still couldn't shake the fear they would see her as a liability and ditch her somewhere.

"I'm, erm, Daniel. But you can, erm, call me Dan," the boy stuttered, giving her a shy smile.

"Hello, Dan." She smiled back at him. "I'm—"

"Victoria," he cut in, then looked horrified at what he'd done. "I'm, erm, I'm sorry. I didn't mean, erm, sorry," he mumbled to his feet. "I heard you tell the soldier your name," he finished, trailing off so much toward the end Victoria struggled to hear what he said even though he walked right next to her.

Jennifer grinned at his awkwardness. "It's okay, Dan."

"Sorry," he muttered again.

"Jennifer's right, Dan. It's okay. You've proven you have good listening skills," Victoria complimented him. She had seen students like him before—people with low self-esteem who needed to be coaxed out of their shell.

He gave her a small nod and smile.

"Are you some kind of teacher?" Jennifer asked, tilting her head to one side as she frowned at her.

Victoria blinked, startled. "What makes you say that?" *How did she figure it out?*

Jennifer shrugged. Or at least she tried to. Victoria's arm across her shoulders made the movement difficult, and it resembled a kind of twitch. "You sound like one. My old chemistry teacher used to talk about people's listening skills all the time," she paused. "Mainly because nobody paid much attention to him in class."

Victoria chuckled. "Yeah, I'm a teacher. I used to be, anyway." She sighed. "Now, I don't know what I am."

"What did you teach, if you don't mind my asking?" Corporal Trueman asked from behind. Victoria realised everyone was listening to their conversation. *Nosey lot.* She didn't want to talk about her old life, but not talking at all would be worse, and she needed something to distract her from the throbbing in her foot.

"I was an English teacher," she announced to the group. "Not a very glamourous job, but I enjoyed it all the same. Well, most of the time. Some of the time," she amended, remembering the troublemakers and spoiled brats that had graced the school halls with their annoying presence.

Sergeant Mollino muttered something Victoria didn't quite catch.

"What?" Victoria turned her head as much as she could to look at him. From what little she could see he looked rather embarrassed, and Victoria imagined she would see a faint blush staining his face if it wasn't so dark. Sergeant Wright turned so she walked backward, the beginnings of a wide grin on her face.

Before the sergeant could speak, the pilot jumped in. "Are you blushing, Sunshine?" she laughed, glee lighting up her face.

"No," he grunted. What had he said? "Look, can we change the subject? Or better yet, not talk at all?"

Victoria didn't think she could stand silence, so she continued. "Sunshine?"

"It's a stupid nickname she gave me," Sergeant Mollino growled, throwing a withering look at Sergeant Wright.

The pilot raised an eyebrow, her smirk deepening.

"It's because you have such a sunny disposition."

"Must be because you're not irritating at all," Sergeant Mollino shot back, his words dripping sarcasm.

"Admit it, Sunshine. You like me."

"Aye, the same way I like golf. Which is not at all."

The pilot frowned. "Did you just compare me to the worst sport in the world—"

"Have you known each other long?" Jennifer interrupted, attempting to soothe the argument.

"No," Sergeant Mollino said, turning away to scan the tree line.

"What the good sergeant meant to say," the pilot said as she turned back to face the direction they were going, "is that we met the day we left Knightsbridge. So, yesterday." She sounded surprised. "Only a few hours ago. I can't believe it."

"Yeah, me too," Jennifer agreed. "So much has happened, it's hard to understand..." she trailed off, her eyes shining in the moonlight. She swallowed as she hitched her arm tighter around Victoria's waist. A heavy silence cloaked the group, dampening Victoria's mood and reminding her of those horrible weeks after she'd overheard Mike and Katherine.

The Indian man cleared his throat in the silence. "I am called Aarav, and this is my wife, Riya." He smiled down at her, squeezing her hand.

"We were married not long ago," Riya said, smiling back at her husband. "I have wanted to see London ever since I was a little girl, and Aarav surprised me for a wedding gift." Her smile vanished. "Of course, we were not expecting anything like this."

"Congratulations," Jennifer said.

"Thank you." Sadness tinged Riya's smile.

"I'm Anthony," Corporal Trueman announced in the lull.

"What, are we introducing ourselves like this is some kind of icebreaker session?" the pilot laughed. "You lot can continue calling me Sergeant Wright."

After Victoria declared her name and nudged Dan and Jennifer to do the same, the idiot spoke up.

"My name is Martin," he said in his obnoxious voice.

"Okay, now that we all know everybody's names, can we stop talking?" Sergeant Mollino said, still scanning the trees around them. "We don't want to announce ourselves to anyone who might be hostile."

"We don't know your name," Jennifer stated, looking at him over her shoulder. He glared at her.

"James," he bit out. "Now, no more talking."

They walked in silence for several minutes, Victoria gritting her teeth against the pain in her ankle. She didn't think she could keep going for much longer. She didn't think *Jennifer* could keep going for much longer, no matter how brave a face she put on. The poor woman grew more breathless and moved more slowly compared to five minutes ago. Victoria was about to tell her to let go when Anthony swooped in and got there first. He moved Jennifer out of the way as he took Victoria's weight, nodding for Dan to help the other woman instead.

"Thanks," Victoria said.

Anthony didn't say anything in return, his eyes never ceasing in their scan of the trees, but he did nod. Victoria let him support her, moving with more ease than she had with both Jennifer and Dan. Bolts of pain still shot through her foot and up her leg every now and then. All she wanted was to get to this air base as soon as possible, rest her foot, and sleep.

Chapter Nine

They had been crouched behind the trees for thirty-five minutes according to Dan and his expensive-looking watch. The night was downright *cold*, but heat tore through Jennifer's tired body with vicious claws. She hoped Corporal Trueman was right. She didn't feel immune to anything. In fact, this had to be the worst she'd ever felt. She let her head fall back against the tree she was sprawled against and looked up at the dark sky. She could barely make out the moon obscured behind thin clouds and thick branches, its dim light offering little illumination. Instead, they had to rely on the small torches the soldiers had. She ignored the anxious faces around her as she massaged her head. Her brain felt like it was wedged in a vice, and she sighed with relief as the tight pulsing loosened a touch.

The two sergeants had gone to scout some buildings at the edges of the forest. Beyond them lay their destination. Jennifer couldn't make it out as gloom pressed in on all sides.

"Jennifer?" Victoria sat next to her, her foot in a bad way. Jennifer let her eyes slide shut—they'd become too heavy, and it took too much effort to keep them open. She turned her head toward Victoria's voice.

"Hmmm?" Even talking required too much energy.

"Don't fall asleep." Victoria said sharply, nudging her—*yet again*—with a pointy elbow.

Jennifer frowned. "I'm not."

"Yeah? Then why don't you open your eyes?"

It was one of the hardest things Jennifer ever did. Her eyelids felt like they were glued shut, and they kept closing before she managed to focus on Victoria, lethargy pulling at them as she fought to keep them open. Victoria's own eyes were wide as she watched Jennifer struggle. God, she was beautiful.

"There. That wasn't so hard, was it?" Victoria smirked as Jennifer threw a glare her way. She knew damn well it had been anything but easy.

She still hadn't thought of a good comeback by the time Sergeant Wright returned. Fatigue blinded Jennifer to her surroundings, and she didn't see the pilot enter their little hiding place amongst the trees—one minute she wasn't there, the next she was. Jennifer couldn't muster up enough energy to be surprised.

"Good news, people," Sergeant Wright said, crouching down in front of the group as they gathered in a semi-circle around her. "The buildings I looked at are all deserted. No crazy infected and no sign of any more hostiles."

Aarav jerked his head in what Jennifer assumed was a nod, his floppy hair hitting his forehead with the rough movement. "Does this mean we can go to the air base now?"

"We need to wait for Sergeant Slow to get back, but if all's well on his end, then yeah."

A mixture of anxiety and hope bloomed in Jennifer's chest. Maybe this air base would finally offer the safety she craved. *What if it doesn't? What if there's nothing left but ashes, like before?* Jennifer shoved those thoughts away, but they kept returning like a buzzing fly that wouldn't piss off. What if infected people had overrun it? *I can't go through that again,* she thought with a shudder, remembering how her euphoria at defeating the infected man had evaporated. *I am so out of my depth here.*

"Erm, can I ask a question?" Dan mumbled, ducking his head.

Jennifer thought the pilot intimidated him with her blasé attitude to everything. Jennifer herself was comforted by the sergeant's carefree outlook. It made her seem in control, like nothing could faze her.

"Sure, kiddo. Shoot," Sergeant Wright said, not paying him much attention as she eyed the buildings Sergeant Mollino had gone to scout.

"When we uh, get to the air base, are we going to erm, stay for a while?" Dan wilted as Sergeant Wright turned to him. He glanced at Jennifer, his eyes barely making contact with hers before he squared his shoulders and looked back at Sergeant Wright. "I think we should. Some of us—" another fleeting glance at Jennifer "—erm, some of us need to rest." He couldn't hold the pilot's gaze for long, and he ended up staring at his feet a few beats later.

The pilot watched him for a couple of seconds, her head cocked to one side as a frown began to develop, wrinkling her smooth forehead. She transferred her intense gaze to Jennifer. "We need to gather information and contact British forces as quickly as we can. If we have time to rest, then sure, why not? But if not, don't fucking complain. If we must keep moving, we keep moving."

Jennifer held her ground, determined not to be impressed by the sergeant's commanding air. "With all due respect, sergeant, I can't keep going for much longer. Victoria needs to rest her foot. We've all been through a lot in the past few hours." Jennifer took a deep breath and wondered where her sudden nerve came from. "If it's safe, we should stay." She thought her tone would waver and betray her nervousness, but her voice was strong and steady, not faltering despite her fatigue.

Both of Sergeant Wright's eyebrows shot up, disappearing under her helmet, before they slammed down as anger swept across her face. Jennifer was saved from her ire and scathing remarks by the arrival of Sergeant Mollino, who chose that moment to stealthily return to the group.

"Okay," he breathed, sounding out of breath. He didn't seem to notice the tension choking up the air. "The buildings I checked were empty. We can keep going."

Still riding the wave of her newfound boldness, Jennifer spoke before Sergeant Wright or Corporal Trueman could. "Good. The sooner we get there, the better." She gathered her remaining strength and pushed herself to her feet, leaning on the tree as dizziness took hold.

Sergeant Mollino frowned at her, then raised an eyebrow at the pilot, who shrugged. "It seems we've been usurped. She thinks she's in charge now." Annoyance and amusement warred for dominance on Sergeant Wright's face, and Jennifer felt her own flash of anger. *They aren't considering continuing, are they?* Exhaustion had turned her legs to mush, Victoria couldn't walk for long stretches of time. The whole group was tired for *fuck's* sake. Couldn't they see pushing on wasn't the right thing to do?

"Now is not the time to start debating leadership," Sergeant Mollino said, scowling at everyone. "You are all in our care, and you will all follow our orders. I hope that's clear enough for you." He reached down and helped Victoria up, supporting her as they limped out onto the open field.

Dan moved to help Jennifer again, but Sergeant Wright got there first. "I've got this one, kiddo. Why don't you follow Sergeant Mollino and keep an eye on our surroundings?" It wasn't a question. Dan all but ran after James and Victoria, sparing Jennifer a little apologetic glance as he dashed away.

"I'm fine," Jennifer snapped as Sergeant Wright moved to support her. She wasn't fine, but she couldn't ask for help when she had so vehemently denied it. *Damn, I feel like I need to sit down already, and I've only just stood up. Way to go, Jen, let your pride get the better of you.*

"Whatever." Sergeant Wright shrugged, like it didn't matter to her whether she helped or not. She watched Jennifer closely as they started walking, however, and she seemed ready to catch her if she faltered. Her words were at odds with her actions, and confusion draped itself around Jennifer. Was the pilot annoyed at her or what?

After several stumbling steps, the pilot heaved a loud sigh. "Look, I know you're tired. I am too. But I'd rather be tired than dead." She gave Jennifer an, *'if you don't agree, you're an idiot'* look, one of her eyebrows twitching upward. "We don't know the situation in this country. We can rest when we have more information and when we know we're in a safe place. Is that good enough for you, O Great Leader?"

Jennifer's face twisted. She had a point. "I'm sorry," she muttered. "I didn't mean to try and take charge. I'm pissed we're going to keep pushing forward when we should rest." She couldn't be bothered to argue. "If this air base is deserted, can we stop for a little while, at least? I wasn't lying when I said I can't go on for much longer." Even as she spoke, exhaustion spread through her body like an insidious fog, its strong tendrils tightening around her muscles as she struggled to keep moving.

"This virus has really taken it out of you, huh?" Sergeant Wright said, her brow furrowing as she studied Jennifer. "I guess we're gonna have to stop. Or I carry you, but no offense, but I'm not lugging your arse all around France."

Jennifer breathed out a laugh. "None taken."

They walked a few more paces before the pilot heaved another loud sigh. "At the rate you're going, we'll reach the base in time for Christmas." Without warning, she pulled Jennifer's right arm up around her neck and wrapped a strong arm around Jennifer's waist, tugging her along. Jennifer winced at the sudden movement, and almost lost her balance due to their increased pace. They staggered a few precarious steps forward before falling into a steady rhythm, marching across the uneven ground.

"You reek of blood and vomit," Sergeant Wright complained.

"Wow, thanks," Jennifer deadpanned, too tired to be insulted. It was true anyway. A thought pushed up through her exhausted mind, demanding attention.

Something important... something to do with what the sergeant had said. Blood? Jennifer froze for a second before she used her limited strength to shove the pilot away from her.

"What the fuck?" Sergeant Wright objected.

The others all stopped in their tracks, and Jennifer saw fear twist their features as they took a couple of steps back. Sergeant Mollino and Corporal Trueman both aimed their guns at her, the sudden torchlight blinding.

"Blood," Jennifer whispered. She had infected blood on her, and she'd touched Dan, Victoria, and Sergeant Wright. She might be immune, but were they? "I have contaminated blood on me, and I touched you," she said, her voice getting louder with each word. "Oh God, what if you're infected now?" She looked wildly from the pilot to Victoria to Dan, taking in the latter two's frightened faces as comprehension dawned. *Have I infected them?* She reached up and started wiping her face with frantic energy, trying her best to scour herself clean. The blood had long since dried, and it fell away from her violent scrubbing in little flakes that drifted to the ground like red snow.

"Hey, *stop*. Here." Sergeant Wright grabbed her wrists and pulled her hands down. Jennifer clenched them into fists as the pilot accepted a canteen and gauze from Corporal Trueman, not registering the pain from her broken fingers. Sergeant Wright passed both items to Jennifer, her steady hands in sharp contrast to Jennifer's shaking ones.

Scrubbing her face and hands, Jennifer couldn't get enough air. *Shit. Have I infected them? Oh God.* Her thoughts whirled around her head in a fierce tempest and she knew she was panicking, but she couldn't seem to calm down. She rubbed the damp gauze up her arms, hissing as it passed over her torn skin. Welcoming the pain, Jennifer cleaned her arm, causing it to begin bleeding again. *I've infected them, I've infected them. Oh God, I've killed them.*

Sudden silence. Her speeding thoughts ground to a halt, leaving her frozen with the horrific realisation she was responsible for someone's death. Cold spread through her limbs like she'd been dumped in ice water, inching toward her chest and stilling the air in her lungs.

"*Hey*." Sergeant Wright's sharp voice cut through the frosty quiet filling her mind. "You need to calm down. You've made yourself bleed, you fucking idiot."

Jennifer looked down at her raw arm, the light from Sergeant Wright's torch illuminating the bright red of her blood, making it look like it shone with its own glow. "S-sorry, I—"

Sergeant Wright cut her off. "If you are infected, and we're ninety percent certain you are, you need to calm down and clean yourself up."

Jennifer watched, transfixed, as her dangerous blood oozed down her arm.

"I need you to listen to me." Corporal Trueman's soft voice sounded far away, but it broke through the cold gripping Jennifer's mind regardless. "I need everybody to listen. It's very unlikely you've infected anyone. Now, I'm not an expert, but I was told the virus has to either pass directly from blood to blood or saliva to blood or be somehow ingested, I think." His warm brown eyes bore into hers, and the cold receded from her bones as she took in what he said. "Even if you got some infected blood on you," he turned to Victoria and Dan, gesturing with open palms, "you'll be all right as long as you wash it off thoroughly, and as long as you don't have any cuts or breaks in the skin." They nodded, relief making their features slack.

"You see?" Sergeant Wright's loud voice jarred the still air after Corporal Trueman's quiet speech. "No need to panic. Everyone can relax now."

The canteen passed around the whole group irrespective of the pilots' assertions. Everyone was on edge, no doubt from being so close to Jennifer. She supposed she couldn't blame them—she knew she would be the same way if their roles were reversed.

Corporal Trueman gave her some fresh gauze to cover her bleeding arm. "Thank you, corporal," she said gratefully. "Not only for the bandage, but, y'know." Jennifer gave a small smile, embarrassed at her actions.

He smiled at her, his eyes shining with understanding. "It's perfectly all right. You thought you'd passed the infection on, and it's natural to panic. There's no need to be ashamed." He made to move away but paused and turned back. "Please, call me Anthony." With another smile and nod, he jogged to the rear of the group and stood guard while everyone washed their hands and faces.

Jennifer cleaned her arm as best she could and covered the worst area with the gauze. The bleeding had started to slow, but it *was* beginning to sting again. Her whole left arm was a painful mess of swollen scratches and cuts. It had only been a day, but she could hardly remember what the smooth, unmarred skin of her arm used to look like.

The group set off again, quiet in the cold night. The rustling of the grass as they passed through was the only sound. Sergeant Wright moved to their flank, her dark eyes serious as she scanned around them, so Dan once again supported Jennifer. She pushed through the pain and exhaustion, the prospect of resting at the air base driving her forward. The quicker they got there, the sooner she could sleep.

Chapter Ten

Jennifer didn't know how long they had been walking, her mind dulled by every arduous step forward. She was so preoccupied with putting one foot in front of the other she didn't realise when they stopped. She kept walking for another step, prompting Dan to reach out and steady her before she could nosedive into the mud.

Startled, Jennifer looked around with wide eyes for any sign of danger and noticed the air base for the first time. *We've arrived.* She blinked up at a thick, shadowed wall. Eyeing it, she hoped the soldiers didn't expect her to climb. She didn't think she could start walking again now she had stopped, let alone scale a damn wall. Just looking at it drained the last of her energy, and she sank to the ground with a small sigh.

Feeling watched, she raised her eyes and found Aarav's. His gaze was like knives digging under her flesh, and Jennifer couldn't name what she saw there. She turned away first, unable to bear the scrutiny any longer. She supposed she couldn't fault him for being suspicious of her.

She shifted her unfocused attention to the group and noticed the two sergeants were absent. *God, how tired am*

I? How many things have I missed? She looked around again in case she had overlooked them, but she didn't spot them amongst the other tired, scared faces.

"They've gone to scout the air base." Anthony's calm voice drifted over from where he crouched on a road.

A *road*. How had she not noticed it? Irritated at her inability to take in her surroundings and annoyed at her eyes for wanting to do nothing but close for a good ten hours, Jennifer turned to properly study the air base.

The first thing she realised was she was in a bad position to properly study the air base. The wall right in front of her blocked her view of pretty much everything else. Darkness shrouded the rest—Jennifer couldn't see any light, and the little illumination the moon reflected failed to pierce the heavy blackness.

Sergeant Wright returned first again, materialising out of the darkness like a leopard, arriving back amongst the group without any of them noticing her reappearance. Jennifer jumped when she saw her crouched next to Anthony and wondered if she would ever get used to the small woman's stealthy way of moving.

Pushing past the fatigue burning its way through her, Jennifer stood and shuffled over to the soldiers. "Is it safe?" she asked with a sharp intensity. Hope surged like the sea in a storm, drowning out her worry that they were going to be let down again, and she struggled to keep from going under. She didn't want to think about having her hopes dashed again. If it was occupied, they *had* to let them in. They wouldn't leave them out here, would they? And it *couldn't* be overrun with infected. Not again. At least healthy people could be reasoned with. Maybe.

The pilot looked up at her, and something she saw in Jennifer's face softened her own, the hard edge disappearing from her eyes. "You look worse than my grandmother, and she's been rotting in the ground for close to twelve years now."

You certainly don't pull any punches, Jennifer thought sardonically. She twisted her face and Sergeant Wright grinned, a wide flash of white amidst the shadows. She had a nice smile. It relaxed her entire face and made her look younger.

"Sergeant Mollino is waiting for us at the entrance to this particular marguerite of hardstands," the pilot announced to the group. "We checked the whole air base and didn't see anyone. The place has a really creepy, abandoned feel," she added with a faint air of anticipation.

Jennifer thought she might be *excited*, like she enjoyed going into dangerous, unknown situations. Dan once again wrapped a thin arm around her waist while Anthony helped Victoria.

Each step was torture, but Jennifer would *not* waver. She pushed through her fatigue, thinking of how proud her parents would be, of how Evelyn would be cheering her on, shouting stupid, cheesy words of encouragement designed to make her laugh. She thought of how Damien would be a solid pillar of confidence, so sure she wouldn't fail, his dimples appearing in his cheeks as he smiled. Amanda would yell with mad enthusiasm as Rachel willed her on in a more reserved manner. Rhys would nod, never doubting her for a second. Her friends, her *family*, were gone, but she would carry on for them.

The solid wall was a constant barrier to their right, a heavy presence that reminded Jennifer of how fucked up her life had become. She hadn't taken it all in before, but *God*. They were in *France*, about to enter a *military air base*. She had never been to France before, and she had never been anywhere remotely military in nature until Knightsbridge.

She couldn't muster any excitement about seeing any of it. She channelled all her attention into willing her lead-filled muscles to keep moving. It was a shock when the wall fell away, a gaping hole appearing instead. Jennifer stared at the emptiness, her weary mind taking an embarrassingly long time to figure out it was an entrance to the air base beyond.

She blinked when a shadow broke away from the wall and strode toward them. Her heart began to beat harder before she finally made out Sergeant Mollino, a scowl marring his rugged face.

"What took you so long?" he hissed, glaring between Sergeant Wright and Anthony before turning his piercing eyes to Jennifer. She was taken aback by his intense scrutiny and wondered why he frowned so fiercely at her. *Does he think I tried to take charge again?* Jennifer thought, bemused. *Held everyone up? Seriously?* She stared back at him blankly until his expression shifted, becoming less harsh as doubt crept in.

"We couldn't exactly sprint here with Miss Sprained Ankle and Miss About-To-Fall-Asleep-Walking, could we?" Sergeant Wright rolled her eyes at him, his scowl about as effective as a chocolate teapot in the face of her nonchalant attitude.

He grumbled something inaudible and motioned for everyone to follow him. Jennifer started moving again when Dan nudged her. Drawing in a sharp breath of cold air, feeling it sting and spread in her chest, Jennifer called upon some deep reserve buried in her bones and started walking again. She couldn't wait to sleep.

The night filled with the sound of the group's shallow breathing as they hurried away from wall, venturing in the opposite direction and across open space instead. They rushed over more mud before Jennifer's boots hit solid concrete. She could make out the vague outline of buildings emerging from the night, dusting off the shadows that clung to them like cobwebs, the smaller ones arranged haphazardly around what appeared to be a large hangar set behind a wide stretch of asphalt.

They ignored the massive hangar, going around it to one of the smaller buildings. James continued to the building, not breaking stride as he marched straight through the front door. The others hesitated for half a second before following.

Inside was as dark as outside. More so, in fact, as they didn't have the light from the moon, weak as it was behind thickening clouds. They fumbled after the sergeant as he strode through the dark corridors, trying to keep up with his rapid pace. They entered a room and stood in blackness for a few seconds before blinding light exploded as someone flicked on the switch. Jennifer screwed her eyes shut as the light stabbed at them like little pins, the glare shocking in its suddenness. She blinked away tears as her eyes took their time adjusting to the brightness.

Chaos swam into focus. They were in what appeared to be a type of office. It looked as if a tornado had blown through, pulling everything up before spitting them out in random directions. Sheets of paper were scattered around. Desks were overturned, their drawers spilling out onto the floor. Computers were smashed up with all the internal drives exposed. A keyboard lay in two pieces in one corner. How did that even happen?

"Are you sure there are no diseased people here?" Riya asked in a small voice, her honey-brown eyes wide as she took in all the destruction.

"Don't worry, Sergeant Wright and I checked. The place is empty," James responded in what he probably thought was a reassuring tone, but it sounded gruff to Jennifer.

"Make yourselves comfortable, people. We'll be staying here for the rest of the night," Sergeant Wright announced, unfastening her helmet straps and pulling it off. Her head looked small without the bulky protection, and her close-cropped fuzzy hair added to her slightness. "Before you all go to sleep, you can help us look through all this shit for anything that might be important. Something like reports or things that look official. Anything like that."

Jennifer almost slid down the wall she leaned against to go to sleep right there on the floor, but she stopped herself. *One more task,* she thought as she forced herself to stay on her feet. Dan shot her a concerned look.

"But won't everything be in French?" Victoria said from her perch on one of the few upright desks.

Jennifer cursed herself for not realising something so obvious. She didn't know any French beyond basic greetings and phrases. Ignoring everyone and curling up to go to sleep sounded more appealing by the second.

"None of you know French?" Sergeant Wright asked, one styled eyebrow arching upward. Jennifer looked around the group and saw everyone shaking their heads. "*None* of you?"

Martin cleared his throat. "Well, everyone speaks English, don't they?"

Jennifer winced.

Sergeant Wright glared at him. "Do you have any idea how ignorant you sound right now?" Her voice pitched low as something dangerous crept into her tone.

"I—I'm sorry, I didn't—" Martin stuttered, flinching as the pilot pointed at him.

"Stop talking." Sergeant Wright closed her thunderous eyes and sucked in a deep breath. When she reopened them, the stormy element had dissipated. "Do any of you understand at least *some* French?"

"Sorry," Jennifer said. "I was never good at languages in school."

"Aarav speaks Hindi and English. I speak Hindi, English, and Bengali. Neither of us know French, unfortunately," Riya said, her tone apologetic.

"No need for you two to be sorry. At least you know more than one language." Sergeant Wright threw a disgusted look at Martin, who stared down at his feet with his jaw clenched, his curly hair obscuring his eyes. The pilot turned to Dan. "What about you, kiddo? You learning French at school?"

"Erm, yeah, but I'm not good at it," Dan mumbled, looking ashamed of himself.

Sergeant Wright asked Victoria, who answered negative.

The pilot looked annoyed, but there was nothing she could do about it. "Fine. Search for things that look official and pass them to me." She picked up a broken drawer and started riffling through the papers in it.

Before Jennifer could move to sort through anything, Anthony came over to her holding what looked like a roll of white tape. "I found this, and I thought we could use it for your broken fingers."

"Yeah, sure," Jennifer said. "Thanks."

Anthony bound her two fingers together with little fuss. There was nothing more than a dull flare of pain as he pulled them close and immobilised them, which faded into nothing before he finished. She flexed her hand, thankful for one less thing to worry about.

Jennifer sighed as she leaned down to pick up a folder propped against the wall. She struggled to get back up again as her camera swung forward and bumped her arm below the gauze. God, she felt ninety-four instead of twenty-four. She couldn't believe it had been her birthday two days ago. Pushing through the wave of sadness accompanying the thought, Jennifer opened the file and stared at words she didn't understand.

She thumbed through the pages, hoping to spot a word or two she could recognise, but nothing jumped out at her. The papers didn't have any kind of official seal on them, so Jennifer didn't think they were what Sergeant Wright wanted. She dropped the folder on the desk next to where Victoria sat and smiled at the blank look on the blonde woman's face as she stared down at a ripped piece of paper.

Victoria let it flutter to the floor with a frustrated grumble, reaching up to massage her head as she picked another torn page from the small pile on the desk. Jennifer grunted in agreement—this was, in all likelihood, a waste of time. Time better spent sleeping. Picking up a thick file from the corner of the desk, she got comfortable on the hard floor, leaning back against the wall and cradling her camera in her lap as she started flicking through the pages. It didn't take long for the words to run together, the tiny font blurring even as she blinked her tired eyes clear.

She felt herself drifting off when someone dropped down next to her. Jennifer startled awake, afraid they were under attack, but it was only Dan frowning at his own stack of paper. Jennifer released a rough breath and gave him a little shove to show her irritation. He looked up at her, confusion filling his young face.

"You nearly made me shit myself, Dan," Jennifer scolded, the lingering adrenaline making her somewhat more alert. "Next time announce yourself or something."

"Oh, erm, sorry," he apologised, not looking sorry at all, a little smile playing about his lips. "You uh, shouldn't be sleeping on the job, though."

"Cheeky little bastard," Jennifer muttered, straightening up her pile of indecipherable reports. She sighed as she started looking through them again. Her eyes became heavy straight away.

"What do you think of this one?" Dan held up several pieces of scorched paper that had been stapled together. It had a yellow, official-looking seal on it, but it was badly singed.

"I haven't got a clue. You probably know more French than I do." Jennifer shrugged, frustrated she couldn't be of more help.

Dan nodded and stood up, dragging his feet as he made his way over to Sergeant Wright, as if afraid she would shoot him down without even looking at his papers. Jennifer watched the pilot's dark eyes skim over the first page, stop, then read it from the beginning again. She pulled James and Anthony to one side and spoke to them in a hushed voice. A spike of annoyance pulsed through Jennifer—no way were they going to keep things secret from everyone.

"If you've found something important, we all need to hear it," she said, her mouth set in a hard line as she frowned at the soldiers.

"Listen—" Sergeant Mollino began, but Sergeant Wright put a hand on his arm and silenced him with a look. He clenched his jaw and took a small step back.

The pilot stared at the singed paper for a few seconds before looking up at the group, her gaze settling on Jennifer. "It's not good news." She stopped and gathered her thoughts before continuing. "The report says Paris has fallen. It says most major cities around the world have. Madrid, Tokyo, New York, Beijing, the list goes on." She paused again to wet her lips. "It doesn't say how it has spread so fast and with such devastating consequences though." The pilot frowned, shaking her head. "It goes on to say when London and the rest of the UK collapsed and panic spread, everything went straight to shit. The military lost contact with the government, lost control. Most people have been left to fend for themselves.

"It goes on about South America—that's where the virus is thought to have originated," she clarified when people frowned in confusion. "It says the place is like a black hole. No reliable information is known at all, but we already knew that. Communication started to break down with that continent several months ago. No one has a clue about what's going on there."

Jennifer nodded. The government hadn't been able to keep that quiet. Rioting, looting, people dead in the streets. *Reports of people attacking and fighting each other*, Jennifer realised. *They were probably infected.* She had thought it odd how the news stopped reporting on it with no explanation. It was the subject of one of the many protests in London, the people demanding answers that never came.

"You probably know a little about it all—social media had leaked a lot of information before the governments of South America had a chance to lock everything down," Sergeant Wright continued. "It compares the UK to South America, saying no new trustworthy information has come out of Britain since London fell."

"So, what does that mean for us?" Victoria interrupted. "Are we still going back?"

"We need reliable, up-to-date information before we do anything," James said as he leaned against a desk and folded his arms.

"Sergeant Mollino is right," the pilot said. "Right now, we rest. I'm sure everything will look better in the morning." She sounded somewhat derisive as she finished speaking, her lips drawn into a thin line. Jennifer hoped she hadn't held anything back.

"Does it say anything about the virus itself?" Jennifer asked, her hands curling around her camera in her lap. She wanted to know as much as she could about the disease, wanted to understand both it and what *exactly* was going on inside her body.

"Yeah, but not in a great amount of detail," Sergeant Wright responded, making a face as she flicked through the pages. "The military was briefed on all of it when it first became apparent there was a problem."

"We do not know about it though," Aarav said with a forceful flick of his chin. "We need to know about it." He glanced at Jennifer out of the corner of his eye, an apprehensive look stealing over his face. She understood his misgivings, but damn, had the man never heard of being subtle? She started to become exasperated with his obvious mistrust.

"Hold your horses, Mr. Impatient." Sergeant Wright directed a placating gesture at Aarav. "From what I can remember, the specialist said the infected person can become symptomatic one or two days after initial exposure. Once the symptoms start, the person becomes contagious." She turned to Anthony. "That's right, isn't it?"

"Yes, it is." The corporal nodded. "You start with flu-like symptoms before progressing to nausea and vomiting, then paranoia, aggression, and finally, insanity. The infected person usually dies due to the inflammation of the brain, I think. The urge to bite manifests in the later stages of the disease when the person is confused and becoming paranoid and distrustful. It's transmitted through blood and saliva, as I said earlier."

"Okay, people. I suggest you find a nice, uncomfortable section of floor and try to sleep," Sergeant Wright grinned as several people's face's fell. Victoria let out a frustrated groan, eyeing the floor with distaste. "What did you expect? The fucking Ritz?" The pilot laughed and moved to the door, sitting next to it as she checked her weapon. Jennifer followed her lead and relaxed back against the wall, finally closing her heavy eyes.

She had only experienced the flu-like symptoms, hadn't she? Nothing more? Did that mean she was immune? She sighed, too tired to think about it properly. As soon as she woke up, she would run through it all. As soon as she woke up.

"I guess I'm taking first watch," James said. His gruff voice was the last thing Jennifer heard before she slipped into the welcoming embrace of sleep.

Chapter Eleven

James bit back a yawn as it threatened to stretch his jaw as wide as physically possible. *Maybe it's time to wake Wright up.* How long had he been scouting the perimeter anyway? He'd been awake for far too long. He checked his watch—half past two in the morning. *Time to wake Wright*, he decided.

He almost made it back to the building when he caught sound coming from his left—indistinct noises carried on the cold breeze, the occasional scraping of *something* against the ground. Boots? James froze in place, crouching low and switching his torch off. He sucked in shallow breaths, and mist formed as hot air greeted cold. Were the sounds caused by infected? More French soldiers? Why had the group earlier even attacked them? Were they hoping to steal their resources? James could only guess at their motives. *Shite. I need to get back.* He peered into the darkness, willing his eyes to adjust faster, to see them, to see *anything*. The blackness was too absolute. Clouds had long since obscured the moon, blocking the small amount of light it managed to reflect.

The weak breeze shifted direction, taking the vague sounds with it. James didn't know how far away the enemy was, nor how many stalked the air base. Trying to make as little noise as possible, he slowly moved toward the building, which stood dark and quiet ahead of him.

He supposed he could make a run for it, but they might hear him, and his position would be compromised. Clenching his jaw, he continued his slow shuffle, making sure to keep to the deep shadows so he didn't stick out like a sore thumb and make for an easy target.

Whoever they were, they were being too quiet to be infected, so James surmised French military. Possibly people from the same group who had attacked them earlier. A wave of white-hot fury coursed through him at the memory, and his hands gripped his weapon so hard he knew his knuckles were white even though he couldn't see them. *Bastards!* Pushing down his rage until it became something cold and solid inside him, James finally reached the doors.

He remained crouched to the side of them, another unmoving shadow in the darkness. He *still* couldn't pinpoint the source of the noise. Had he imagined it? No, he had to assume people were out there, and he had to warn the group. The enemy would clear the buildings as they moved forward, which would give James the time he needed to get to the others and for them to make their escape. They didn't have the ammunition for another extended firefight, but luckily, he and Wright had found a couple of bodies earlier as they searched the buildings, and they had stolen their car keys. If they came under attack, they had a plan to take the two cars and get out as fast as possible.

With another futile glance around, he inched open the door until it was wide enough to squeeze through. He carefully shut it behind him and hurried through the dark corridors back to the group, all too aware of the clock ticking down until the enemy reached them.

Wright was already awake when he entered the office room. He frowned at her as she flashed a wide smile his way, bright even in the dim light of the torches. They had switched off the main light so people could sleep.

"What took you so long, Sunshine?" Wright whispered, conscious of the civilians. "I've been waiting to take over the watch for ages."

"You're not going on watch," James muttered as he nudged Trueman awake. The tall man came alert the second James touched his shoulder, sitting up and grabbing his weapon with no fuss. James wished he could wake up half as smoothly. He put a finger to his lips and held out his other hand to help pull the corporal to his feet.

"What's that supposed to mean?" Wright questioned, side eyeing him as she checked her weapon and stood up. "What's happened?"

"I heard movement outside," James said as he gestured for them to wake the civilians. "Too quiet to be infected. I'm thinking French military, possibly from the same group who attacked us before."

"Did you see how many there are?" Wright asked as she started waking up the civilians.

"No, I didn't see anyone." James didn't like the way Wright's eyebrows rose as she looked at him. "We can't take the chance it's nothing," he said defensively, willing her to agree.

She did. "You're right. Fuck. I knew we shouldn't have stopped."

"What's going on?" Victoria asked, her voice rough with sleep.

"We're leaving," James said as he helped Martin to his feet. "I heard soldiers sweeping the buildings. We need to go before they get to this one." He eased open the door and peered down the long corridor. Empty. Silent. *Good.* He turned back to the group and saw the fear shining out of their eyes as they stood watching him anxiously. James thought they all looked like ghosts, pale and ephemeral in the faint glow saturating the room, their shadows warped and distorted in the shifting torchlight.

Shaking the disturbing image from his head, he met Jennifer's resigned gaze. "Are you okay to walk by yourself?"

She hesitated a second before nodding. James eyed her a moment longer, taking in her drooping shoulders, her heavy-lidded eyes, and the way she swayed slightly even as she stood still. He would have to take her word for it.

James motioned the kid forward. "Dan, is it?" The boy jerked his head, licking his dry lips and drawing in a deep, shaky breath. "We need to be free to use our weapons if the worst happens, so I need you to help Victoria, okay?"

The boy nodded again and shuffled over to Victoria's side. "You two follow after me, then Jennifer and Martin, then Aarav and Riya. Understood?" James barely waited for their confirmation before turning back to the door. He did catch the fright-filled look Martin directed toward Jennifer, though. The man needed to grow some thicker skin. "Sergeant Wright and Corporal Trueman will bring up the rear. You'll all be safe as long as you stay between us."

James levelled his weapon and torch and crept past the door, clearing the right and moving left. Exiting via the side entrance was their best bet at remaining undetected. He crouched close to the wall as he stole forward, his boots scarcely making any noise on the laminated floor. The same couldn't be said of the civilians. They all breathed heavily. Someone scraped a boot along the floor, resulting in a loud squeak that resonated up the corridor. James had to fight down the urge to punch who ever couldn't lift their feet properly. Didn't they understand the concept of being quiet? They had barely left the office, and his stress levels were already rising. Stupid civilians. How was he supposed to protect them if they went about announcing themselves to the enemy?

They came to a corner at the end of the corridor. James stopped and crouched, signalling the others to do the same. The hand signals weren't rocket science—the civilians would be able to understand. He hoped.

James listened as hard as he could for any signs of movement around the corner, but only heard the strained breathing behind him. Taking the silence as a good sign, he signalled '*come*', and Trueman moved toward him.

If people were around the corner and James ended up getting shot, Wright and Trueman would need to keep the civilians calm and shepherd them to safety. With a deep, steadying breath, James rounded the corner, quickly moving across it to the opposite wall as he scanned down the corridor. Empty. Good.

He remained crouched against the wall with his weapon raised as he signalled Trueman to move forward with the civilians. His heart beat loud in the silence, so much so he thought the others might hear it.

James joined Wright at the rear of the group, keeping an eye on their six so they weren't caught by surprise. Getting shot in the back was the last thing he wanted.

They shuffled forward as one, clearing the shorter corridor in no time. The civilian's collective cool-headedness pleased James. They all moved in an efficient manner, no jostling or shoving or stepping on each other's feet. When they stopped at the next corner, they all immediately crouched. *Good. We'll survive this shit storm yet.*

At the intersection, Wright moved up as Trueman cleared the corners. They rotated in the same manner until they came to the exit they were aiming for.

James left everyone a little way down the corridor as he moved to the door. *Please be unlocked, c'mon.* They should have tried it when they found it, but they had decided to head back to the civilians instead. James cursed their lack of foresight. He let out a breath and tried the handle. It moved down without resistance, but the door itself wouldn't budge. *Shite! Just my luck.* He considered breaking it down, but that would create a lot of unwanted noise. Sighing, he signalled Wright over.

"Door's locked. Got any suggestions?"

Wright frowned at the solid door, absentmindedly biting her lip as she thought through their options.

"You know how to pick a lock?" she asked, raising an eyebrow at him. He shook his head and her lips thinned. "And the only other way out is through the front doors back the way we came."

"Yeah, we could—"

"*Shhh.*" Wright cut him off, frowning as she leaned closer to the door. Her eyes lost focus as she listened.

James also leaned forward, straining his ears to hear anything. Faint voices drifted through the door. *They must literally be on the other side if we can hear them.* Before James could signal a retreat, the sound of keys entering the lock reached him, and the handle started turning.

James reacted—there was no time to think. They weren't going to be blindsided like they were at the helicopter. As the door started to swing open, he grabbed it and yanked, throwing himself into the person stepping though. The man grunted as they fell heavily to the ground, and James's weapon banged into his leg as it swung on its straps. The light from the torch spun in a disorientating way.

James wasted no time slamming a fist into the man's face. The enemy grunted again, louder, but managed to block him as James made another swing. The man jammed James's right arm down and tried to roll them over, but James leaned his full weight on him and squeezed the man's throat as hard as he could with his free hand.

The enemy managed to break his hold, rewarding James for his sloppiness with a punch square in his left eye. Pain radiated across his cheek. During those precious few seconds of confusion, the man flipped them over and wrapped both hands around James's neck, tightening his fingers and denying him oxygen. James kicked his legs and bucked his hips, desperately trying to throw him off, but the bastard only strengthened his sweaty grip. James's vision started to dim around the edges, but he *wouldn't* let panic take over. He'd been trained better than that. In one last ditch attempt to stop the man from asphyxiating him, James lifted his arms above his head and slammed them down hard into the man's elbows.

The vice around his throat loosened.

As the man fell forward slightly, James lifted his head off the ground and smashed it into the bastard's face. His helmet took the brunt of the impact as he broke the man's nose. Blood spurted as he reared back, blindly swinging a fist in James's general direction. He missed. James pushed him away and sat up, his throat burning as he breathed in great gulps of sweet air.

He reached for his knife as he clawed back some equilibrium. In the brief calm, James became aware of both Wright and Trueman struggling with their own assailants, but a cursory glance was all he got.

James threw himself on the enemy again and stabbed down, aiming for his carotid artery. With an enormous amount of luck, the enemy somehow caught his wrist, halting the knife's downward arc into his neck. James leaned forward, putting all his weight down onto the knife. The man bared his teeth as he struggled, the blood from his nose appearing black in the limited light. Fear flooded into his eyes, and his arms began to shake. Adrenaline burst through James at the sight of the man's stress. With one last push, the knife sank deep into his throat with little resistance.

Warmth sprayed over James's hands for the second time that night, and he wrenched the knife out as the bastard convulsed, his fingers ineffectually clawing at the wound.

James wiped his blade and hands on the dying man before pushing himself to his feet. He saw Trueman dispatch the person he fought, and Wright climbed to her feet a little way away, two men lying dead at her feet. *Two? What the fuck? She's so small, how did she...?* James shook his head and accepted the fact she was a little, lethal woman who could more than handle herself.

"Everyone okay?" James panted. His throat felt like someone had shoved sandpaper into it.

"Yes, sir," Trueman replied as he too fought to control his breathing.

"Wright?"

"Absolutely fantastic. Nothing gets the blood pumping like a good old wrestle with two men." She casually brushed some dirt off her sleeve and winked at him.

James stared at her incredulously, and she smirked. Stepping over a body, she moved back through the door and beckoned the civilian's out. "Okay, people, there will be more where this lot came from." She nudged one of the bodies with a foot. "We need to move extra quickly and quietly, okay?"

The civilians nodded, their eyes wide in the torchlight. If they hadn't understood the gravity of the situation before, they certainly did now. James brought his L85 back up, checking both the weapon and torch for any damage. Wright took the lead, the group following like lost ducklings that had imprinted on her.

She wound them around the opposite building, heading for one of the car parks. They took extra care to stay in the shadows.

They hadn't gotten far when Wright signalled '*halt*,' immediately followed by '*crouch*.' James's breath came in agonising puffs as she switched off her torch and signalled '*enemy*.' Sweat prickled his forehead, and one lone droplet slid away from under his helmet, down his face, and lost itself in the growing stubble. The trail it left behind burned, and James wondered how perilous their situation had become. As if mad, murderous, infected people weren't enough.

Wright signalled '*nine*.' James knew they had to find a way to circle around them without getting spotted. Nine was too many to handle, especially with their limited ammunition and the civilians to protect.

James edged up to Wright, turning his torch off and making sure to stay out of sight. The enemies sidled up to the building with their weapons raised. *They must have heard the fighting*. James clenched his jaw and squeezed his eyes shut for a brief second. He could draw their fire while Wright and Trueman got the civilians away. He saw the car park—the light grey concrete stretched off into the night, and the cars looked like shapeless, shadowed lumps dotted haphazardly across it.

James filled his lungs with cold air, remaining motionless as it blazed down his throat. He paused as the sting faded, hoping to somehow keep a hold of the calm moment before he most likely went and got himself killed. Death had never really bothered him—everyone died at some point. The *manner* of his death was the important part. His father had slowly wasted away in agony as the cancer tore through his weakened body. James did not want that to happen to him. If he died giving these people a decent chance to escape and live, that was good enough for him.

He released a measured breath, feeling the burn flare up again. "Listen, and please don't argue," James rasped. Wright half turned to him, a sombre look settling over her face as at his urgency. "I'm going to create some kind of distraction to draw them away." A frown settled over Wright's features and she opened her mouth, no doubt to argue. "*Please listen.* I draw them away, and you and Trueman get the civilians to the cars and out of here."

He stared at her imploringly, hoping she wouldn't fight him on this. No such luck. "If you think, for one fucking second, I'm going to let you go on a fucking suicide mis—"

They were running out of time. He had to act, or else he wouldn't be able to make it to another location before the enemy came upon them. "There's no time to argue. Get them to safety." James spun on his heel and rushed back the way they had come, ignoring the confused and alarmed faces he left in his wake.

He darted past the dead bodies of the soldiers they killed, skidding around the building and almost falling over as he carried too much speed into the corner. Quickly righting himself, he ran down the length of the other side of the building, not bothering to be quiet. He slid to a halt at the end, flattening himself against the rough exterior as he attempted to get a grip on his frenzied breathing. His throat tore itself apart from the inside out with each breath, but he embraced the pain, focusing on it as he readied his weapon. It grounded him and gave him the clarity he needed for what he was about to do.

Here we go. Oddly calm, James burst out from behind his cover, firing short bursts in the direction of the enemy soldiers as he continued moving away from the building and over to the adjacent one. They responded instantly, nine weapons spitting death in his direction. James had never been the subject of such concentrated violence before, and he had been in the army for a long time.

He made it to the momentary safety of the other building, not quite believing he was still alive. He gathered his breath, not allowing himself to think as he broke away from the wall and fired at the enemy whilst running in the opposite direction. If he stopped to think about his plan he would likely go into shock, and it would be the end of him.

Bullets embedded themselves into the wall next to him, and little puffs of dust rained down as he flinched away, almost falling. Cursing himself as he stumbled, James twisted around and squeezed the trigger once more, conscious that at any moment he would run out of bullets.

Something solid slammed into his left shoulder with enough force to spin him around. White-hot agony erupted as he crashed to the ground. *I've been shot, I've been shot.* The words repeated over and over in his mind as he lay still for what felt like an eternity, breathing in the mud and dust around him.

The cold of the ground and the heat seeping from his shoulder warred with each other, and the juxtaposition jarred James out of his stupor. He heaved himself to his knees, becoming acutely aware of how close the enemy's yelling was. A loud explosion of gunfire blew apart the wall above him. He launched himself to his feet and began running again.

More yelling and gunfire followed him as he rounded the building. James didn't dare stop, not even for a second to catch his breath. He sprinted down the length of the building and over to the next one, his shoulder screaming with every beat of his racing heart. Burning blood poured out and soaked his clothing. It didn't offer any warmth—cold stole into his bones and froze his marrow.

He didn't think about what direction he ran in. *Have to keep moving, have to keep moving*, the four short words spun around in his head like a stuck record. Buildings flashed past before they abruptly disappeared. He stumbled to a halt, finding himself surrounded by tall trees, their bare branches unmoving in the still night. They looked almost unnatural, frozen in the darkness. How far had he run? The air was silent, no loud shouting, no sharp bursts of gunfire. Had he managed to lose them? His heavy breathing punched through the quiet as he turned in a circle to get his bearings.

He could make out buildings in the distance. The air base. He hadn't run as far as he thought. Strength gone, he slumped against a tree, unable to stand unaided as weakness rushed through him in a wave. He slid to the ground as he pressed a hand to his shoulder, hissing as the pain flared and burned like the sun. He couldn't find an exit wound, meaning the bullet was still lodged deep in the tissue. A horrible grinding sensation reverberated from his shoulder when he moved to feel the point of entry, and the amount of blood spilling out alarmed him. He was *freezing*, shivering against the tree while his rapid breaths became shorter and shallower. His heart pounded furiously in his chest, like it knew he was dying but stubbornly refused to give up, pumping blood around his body and out through his shoulder. It would stop soon enough. Even the most resilient collapsed after pushing too hard.

Wright and the others would have had ample opportunity to get away. They had to be long gone. James told himself they were safe, his sacrifice wasn't in vain, his death would *mean* something. Contentment flooded his body even though he had no idea if he was lying to himself or not.

He reached up and removed his helmet—the thing was too heavy. The rush of cold air over his sweaty head was *not* welcome, and it set off another bout of shivering. He didn't like being cold. He wanted to feel the sun on his skin one more time, feel the heat soak through every inch of him, feel the icy cold chased out of his bones.

His earlier contentment fled in the face of his overwhelming desire to see the sun again, and he fumbled with his first aid pack, determined to bind the wound and live long enough to feel warmth once more. Only for a minute.

Getting a bandage in place was easier said than done. The pain threatened to make him black out whenever he moved the wrong way. Gritting his teeth, James slowly removed his body armour and outer jacket, enabling him to reach around easier. He got on with it, powering through the agony. The result was plain shite, but it would stem some of the bleeding.

James collapsed back against the tree, his heart still hammering out a frenzied beat in its house of bone, stalwartly keeping him alive. The ever-present cold wouldn't leave him alone, and suddenly it was too much effort to keep his eyes open.

He didn't know how long he sat there drifting in and out of consciousness. When he came around again, the smell of rain hung in the air like the heavens were about to open at any moment and drown him in a torrent of freezing water. As if his situation couldn't get any worse. He no longer felt cold. He no longer felt anything. Had his heart slowed? James didn't think so. It didn't know how to accept its fate.

It was still dark. *No sun after all then*. Thick clouds continued to obscure the moon and stars, so he wouldn't even get to see them again.

Light. It was small, weak, barely penetrating the heavy darkness. It swayed from side to side and bobbed up and down. A torch? James frowned, straining his eyes as he tried to focus on it. Someone jogged toward him. *Well, they've already killed me. They'll probably leave me here.* His slow thoughts ground to a halt when he finally saw their face.

Was he dreaming? Wright's smooth features scrutinised him, taking in his bloody bandage and ghostly pallor. "Are you real?" James whispered, frightened of her answer. Scared she'd say no. Scared she'd say yes.

"Oh yeah, Sunshine. You're not getting rid of me that easily," she said. She smiled her big, bright grin, and it didn't matter that the sun wasn't up yet. Her smile worked the same.

His lips twitched upward as she continued to beam at him. "Ah, he *can* smile," Wright exclaimed, shifting to pull his right arm up across her shoulders while she grabbed him firmly around the waist. "I was beginning to wonder."

"Very funny," he gasped out, almost falling unconscious again as she pulled him up. His tired heart thumped in his ears, protesting the sudden exertion.

"How... I mean... you're so small..." his voice trailed off, cohesive thought and speech too difficult.

She frowned up at him as they started shuffling forward, travelling at a snail's pace because James couldn't achieve anything more. Before he could mourn the loss of her smile, however, it came back in full force as she laughed at him.

"You mean, how can I lift and support you since I'm only five foot two and you're a big lumbering giant?"

He nodded weakly, letting the sound of her voice wash over him. It gave him hope he was going to be okay. Hope was dangerous, though—the rational part of him knew he'd lost too much blood.

"I'm actually a Terminator sent back in time to stop this virus and save your sorry arse." She delivered that bullshit in such a serious tone and with such a solemn expression James almost believed her.

He snorted. "The Terminator films were about AI's and machines, not viruses." He had to pause to catch his breath, but she waited for him to continue instead of interrupting. "And you've done a piss-poor job of stopping the virus."

She gasped, looking genuinely affronted. "Well, at least I've saved your sorry arse. Although, if you keep insulting me, I might put you back where I found you."

James grunted out a laugh but fell silent afterward. He needed to focus on remaining upright, on putting one foot in front of the other to get to wherever Wright had stashed everyone.

They didn't walk long. James estimated five to ten minutes, even though it felt like much longer. He didn't even realise they arrived at the group until Trueman fussed over his wound like a mother hen, tearing away his pathetic excuse for a bandage and applying more pressure. The abrupt, searing pain cleared the fog filling James's mind.

He tried to count the civilians to make sure they all made it, but Wright and Trueman bundled him into the back of a car before he could count past Dan and Victoria. Trueman climbed in after him and continued putting pressure on his shoulder while Aarav and Riya jumped into the front. The rest disappeared into the other car.

Aarav started the engine and followed the other car down the road. "Can you put the heating on, please?" James asked, becoming aware of the cold again as Wright's smile wasn't there to chase it away.

"Of course," Aarav nodded, putting it on full blast.

James sighed as the warm air hit him and closed his eyes as he relaxed into the seat.

After what seemed like several minutes of steady heat, he still felt cold. Ice had slipped under his skin and pieced his organs. If he didn't get to a hospital soon, he wasn't going to make it. *Wait,* he thought, his mind sluggish and slow to respond, *there are no hospitals anymore. The world ended, didn't it?*

"Sir, I need you to stay awake." Trueman slapped him, the impact scarcely registering across his numb face. "Sir?"

"If you hit me again, Corporal, I'll break your arm," James mumbled, barely conscious.

Trueman smiled at him—*smiled*—and focused on his shoulder again. "We've been driving for about an hour now, sir. I've managed to control the bleeding, but you keep losing consciousness. I really need you to stay awake. Fight it, sir."

They had been driving for an hour? What the fuck? "Where are we going?"

"A military hospital, sir." The reply sounded far away, like they were shouting to each other from opposite ends of a football pitch. "Hopefully, this one is still manned, and it hasn't been looted for medical supplies. It *is* a bit close to Paris, but it's a risk we've..." The corporal's voice became fainter and fainter until it eventually vanished altogether.

Chapter Twelve

They slowed to a stop on the empty road, and silence filled the car as Sergeant Wright cut the engine. Victoria blinked about warily, forcing her tiredness down as she sat up straighter. The last couple of hours passed in a blur of faded black trees, faded black road and faded black sky. It had rained once, briefly breaking the monotony before that, too, faded.

Victoria kept dozing off only to jerk awake a short while later, too tense to fall completely into the vulnerable depths of sleep. Every time she awoke, she noted the slow rise and fall of Jennifer's chest, her even breathing at odds with the small frown marring her features. Her hands held her camera in a vice-like grip, as if she thought some-one would snatch it away while she slept. The poor woman had been out since they left the air base, but Victoria didn't think it was a restful sleep. Dan, on the other side of Victoria, had made a valiant effort to stay awake, his eyes wide as he alternated between staring out the win-dow and checking on Jennifer. He had succumbed to slumber about an hour into their impromptu road trip, struggling against it all the while.

Martin also slept most of the drive. He was so quiet Victoria almost forgotten he was there. *Makes a change from the other day,* she thought as irritation crept up her spine. He'd blathered on about how *horrible* and *traumatic* his ordeals had been, as if no one else had gone through any pain and horror. Victoria fought so hard to keep herself together, to keep a civil face and *not* lash out at him, especially after what she'd been through.

No. No, she couldn't think of that. *Focus on the here and now.*

Sergeant Wright rubbed her eyes and sucked in a deep breath before she opened the door. "Out," she said, the word bitten short as she fought back a yawn.

Martin and Dan woke up when the car stopped, and they sluggishly climbed out, both stretching and blinking away sleep. Victoria nudged Jennifer, who came crashing back to consciousness as if Victoria punched her in the ribs. She banged her head against the window and swore loudly before she went still as she took in their surroundings.

"Could you make any more racket?" Sergeant Wright's hissed words drifted over from the other car.

Jennifer glared at Victoria as she rubbed her head, but Victoria remained unrepentant. It wasn't her bloody fault the other woman reacted in such a way. Instead, she raised a stern eyebrow and shuffled out of the car, hopping on her good foot. Her right ankle had swollen painfully, and she dreaded the moment she would have to remove her boot.

She heard indistinct grumbling behind her as Jennifer pushed herself out of the car, looking like she hadn't had any sleep at all. She still gripped the camera with fingers of steel. Dan smiled at Jennifer's grouchiness as he helped Victoria move over to where everyone gathered next to the second car. Sergeant Wright and Corporal Trueman fretted over Sergeant Mollino, who had passed out on the back seats.

Victoria thought Sergeant Wright's insistence to go back for James was commendable, but ultimately fruitless. Surely, he hadn't survived. She remembered the way the loud cracks of gunfire had echoed through her bones as they ran to the cars, remembered how it had all been directed away from them. To say she'd been shocked when the two sergeants came stumbling back to the group was an understatement.

"Okay, listen up, people." Sergeant Wright straightened, looking more serious than Victoria had ever seen her. "We're outside a military hospital. We're *exceptionally* close to Paris right now, so close we're practically in the city, so we need to find out if it's still manned or if it's been abandoned or overrun, and we need to do so *quickly*, for us and for Sergeant Mollino. He's stable at the moment, but he could do with some medical atten—"

Two beams of light burst out of the pressing darkness, cutting Sergeant Wright off. She made no move for her weapons, raising her hands and motioning for the others to do the same.

The heavy silence weighed down on Victoria, who froze like a deer in headlights, her muscles locking in place as she clutched Dan tightly. Had the soldiers from the other base followed them here? Dan's grip around her waist anchored her and reminded her she still drew breath. If their assailants wanted them dead, Victoria had no doubt they would be.

One of the disembodied lights moved to the car, chasing away the shadows and revealing the severity of Sergeant Mollino's condition. He looked like he was knocking on death's door—his closed eyes two bruises standing out on a bloodless face.

"We're not your enemies," Anthony told the light, his voice soft but insistent. "Please. We need help. He was shot, and I think he's gone into hypovolemic shock, but my medical knowledge doesn't extend much beyond first aid. I've done all I can for him."

Victoria's eyes adjusted to the onslaught of light, and she saw the outline of people behind the brightness. She implored those shadows to understand, to take them in. They needed all the help they could get.

No one spoke. Victoria felt like she should say something, anything, to ease the strain, but nothing came to her frozen mind. The oppressive silence blanketed them all, and it seemed Victoria would suffocate under it, the stillness stealing her words.

"You are English, yes?" A male voice spoke, cutting through the tension that grew like poisonous weeds.

"Yes," Sergeant Wright responded, taking a small step in the direction of the voice. "We were told to evacuate our country and regroup, but everything went wrong, and now we really need your help."

Another short silence stained the air before the two shadows began to speak to each other in French. Victoria looked at the pilot and tried to guess what they talked about based on her reactions. A pointless endeavour. The woman stood still as a statue and her face could have been cut from marble for all the expression it held.

The two lights shifted away from them as abruptly as they had blinded them, and the man who had spoken stepped forward. "I am Romain Dubois. We will take you in, but you must give up your weapons until we have discussed your situation with the Commandant." His voice was taut and his accent thick, muffling the words and making him difficult to understand. "Is this acceptable?"

Everyone waited for Sergeant Wright to speak, tension thickening in the spaces between people. After several seconds that seemed to stretch into eternity, the pilot sighed. "We agree to those terms." Her clipped tone made it obvious she wasn't happy. Perhaps Victoria should have had more reservations than she did, but she was simply glad they were being taken in.

One of the shadows got into the car with James and Anthony and drove off. The rest of them walked. *Bloody walked.* Victoria supposed it didn't take much time to reach the hospital, but if asked about it she wouldn't have been able to answer. Her world boiled down to the pain in her ankle, and the sharp pulsing that shot through her with every step even though she leaned on Dan. By the time they stopped, her right leg throbbed in time with her heartbeat as she fought back tears.

They were taken to a large ward, the walls an unappealing off-white colour. One of the lights flickered, and one of the beds had a dried bloody handprint on the railing. *What happened here?* Dan helped her up onto one of the beds near the door, and she closed her eyes as the pain abated somewhat. Jennifer sat down on the bed next to her, her eyes dull as she looked around the room.

The man who spoke to them at the cars looked unkempt, with greasy dark blond hair and a patchy beard struggling to grow. He seemed quite jittery as well, throwing mistrustful glances their way as he spoke, his hands never stilling. He was shorter than the man he started talking to, who arrived as Victoria sat down. This new man was calm where the other was jumpy, dark where the other was pale. He was broad and solid and looked like nothing fazed him. His brown eyes betrayed no emotion as the smaller man talked, his impassive gaze flitting over each person before settling on Sergeant Wright.

An urgency clung about the pilot, sticking to her like chewing gum to the underside of school desks. Victoria watched Sergeant Wright glare around the room before she shifted her intense scowl over to the French soldiers. As she opened her mouth to no doubt snap at them, the tall, solid man spoke.

"Your soldier is in good hands. Capitaine Roux is one of the best trauma surgeons I have ever seen." He had no accent, his smooth voice washing over Victoria like a stream over rocks, gently soothing her. *Maybe we're going to be okay.*

"The civilians will be all right here?" Sergeant Wright asked curtly, her earlier tiredness gone and replaced by a tension holding her rigid. *It looks quite unnatural,* Victoria thought. She associated the pilot with loose, flowing motion.

"Yes." The tall man nodded.

"Then take me to Sergeant Mollino."

The tall man nodded again. "You can all sleep here," he said to the rest of them. Both he and the pilot strode from the room, leaving the jumpy man standing by the door. He looked momentarily lost before he gave them one last suspicious glance and left, closing the door on his way out. His stride was nowhere near as confident as the other two soldiers'.

There were five beds and seven people. Aarav and Riya doubled up, and Jennifer and Dan went top and tail. Nobody talked as Martin turned off the lights and they settled down. Victoria wanted nothing more than to join the others in the wonderful land of unconsciousness, but the pain prevented her from properly drifting off.

After a short while, Victoria finally managed to fall into a light, fretful doze. She cursed her *stupid* ankle every time it denied her true oblivion.

What felt like several hours passed in the same manner, and soon soft morning light filtered through the gaps in the cardboard over the windows. The door opened on loud hinges and a man stepped through, switching on the light as he moved further into the room. The disappearance of darkness drew the others from their sleep, and the room filled with the sound of creaking springs as people shifted on their beds, rubbing their eyes sleepily.

When the man looked at her, Victoria waved him over. His eyes were a startling hazel, especially for someone with such darkly tanned skin. He kept his black hair shaved close to his head and had an angled face with a sharp jawline and cheekbones. He smiled tiredly at her as he walked over, his eyes crinkling at the corners.

"Can I help you with something?" he asked in an accent thicker than the tall, commanding man, and his voice was a touch higher than Victoria expected.

"Sorry to bother you, but can I have something for my ankle? Some painkillers would be great," Victoria whispered as Jennifer—the only person still sleeping—burrowed deeper under her covers.

He nodded as he sat next to her on the small bed, motioning for her to lie back against the headboard and stretch her leg out. Victoria held herself rigid as he removed her boot and let out an explosive breath after he peeled away her sock. Her ankle had swollen, painfully so, and the bruise had darkened to a deep black.

The man tutted when he saw it, frowning as he examined her foot and leg. His bright eyes flicked up to meet hers briefly before dropping back down. "I will be right back," he said with one final look at her ankle. He strode back after a few minutes with what looked like a lumpy cloth. He grabbed her pillow and used it to gently prop her foot up. "Ice," he said and cautiously pressed the lumpy cloth down over her ankle, pausing when she flinched as the coldness assaulted her.

After several tense seconds, he pressed the ice back down on her ankle, and it felt fine beyond the initial shock. The man smiled at her, and Victoria responded, despite the pain. Her ankle would finally get the chance to heal. "I'll come back in about fifteen minutes to bind it and check you for bites."

He stood and moved to check on the others. Victoria settled back onto her pillow, letting her foot slowly relax. She assumed he was a doctor, perhaps the trauma surgeon mentioned earlier. He was attractive, she noticed with a sigh-turned-grimace. Thinking about attraction led to thoughts of Mike and Katherine. The raw pain from her past persisted, the bad memories roughly shoving the good ones aside and demanding attention instead, like some spoiled brat. The trial had been exhausting, and Victoria had begun to doubt she would ever taste freedom again.

She sat in silence, lost in her dark past until the doctor returned. She shoved her dark thoughts down and focused on his hands as he worked, his touch gentle but firm. Her ankle was immobilised, and she was found to be bite-free. "That should do for now. Rest, and try not to put any weight on it for a while."

"I'll do my best," Victoria returned his smile, and he nodded at her as he left. She settled down to finally sleep, choosing to think about the doctor instead of her horrible last few months.

Chapter Thirteen

Jennifer came awake leisurely, rising out of the dark depths of sleep without causing a ripple as she breached the surface. She lay for a while, not moving, listening to the peaceful silence encompassing the room. She didn't want to break the soft bubble that encased her.

Eventually, she blinked open her eyes and rose from her small—and frankly uncomfortable—bed, leaving her camera on the pillow. The need to get out of the stuffy room grabbed her and wouldn't let go. The other beds were empty. She must have slept for a long time.

It didn't take her long to find an exit, and she checked to make sure the door was locked. It was. *Good*, she thought with satisfaction, content to look out the window for a while. A feeling of security wrapped around her like a blanket.

She watched the clouds drift across the bright blue sky, her thoughts back with her friends as she day-dreamed about how her birthday should have gone. The sun hovered high in the sky when she heard footsteps approaching from behind. She whirled, her heart jumping into her throat. *I guess I'm becoming paranoid.* It was only Anthony, lacking his armour and looking refreshed in a dark green t-shirt and combat trousers. He stopped a few paces from her when she turned, holding up his hands with a reassuring smile on his thin face.

"I didn't mean to startle you," he said, cautiously walking closer.

"No, it's okay," Jennifer replied, trying to alter her breathing subtly so he didn't figure out how much he had surprised her.

They gazed out the window for a few more minutes in silence. Jennifer let the calm soak through her and allowed herself to believe she was safe here, in the warmth of the building with the soldiers protecting them. For a moment, a second. She saw through the illusion, though. The handgun strapped to Anthony's waist shattered her fantasy.

"You, um, might want to think about having a shower," Anthony said sheepishly as he glanced at her out of the corner of his eye.

She turned to look at him, raising one of her eyebrows in a stern expression. She knew she needed to wash—her brief scrubbing with the gauze and canteen was not enough to scour away all the grime and sweat—but it was funny watching Anthony squirm. He was too polite.

She couldn't hold her offended look for long, though, and ended up grinning at him. "I know. I feel really disgusting right now, believe me." She barely suppressed a shudder at the thought of everything she had been through. "Can you tell me where the showers are?"

"I'll walk you," he said, as if he thought he needed to redeem himself for a perceived insult.

They walked down a corridor before Anthony spoke again, a little crease between his brows revealing his disquiet. "How are you feeling?"

Jennifer thought for a moment before answering him. She didn't feel tired or sick, nor did her head or hand or arm ache. Not *that* much anyway. She felt better than she had in days. "I feel really good," she said as a slow smile spread over her face. She took in Anthony's sceptical look and let out a small laugh. "I know, it's weird, right? Yesterday I thought I would feel tired and horrible for the rest of my life, but today... I don't feel like I can run marathons or anything, but yeah, I feel good."

They walked the rest of the way in companionable silence. Jennifer felt at ease with Anthony despite only knowing him a short time. Something about his soft eyes and relaxed but capable bearing that reassured her.

He left her at a door with a small bow of his head, and Jennifer smiled to herself. *That man is far too... what's the word? Gallant for this day and age.*

Jennifer entered a large patient bay. She was confused for a moment, but as she looked around, she noticed the other door off to the right. It led to a bathroom larger than she expected and with lime green panelling covering the walls. A small pile of clean clothes and gauze were neatly folded on the closed toilet. Her smile widened, and she was grateful for Anthony's foresight. He had an agenda when he sought her out, but Jennifer found she didn't care.

She stripped and turned the water on, welcoming the hot spray over her battered body. She didn't know how long she stayed in there, the water washing away the past. It was cathartic, in a way, the warmth beating out the cold, draping itself around her, soothing her worn muscles. It reminded her of when she had been ill as a child and her mother made her the best hot chocolate and wrapped her in an all-encompassing hug.

The sound of the outer door banging open jerked Jennifer out of her nostalgia. "You still in here, Miss Immune?" Sergeant Wright's loud voice was almost painful after the quiet serenity of the past... How long had she been in the shower? "You do realise you've been in there for almost forty-five minutes, right? I'm not letting you steal all the hot water."

Jennifer bit back a sigh and turned the water off. Goosebumps rose on her skin, and she quickly wrapped the towel around herself, grabbed her clothes, and stepped out of the bathroom. The pilot would see her naked over her dead body. She would never hear the end of it.

Sergeant Wright grinned at her as she walked past and into the shower, but Jennifer ignored her and focused on drying herself as quickly as she could. She had always hated those freezing moments between exiting the shower and getting dry again. The clothes Anthony left for her were like the ones she had been wearing from Knightsbridge—black boots, black combat trousers, and a dark blue t-shirt. She stuck the new gauze over her arm as Sergeant Wright's shower stopped, and the pilot waltzed out wrapped in a towel of her own.

Jennifer averted her eyes and focused on tying her laces. She hoped she wasn't blushing *too* much. "How's James?" she asked, hoping to fill the silence with words.

"Captain Roux said he's lost a lot of blood, but he'll pull through. The bullet had lodged deep in his shoulder and he'll have difficultly regaining a lot of movement, but I'm sure the stubborn bastard will be fine." Sergeant Wright sounded *proud*, and Jennifer sneaked a glance at her to see a grin taking up most of her face.

Jennifer waited for the pilot to get dressed as she didn't know where to go. She began to feel little pangs of hunger, but she still didn't think she would be able to eat much.

They left the room together, Jennifer trailing half a step behind the pilot as they strode down a corridor. Sergeant Wright walked quickly for someone so short. *She's like a little rocket,* Jennifer thought as she struggled to keep up.

"Trueman said you were feeling better?" The pilot raised a cynical eyebrow, her eyes lingering on the fresh gauze covering Jennifer's torn arm. She thought it looked better than yesterday—the skin was scabbed over and healing well. Why did they doubt her? Did she still look awful?

"I am, yeah. Much better," she said, nodding to emphasise how good she felt. "Did I really seem that bad?"

Sergeant Wright snorted. "You looked like a breeze would send you flying." Jennifer sighed. That sounded about right. The pilot stopped walking abruptly, and Jennifer continued for a step before she realised the shorter woman no longer moved. Turning, she saw Sergeant Wright frowning at her. Her piercing eyes made Jennifer feel exposed. "How are you feeling, *really*?"

Jennifer sighed after a pregnant pause. "I still don't really have much of an appetite, and I do feel a bit run down, but honestly, I feel great compared to the past few days." There was no point in lying to her.

"I'm glad you're being honest. We need you running at one hundred percent so we can use you to find a miracle cure." She nodded brusquely and continued walking.

Jennifer stood rooted to the spot for a second before her limbs unfroze and she jogged to catch up. How had she not thought of using her blood to find a cure? She had been so wrapped up in feeling shitty it hadn't even crossed her mind. She could help people. Put an end to all the madness. Would it be painful? But wait, she was getting ahead of herself. They weren't even sure she *was* immune.

They halted outside some plain double doors, and the pilot turned to face her. "Listen, don't bring up the immune thing around the French soldiers okay? I haven't told them yet—we haven't been around them long enough to guess at how they'll react. They might welcome it and be happy this virus can be stopped, or they might not believe us and could potentially try to kill you. Yeah, they helped James, but who the fuck knows what they'll do when it comes to the virus?" Sergeant Wright shrugged as if it were no big deal and sauntered through the doors, leaving Jennifer staring after her, more than a little concerned.

After a brief pause, she followed Sergeant Wright into a room which turned out to be an average sized cafeteria. Round tables filled the space, and a long counter to the left of the entrance stretched down half of the room, separating them from the cold kitchen beyond. There were several tall windows opposite the counter, and Jennifer imagined they let in a lot of light during the summer, but the curtains were drawn, plunging the room into perpetual gloom staved off only by the clinical glow of the overhead lights.

Everyone was there except Anthony, sitting and eating cereal. Dan looked to be inhaling his. He smiled when he saw her, his cheeks bulging like a hamster as he pointed to the seat next to him. Jennifer sat down and smiled as he pushed a bowl in front of her. What little appetite she had fled when she looked down at the soggy cornflakes. She ignored the faint nausea and ate a spoonful, conscious of Dan's watchful gaze. The cereal felt heavy on her tongue and tasted so bland she would have had a better time eating cardboard.

"Are you all right?" Victoria asked.

Jennifer smiled at the blonde. "Yeah, thanks for asking."

Victoria nodded and returned to her food. It seemed a sombre mood hung over everyone today. *Probably because of James.*

Aarav and Riya chatted quietly in their own language, but everyone else ate in silence. Jennifer noticed Martin sitting by himself at a table apart from the others. She knew the extent of Victoria's contempt for the man, but honestly, it was a little over the top. So, he was a bit self-involved. Who wasn't? Hell had come for everyone. No need to make it worse for the poor guy by excluding him.

Jennifer stood up with her bowl, and before she could remember she wasn't great at making small talk with new people she walked over and sat down at his table. She didn't need to look at Victoria to know surprise had etched itself across her face.

Martin's eyebrows rose as he stared at her with uncertainty. Did fear crowd his face as well? *Does he seriously think I'm going to attack him?* Jennifer smiled widely at him, hoping to put him at ease. If anything, it seemed to make him more anxious, his messy hair almost vibrating with tension.

"Hi," she said, holding out her hand. Embarrassment sparked a fire through her body as Martin made no move toward her. She sat there with her arm extended for a few uncomfortable beats before he tentatively reached out and shook it. He had a weak grip, and he let go almost as soon as he touched her.

"Hello," he replied, coughing into a fist.

He spoke to me. Progress. Jennifer forced down a few more mouthfuls of cereal, hoping the man would relax. Did he not understand the concept of immunity?

She couldn't eat anymore, her stomach roiling in protest, so she pushed her bowl away and crossed her arms on the table. She noticed the way Martin's eyes kept darting to the gauze, and she wondered what happened to make him so nervous.

Deciding the question was too personal, she opted for something more generic. "Martin, right?" Jennifer waited for his short nod before continuing. "So, what did you do before all this happened?"

He gave her a funny look. "You really care?"

"I wouldn't have asked if I didn't."

He stared down at his own bowl of cereal as he replied. "I was a taxi driver." He lapsed into silence, idly pushing cornflakes around with his spoon.

"You must have met lots of interesting people. How long have you been doing it?" He still seemed uncomfortable, shifting in his seat as he set down his spoon. The cornflakes were as soggy as her own. A lost cause if she ever saw one.

He snorted softly. "Interesting is one way to put it. Eleven years," he said. Jennifer got the distinct impression he didn't want to continue the conversation. Well, he talked to her at least, so it was a start. She didn't want to be wary of him doing something to her because of some misguided fear she had the infection.

She looked up and caught Aarav's eye. He gazed at her flatly, his dark eyes boring into her own before he turned back to his cereal.

Might as well nip this one in the bud too, she thought as she stood up and walked back to the other table, sitting down between Dan and Victoria again. Dan side-eyed the bowl she left, and she felt a faint twinge of guilt for not being able to finish it. Mentally shaking her head at herself, Jennifer stared at Aarav until he sensed he was being watched and raised his head to look back at her.

"If you have a problem with me, you should tell me now." Jennifer cut straight to the point, not wanting to mince words. The beginning of a headache stirred behind her eyes, and her good mood from waking up refreshed quickly evaporated.

"There is no problem. I will be watching to see if you turn crazy, and then I will do whatever I have to do to protect my family," Aarav said in a matter-of-fact tone. Everyone stopped eating and watched the two of them. Jennifer noticed the pilot wasn't there anymore. *How did I miss her leaving again?*

She opened her mouth to tell him in no uncertain terms she *wasn't* about to go crazy—she was *immune* for crying out loud—when Riya swatted him on the arm. He jumped and looked at her in surprise. She started speaking in her language, gesticulating first at herself and then at Jennifer. Aarav looked in turns contrite and angry as she spoke, her rant lasting several uncomfortable minutes. By the end, Aarav scowled down at the table and Riya looked embarrassed.

"I'm sorry about that," she said. "We know you are immune, and you mean no harm." She glanced at Aarav who nodded, still glaring at the table. "We have seen a lot of awful things recently, you understand. He's just being careful."

"Yeah, I understand," Jennifer said quickly, not wanting to start another argument. Riya missed the glare Aarav shot her way, and Jennifer clenched her hands into fists under the table. *Great, now he probably resents me for causing an argument with his wife.*

The low hum of husband and wife conversing filled the room, and Jennifer let it wash over her as she stared down at the table. Her broken fingers caught her eye, the binding damp from her shower. She would have to change it. She made no move to get up, though, her earlier apathy from Knightsbridge curling through her, its insidious nature making it difficult to resist. She continued to sit quietly while everyone finished eating.

She fought down painful thoughts of her family and friends. *God, has it only been a few days since everything fell apart?* It didn't seem real. Instead of letting the lethargy get any more of a foothold, Jennifer turned back to what the pilot had said about using her blood to find a cure. Could they do it here? What happened to all the patients anyway? The staff? Were they all dead?

Her hands clenched again as she worked herself up. She wondered when she'd become so nervous. Thankfully, her swirling thoughts were interrupted by the arrival of Sergeant Wright and four French soldiers, two men and two women. The pilot marched through the doors like she owned the place, and calm swept over Jennifer. The smaller woman had shown she was capable and could keep a clear head in times of crisis. Jennifer relaxed as the soldiers grabbed something to eat.

The commanding soldier from last night stepped in behind Wright, his solid presence more comforting than intimidating even though Jennifer didn't know him. His dark skin looked rough, stretching over a hard face that was all sharp edges. The other man was someone Jennifer hadn't seen before, his hazel eyes startling in someone with such bronze skin. The two men looked quite similar, like they were related.

A woman with brown hair pulled into a ponytail followed them, her eyes crinkling at the corners when she looked over Jennifer's group. Her mouth looked like a smile always hovered close by, ready to curl her full lips. When the woman's warm eyes touched Jennifer's, her breath caught in her chest, and she smiled back. Kindness and sympathy radiated from her like sunlight glinting off metal, bright and warm and difficult to look at. Jennifer was grateful for it all, but it also reminded her of the past few days. She didn't want to think about any of her past as she stared at the woman.

Her eyes found Jennifer's again, like she could sense her gaze, and her smile deepened. Heat diffused through her cheeks. *What is this? Get yourself together, Jen.* Pushing her reaction away, she turned to the final woman.

She followed behind everyone, her disapproving gaze sweeping over the group. Her strawberry-blonde hair was tied back in an impeccable bun, and her lips were pursed as she observed everyone, her eyes the colour of steel. The soldiers sat around a table adjacent to Jennifer's and started digging into their food.

The commanding soldier didn't eat. Instead, he put down his bowl and spoon with precision—Jennifer got the impression every move he made was calculated and wasted as little energy as possible. He angled himself so he faced Jennifer and the others, and carefully weighed his words before speaking.

"I am Commandant Marcel Phillipe," he introduced himself, his smooth voice unexpected from such a rough-looking man. "You are all welcome here for as long as you wish to stay. We will help to keep you all safe, and we will try to get you back in contact with UK forces as soon as we can, although it is not looking promising. Your country has fallen hard." He paused for a moment, looking at them sympathetically. "You can move around this wing freely, but please don't leave the building for any reason without a soldier present. I will be honest with you—all communi-cations are a mess, and we have heard no proper com-mand. We don't know the status of France. The hospital was evacuated, and in the ensuing chaos, we've managed to secure this wing. It is not safe outside."

An ominous silence settled over the room, thickening the air and making it difficult to breathe. Jennifer dragged some into her empty lungs, making them expand as far as they would go before expelling it all in a rush through her nose. *In and out.* The whole world had *actually* fallen apart. *In and out.* She had to resign herself to the reality of never finding out what happened to her parents. *In and out.* This was her life now. *In.* A rush of motivation flooded through her as determination settled deep within her bones. *Out.* She would help find a cure. *In.* She would help rebuild what she could. *Out.* She would make her friends and family proud. She wouldn't give in to the looming numbness.

The hazel-eyed man leaned forward with a strained smile on his lips, like he wanted to tell good news but didn't quite know what it was. "I am Capitaine Louis Roux. Captain or Doctor is fine also." He cleared his throat. "Your soldier was badly injured and will need to stay here for as long as it takes for him to recover." His English wasn't as perfect as Commandant Phillipe's, but it was still good. Jennifer certainly couldn't complain—her grasp of foreign languages had always been appalling. "Do not worry. He will be fine. I saw to most of your injuries last night, but if you have any other queries, please ask." He flashed everyone another smile that didn't quite reach his eyes and turned back to his bowl. Jennifer noticed he devoted more time to pushing the food around than he did to eating. She wondered what his story was.

I might as well see him about my hand, she thought. She moved to stand but froze halfway up, remembering what Sergeant Wright said. *What if he asks about my arm?* She didn't want to start a fight. Well, too late. She couldn't continue half-standing without looking like an idiot. She straightened, trying to make it look as smooth as possible.

Jennifer ignored the warning look the pilot threw her way as she walked over to Captain Roux. "Hi." She smiled at him. He pushed his almost full bowl aside and turned to face her, another fake smile twisting his otherwise handsome face.

"Is this about your arm? The others said you'd cut it falling over. I gave your corporal some new gauze."

Ah, they had fed them a fake story. "No, not my arm. Thank you for the gauze. Could you have a look at my hand? I broke my fingers punching someone." She held her hand out to him. His touch was gentler than she thought it would be.

"This looks fine," he said after a short examination. "I will get some proper bindings for it."

"Before you do," Sergeant Wright said before the doctor could leave, "can you tell us anything about this virus? And immunity? Could, I don't know, someone be immune, perhaps?"

That had been the furthest thing from subtle Jennifer had ever heard, but the other soldiers didn't seem to notice anything amiss.

Captain Roux grimaced. "Unfortunately, I am a trauma surgeon, not a virologist or immunologist. I have not studied viruses since medical school. I can't really tell you anything more than what you probably already know—it is virulent for sure, as soon as the symptoms start, it can be transmitted. I know it was, erm, how do you say the word? Zoonotic? Yes, zoonotic in origin." He must have seen the blank looks from everyone as he rushed to clarify. "It is when a disease is passed to humans from an animal. This virus is thought to be related to the rabies virus and was passed on to us when an infected animal bit a human. I don't know if it is an entirely new virus, or if it is a mutated form of an already existing one. We need a specialist to know more."

"But can people be naturally immune?" the pilot pressed. She sounded tense to Jennifer.

"All healthy individuals have an innate immune system which is triggered in response to a pathogen," Captain

Roux said. "The virus has evolved to evade our defence mechanisms, though. Thinking about it, however, I guess there may be a small selection of the population whose immune systems can still fight it. Maybe they can recognise some product of the virus the rest of us can't." Captain Roux pursed his lips. "Immunity is individual. Some people won't catch a disease at all. Some catch it and recover while others die. Still others can be carriers, where they have a disease and can infect people but they themselves don't suffer from it. But you must remember there are diseases that are almost always fatal," he warned, emphasising the point with his hand, jabbing the table with a finger. "I would not get your hopes up with this disease, Sergeant Wright. It has brought the world to its knees like never before."

He nodded apologetically and rose from the table, leaving the room to retrieve better bindings for Jennifer's hand. The silence he left behind had a weight to it. Jennifer's brows knitted together as she picked at the gauze covering her arm, confused and worried. *Am I immune or not?* She looked at the faces surrounding her, some troubled, some hopeful, others stubborn or simply impassive. In that moment, seeing all the different emotions swirling around, Jennifer decided she would consider herself immune. She had to have hope. *They* had to have hope.

What was the point of surviving without it?

Chapter Fourteen

James struggled against waking, the remnants of his dream fading even as he clutched at them. Something about the sun and a smile. The further the dream slipped away, the colder he felt.

He lay on a shallow, uncomfortable mattress. He tried to relax on the thin surface, lifting his hand from underneath the warm blanket to rub his face. He winced as he touched the bruise blackening his eye and groaned as the pain in his shoulder loudly announced itself. Agony pounded an offbeat rhythm throughout his body, and he longed for unconsciousness to claim him once more.

When it became apparent that wasn't going to happen anytime soon, James turned his attention to taking stock of his injuries. His shoulder hurt the most by a fair margin—the pain there threatened to overwhelm all else. He gritted his teeth and breathed as evenly as he could, trying to concentrate on the lesser hurts.

His throat ached, like nails had scraped it all from the inside, and the left side of his face—chiefly the eye—was tender and sore. The rest of him was battered and bruised, and a pervasive fragility coated every inch of his body, like his skin would crumble at a touch.

He remembered the air base and leading the enemies away from the civilians. He remembered getting shot. Getting fucking shot. Typical.

The gunshot wound worried him. He couldn't move his arm when he tried, and he had to stop immediately as another wave of pain washed over him. Had he been given any form of painkiller at all? It didn't feel like it.

He blinked open his eyes, squinting against the bright light emanating from seemingly everywhere. The room was unfamiliar—the white walls appeared too bright in the light, and a thick black sheet covered the single window. Where was he? A hospital? It looked like a hospital room. Images of his father's last weeks accosted his mind, and it took every ounce of willpower to force them out of his head. He *hated* hospitals.

He rubbed his face again and registered the growth of hair there. How long had he been unconscious? What happened? Was everyone all right? He made to sit up, but the room spun, and he almost passed out, nausea rising as he pulled in several deep breaths of cool air.

He relaxed back on the thin mattress, not moving. It was too painful.

Would he be able to use his arm again soon? He *needed* both arms. With a long exhale through his nose, James turned his mind back to his surroundings in a futile attempt to ignore his shoulder and the worry gnawing at him.

He wasn't in his armour anymore, only his boxers. No wonder he felt cold. He had an IV line going into his right hand, and other wires connected him to a heart rate monitor, the beeps steady and strong. A sling cradled his left arm, and thick bandages covered his shoulder. *Maybe that's why I can't move it.*

The door creaked open, and a woman stepped through. Her light brown hair was pulled into a short ponytail, and she carried herself with a certain amount of grace, not unlike Wright. *Where is she, anyway?* As the woman got closer, James tried to sit up again but another dizzy spell put that idea to bed.

"Do not, ah, strain yourself," she said. She had a French accent, her voice soft, almost musical, flowing through the air like fingers over silk. She was quite nondescript, and her eyes were a similar colour to her hair. She wore a uniform and had a weapon at her waist. "I have been looking at your vitals, yes?" She moved to the bottom of his bed, making notations on a clipboard she picked up from the foot of his bed. "Your friends will be happy you are awake."

"Where are they?" James asked.

"It is midday. They will be eating." She smiled at him and put the clipboard down on the table next to the light. "I will, ah, get Capitaine Roux and Sergeant Wright."

She turned to leave, but the need to know the extent of the damage burned in him. "Wait, please. My shoulder, how bad is it?"

The woman looked at him with sympathy, and James felt his heart sink. "Capitaine Roux will tell you more, but you will have a hard time moving it. I will be back with him." She swept back out through the door, and the room suddenly seemed colder. James pulled the pathetic excuse for a blanket further up his chest, clenching his jaw as worry began to eat away at him again.

He didn't have to wait long for Wright and a man he assumed to be Captain Roux. Wright's massive grin took up her whole face. It banished some of the cold, and the small knot of apprehension in James's stomach loosened a wee bit.

"Welcome back to the land of the living, Sunshine," she said as she sat down on the end of his bed. He had to hastily move his feet lest she crush them.

"How long have I been unconscious?" James asked, his need for information bubbling up within and spilling over, like a fizzy drink someone had shaken before opening. Fuck, he missed pop.

"Three days," Wright answered. "You took your sweet time waking up. Maybe I should call you Lazy instead of Sunshine."

"Aye, right." James scowled. "Why don't you get shot and almost bleed to death? We'll see how long you take to wake up then."

"Who says I haven't?" Wright smirked down at him, an eyebrow rising in amusement.

He chose not to respond, giving her a flat stare before turning to Captain Roux, who stood awkwardly by the side of the bed as he waited for them to finish talking. "How bad is it?"

The man smiled at him. James thought it was meant to be friendly and reassuring, but he just looked tired. *Shite, how much have I missed?*

"I am a trauma surgeon, and I was the one who operated on you. I successfully removed the bullet lodged in the muscle—"

"That's good, isn't it?" James interrupted. His father's wasted face flashed up in his mind—he *really* didn't want to be here a second longer than necessary.

"Yes, that is good," Captain Roux said slowly. He wet his lips as he took a deep breath. "But the damage to the bone and muscle and tissue is extensive. You will have lost a lot of mobility to your shoulder. Regular physiotherapy will be required to regain movement, and while it is not my area of expertise, I will help in any way I can. Sergeant Wright has also volunteered to assist."

"It's going to be fun, Sunshine."

James didn't know what to think. Regular physiotherapy? Where would he find the time for that? He needed to protect the civilians and make sure this place was secure. With the constant threat of enemy combatants and infected people, he couldn't afford to be injured. Maybe it wasn't as bad as the captain thought. Maybe the man was simply being cautious. Aye, that sounded plausible. Didn't it?

A burning desperation flared deep in his gut at the thought of never regaining movement. Sweat prickled the back of his neck. He was abruptly back at the air base again, running from the enemy. He felt the bullet pierce his skin once more, felt the sudden force slam him around as pain and blood spurted out. He lay on the cold ground again, the warmth pouring out of him like it was desperate to leave, and he couldn't stop it. Couldn't stop it. The cold tightened around him, smothered him, crushed him—

James blinked rapidly, his breathing out of control. He became aware of a fast beeping sound, and the captain's mouth moved, asking questions he didn't know the answer to. James focused on Wright instead, taking in her frown as she looked at him with her big dark eyes. She was like a life raft, and he was sinking, drowning, struggling to stay afloat.

After several deep breaths, his hammering heart slowed down, and he felt more like himself again as tension drained from his muscles. *What was that?* Wright still frowned at him with concern clear on her face, and James looked to Captain Roux—maybe he had some answers.

"I think you have had a panic attack," he explained, his hands hovering close to James like he didn't know what to do with them. "It is understandable—you have been through a traumatic event—"

"I've been in the army for fifteen years, Captain. I've seen my fair share of shite, and I've never had a panic attack before."

"Have you ever been shot before? Been very close to dying?"

James stayed quiet. Yes, he fought on battlefields before. Yes, he had been shot *at* before. He'd seen friends shot, some fatally. Fucking Andy and his complete disregard for his own safety. He still missed him. But no, he himself had never been shot before.

Shaking his head, James shoved the brief *incident*—he wasn't going to call it a panic attack—behind him and looked at Captain Roux. "Can I have my clothes back? And some painkillers?"

The captain nodded. "Of course. I'll be right back."

The doctor left him in the cold room with Wright. Embarrassed by his *incident,* James picked at a piece of thread on his blanket, staring at it so hard he was surprised it didn't burst into flames. As the silence threatened to become too much, Wright stood.

"Listen, Sunshine." She paused. "James. I know this is hard. I know you're probably scared, even if you won't admit it. I also know we will do everything we can to get you fit and healthy again. You have my word."

James looked up at her and saw sincerity shining out of her eyes. Something swelled in his chest, and he had to take a deep breath to dispel the strange sensation. He cleared his throat and grunted out a thanks, wishing the weird conversation would hurry up and end.

It appeared Wright shared his sentiment. "Right, well, sorry I didn't bring you a fruit basket, but I couldn't find one. I guess they aren't in heavy demand during the end of the world. Shocking, I know."

"No that's not it. You didn't want to waste any money on me. I'll try to understand." James pretended to be upset as he felt more at ease.

"Yeah, you got me. Who would want to spend money on a miserable bastard like you?"

Talking with Wright felt good, and James relaxed into the teasing conversation, letting his worries and fears fall to the wayside as he focused on her. He tried to think of a witty comeback to one of her more sarcastic remarks as the captain returned.

"Your friends are all glad you are awake," he said. "Do you feel up to seeing them?"

"Captain, the sooner I get out of this bed, the better I'll be." James pushed himself into a seated position but stopped as the room spun. Squeezing his eyes shut and gulping down air, he succeeded in pushing the nausea away before he vomited everywhere. *Outstanding move there, James,* he thought as he steadied himself.

"Ah no, Sergeant Mollino, please lie back," Captain Roux's anxious voice reached him from what seemed like a long way away, and James wanted to relax back and let the horrible sick feeling pass. But he wanted to get back on his feet more. With a firm shake of his head that threatened to send the room spinning again, James scowled up at the captain, who leaned away from him.

James pushed the blanket aside and swung his legs out of the bed. His feet hit the cold floor and the shock of it helped clear his head. *See? I already feel better.*

He felt a slight tugging on his arm and belatedly remember the IV line. He looked up at the captain for help—he would pull it out himself but, well, he only had one working arm.

"You're still on intravenous antibiotics," Captain Roux said strictly. "Your friends can come to you."

James scowled. He *really* wanted to get out of here. "Well, I'm discharging myself, doc."

"I strongly advise against that. You need to give yourself time to recover."

"Time is something we don't have anymore," James said. "Please take it out, or I'll do it myself." He wouldn't, of course—not only was it physically beyond him, he also didn't know how to without causing more damage.

Captain and Sergeant engaged in a brief battle of wills, one frowning, the other sweating with effort. In the end, the captain carefully removed the line and patched his hand up with a plaster, muttering to himself in French all the while.

With a deep breath, James stood on shaky legs, his muscles protesting after not being used for so long. After several tense seconds, the wobbly feeling dissipated, and some strength returned to his weary body.

He swallowed the two little painkillers the captain handed him dry, as the man hadn't thought to bring some water with him. He closed his eyes, hoping the tablets would kick in straight away, but the pain continued to thrum through his body.

He would have liked to brush aside the captain's helpful hands, but he knew he wouldn't be able to get dressed by himself. He wished Wright wasn't there to see him struggle. He glanced at her, expecting to see a flash of white teeth showing through a smirk, but she wasn't even looking at him. She seemed engrossed in cleaning her nails. Gratitude lodged in James's throat.

It took longer than he hoped it would to get dressed in his combat trousers and an oversized grey t-shirt, his injured arm tucked awkwardly against his chest in the sling. When he was finally ready, he felt like going back to sleep. Ignoring the desire to lie back down, James stood up straighter and started for the door. His steps were halting at first, the captain hovering by his side like a concerned parent, but he quickly gained confidence and became more surefooted. By the time he reached the door, he walked with almost no hesitation.

The journey to the cafeteria was a short one, but his muscles thought he had been walking for miles. He paused at the doors and gathered his strength, attempting to appear as if he hadn't been shot and bedridden for days.

He couldn't let the civilians see him as frail. Ignoring the concerned look from the captain and the understanding one from Wright, James pushed open the door and strode into the room with as much energy as he could muster.

Everyone welcomed him with bright smiles and a chorus of cheers as they stood to greet him. He fought down his own wide grin, allowing only a small smile to tug at his mouth. He had to show them he had merely done his job—he was still calm and collected, even though gratefulness blazed through him like a forest fire. It was nice to have them appreciate his sacrifice.

Aarav reached him first and vigorously shook his hand. "Thank you, Sergeant Mollino. You saved our lives. I'm glad you're back on your feet."

"It was my duty," James said, feeling his face heat up. He'd never really figured out how to deal with compliments. He tried not to show his embarrassment as he nodded at everyone. "You're all okay?"

"Never better," Victoria said, and everyone agreed.

"I'm glad you're going to be all right, sir," Trueman said as he clapped James on his good shoulder.

James didn't want to mention the long road to recovery still ahead of him, so he nodded again and sat down at the table instead. "What do I have to do to get some food around here?"

"One second, sir." Trueman rushed off toward the kitchen as everyone sat down again.

Captain Roux checked his bandage. "This looks good for now. I will leave you to see your friends and look at it again later," he said, another false smile sitting awkwardly on his face. With one last nod at James, the captain left the room.

The painkillers finally kicked in. The constant sharp pain in his shoulder dulled to the point where he wasn't as aware of it as he had been a few minutes prior.

"I'm, uh, glad you're alive, erm, sir," Dan said, fiddling with his knife and fork.

"I'm glad I'm alive too, kid." James smiled at the boy, surprised by his shyness. When he'd last spoken to him the boy hadn't seemed shy then, had he? He couldn't recall.

Jennifer appeared to be much healthier than he remembered ever seeing her. She had colour in her cheeks, and she wasn't weighed down with fatigue. "Is everything all right with you?" James asked her, feeling a burn for information spark up again.

"Yeah, I feel great." Jennifer smiled at him, and it didn't appear to be forced in any way. What did it mean? Had her body defeated the virus? Had she even been infected in the first place?

"That's good," James said as Trueman placed a glass of water and two slices of toast in front of him. James looked down at the disappointingly bland meal. "No coffee?" He would do unspeakable things for some coffee.

"I'm sorry, sir. They never had any here," Trueman blasphemed. "There wasn't a lot to begin with due to the food product scandal and the global shortage. I think water is all you can have for now, anyway."

James pushed down his disappointment and focused on his hunger, which rose up out of nowhere. He picked up a slice of toast and took a massive bite out of it, barely chewing and swallowing before he shoved more into his mouth.

Wright watched him with faint disgust, and he met her eye as he ripped off another bite. She rolled her eyes at him and turned to her own meal, more toast.

"So, what happened?" Riya asked, curious. "Honestly, I did not think you would live."

James washed down his toast with some water as he gathered his thoughts. "We didn't have enough ammunition to engage all enemies and get you to safety, so I decided to create a distraction."

"Stupidly decided to create a stupid distraction," Wright cut in, frowning at him in a way that reminded him of letting his great Aunt Molly down as a child. She had never been happy with anything he did. He used to dread going over to visit on Sundays.

James frowned back at Wright, who shrugged as if she was right. "My distraction worked, didn't it? You were able to make it to the cars."

"Yes, but it still doesn't change the fact that what you did was fucking stupid. You got *shot*, you idiot."

Well, he couldn't argue with her there. His shoulder twinged with the memory of the bullet tearing into it, and James felt simultaneously hot and cold like he had as he'd lain on the frozen ground, his warm blood flowing out. He heard his heart screaming in his chest, getting weaker and weaker as it fought to keep him alive. There was no sun, no warmth—

"Sir? Are you okay?" Trueman's soft voice jarred him back to reality, and he looked around wildly for Wright. She pressed a hand onto his arm and squeezed. The warmth of her touch grounded him, making him feel safer. He steadied his breathing and hoped the civilians wouldn't read too much into whatever the fuck that had been.

Pushing aside *incident number two*, James cleared his throat. "I'm fine," he said, trying to ignore the concerned looks coming from every direction. He didn't need their *sympathy*. They were supposed to turn to him for *protection*, not to dump their pity on. He needed to change the subject, stop everyone from noticing how out of sorts he was. He pulled his arm away from Wright and sat up straighter. "You said I've been out for three days. Anything I should know about?"

Wright went from troubled looks to all business so fast he almost got whiplash. "First of all, we haven't informed the French about Jennifer yet, so don't go blabbering about how she's infected and immune. We need to get her to a specialist so they can synthesize a cure. Secondly, the world has literally gone to shit. Governments have collapsed, quarantine zones and safe zones have been destroyed, and infected people are running free. It's chaos. There doesn't seem to be any kind of command structure anymore."

"What about the plan to regroup here and hit back?"

"I'm sorry, Sunshine, but there's nothing to hit back at in the UK." The pilot looked angry, her hands balled into fists atop the table. "It's..." She paused for a moment before continuing. "Before communication broke down completely, we found out the safe zones we created never got the chance to get off the ground, riots are running unchecked around the world, and militia groups and religious fanatics are springing up like weeds, trying to take advantage of the mess that is now Planet Earth. So, we have to contend with crazy people as well as crazy infected. The Commandant and I agreed to fortify what we can of this place against both and ride out the worst of it here. Eventually, things will settle down. That's when we can find a specialist for Jennifer. The infected people will die of dehydration or hunger or the disease itself, and then we'll just have the normal bastards to deal with."

James stayed silent as he processed the information. It didn't seem real—not too long ago he'd planned his visit to London, excited to meet up with some friends he hadn't seen in a while. *What was that? A fortnight ago? Did they make it okay?* He hoped they were still alive. There was no way to find out. A burden heaved itself over his shoulders as he looked around the table. The civilians would rely on him to keep them safe. He had done his best to protect his friends with the information he had, and he would do his best with these people as well. But what if it wasn't good enough? Especially with only one good arm.

Jennifer's voice pulled him out of his dark thoughts. "The French soldiers have been very accommodating," she said as she ripped her toast into little pieces. Who ate like that? "The Commandant seems like a reasonable man. You'll probably meet him later. You've already met Captain Roux."

James hummed around a large bite of toast. He'd eaten almost all of his portion, yet hunger still echoed in his stomach. Was there more, or were they on rations?

"There's only three others here," Jennifer continued. "A man who goes by Dubois. Am I pronouncing it correctly?" she asked Wright, who nodded in response. Jennifer sighed. "I tried to get his attention earlier, but he glared at me and stormed off. I thought maybe I didn't say his name right." She shook her head. "Anyway, he seems pretty miserable, and he doesn't seem to like us very much."

"Yeah," Victoria agreed. "He's always glaring at us from afar, and he always stalks away muttering to himself in French when we try to speak to him."

"I'll keep that in mind when I see him," James said, making mental notes on the different soldiers. *This Dubois character may need watching.*

"Alexia is nice. Out of the French soldiers, she's the one who's spent the most time with us, playing board games and stuff." Jennifer sounded like she was going for casual when she mentioned Alexia, but the faint blush creeping up her neck told a different story. "And then there's Elise. It's not that she doesn't like us, I just think that's the kind of person she is."

"What do you mean?" James asked, confused.

Victoria took over the explanation. "She comes across as quite disapproving. But not of us, more like in general."

"Okay," James nodded. Alexia must have been the woman to check his vitals earlier. She had seemed friendly, not critical. "Is there anything else I should know?"

"Jennifer's pretty much covered the basics," Wright said. "Commandant Phillipe is the man in charge, obviously. Then there's Captain Roux, who's more of a doctor than a soldier. The other three don't have ranks. There had been more when they retreated here during the initial outbreak, but now there's the five of them. Surprisingly, the hospital apparently didn't see a lot of fighting. They killed the infected in a short amount of time and managed to secure the building." Wright paused. "Well, this wing anyway."

James nodded. He wondered when he would get the chance to meet the rest of them. He assumed they must be busy, covering the hospital with so few soldiers. Which brought him back to security and making it as safe as possible. "You said you were fortifying this place?"

Wright grimaced. "Not the whole hospital, just this wing, like I said. The place is too big for the seven of us to properly control."

"We've gathered weapons and supplies here and in one of the trucks in case we need to leave quickly," Trueman said. "We also run regular patrols of the surrounding area. So far nobody has encountered any hostiles, infected or otherwise."

"I want to help," Aarav spoke up, a determined look on his young face. Riya gripped his arm and spoke frantically in her language. James didn't need to understand her words to know what she said. He was going to say no as well, but he remembered his intention to teach these people as much as he could.

Wright leaned in and pitched her voice low as the young couple continued their argument. "He's been asking several times a day since we got here. I said I would discuss it with you first before we made any decisions. What do you think?"

"I think we should train them all." Training them would make it easier to protect them. "At least in the basics."

Wright nodded, a thoughtful look on her face. "It would certainly make our jobs easier," she said, unknowingly repeating his thoughts. "What are you thinking? Self-defence? Basic weapons training?"

"Aye. With the way the world is now, they're a liability." James was going to have try to drill fifteen years' worth of military discipline and self-control into them over the next few days—maybe weeks if they were lucky. "If we encounter any hostiles, they should know how to defend themselves. We can't always be there for them."

"I agree, sir," Trueman said from James's other side. "I think we should begin immediately. We can start with doing a few exercises to test their fitness?"

"That's a good idea." Wright smiled. "We'll clear away some tables and do it here. This is going to be fun," she added as her smile transformed into a smirk. The pilot clapped her hands together as she turned away from James to address the rest of the table. "Okay, people, listen up. We have decided to train you all—"

"What?" Riya cut her off, a shaken look twisting her round face. "Are you sure that is the best course of action? Is it safe?"

"It's a lot safer than leaving you all *un*trained," Wright countered, both her eyebrows rising as if she was surprised they were still discussing the issue. "Don't you want to know how to look after yourselves? We can't hold your hands forever, you know."

"I'll do it," Dan said enthusiastically. He blinked after speaking, looking shocked at his own excitement. He seemed to shrink as everyone turned to him, as if he were a punctured balloon deflating under the weight of so many eyes.

"Yeah," Jennifer said, her brows furrowed. "We need to know what to do in case you aren't there for us. We have to adapt to this new world."

Riya looked sick while her husband eagerly nodded. Victoria agreed with determination, and Martin with reluctance. *They act like it was up for a vote. Do they not realise this was non-negotiable?*

"From now on, we will consider you all new recruits," James said with a stern voice. "You will do as we say, when we say it, and it is not up for discussion. We are training you all so you can handle yourselves in life-or-death situations. You will listen to us—our instructions may save your lives one day. You'll need to learn a lot of new skills in a short amount of time. Trueman is going to assess your fitness, and we'll go from there. We'll give you some basic weapons and hand-to hand training over the next few weeks. We'll see about more advanced stuff afterward, but we'll cross that bridge when we get to it."

Everyone nodded and turned back to their meals. Silence descended on the group as they no doubt conjured up horrible scenarios of military training. James shook his head as the air in the canteen became strained. They *needed* to be trained. Whether they liked it or not.

Chapter Fifteen

Jennifer fiddled with her toast as she contemplated her life. Never in a million years had she thought she would be going through military training. As daunting as it seemed, she knew it would be good for them. It served as a reminder of the world outside the hospital, though, and a miserable atmosphere settled around the group like a poisonous gas, choking any levity from existence.

Wright fake-cleared her throat. "Stories! Little stories about inane things while we finish our food. Keep it light, yeah?" It seemed she felt it too.

When no one responded, Wright cleared her throat again. "C'mon, people. I don't want to stare at your miserable faces all lunchtime. I'll start us off," she said. "I have family in Canada. Part of the reason I can speak French. One day, my grandma really wanted to see this new horse one of her friends had bought. We all agreed to tag along— it would be a nice day out, and I didn't want to be sitting around with nothing to do. But guess what?" She paused for dramatic affect. "It took us five hours to get there. Five *fucking* hours. I was sick of my life," the pilot laughed. "I never appreciated how big Canada is until then."

"Did you see the horse?" Riya asked.

"Yeah, eventually, and it was underwhelming," Wright laughed again. "I've hated horses ever since."

"I've never been horse riding before," a small voice piped up. Jennifer turned to look at Dan, his young face pale in the harsh fluorescent lights. "Never been to Canada either."

"Well, kiddo, horses are bastards, so you're not missing out there." Wright grinned. "Canada is a beautiful country, though. You should try to go if you can."

Nobody said the obvious. *We'll have this moment. We'll pretend everything is fine, and we'll talk about happiness and dreams and aspirations, and hold onto this when things get bad.*

"I, erm, I think I'd like it." Dan smiled. Jennifer felt a flood of contentment—children should be able to smile freely. The last time she could remember Dan smiling was when they played pool. "I've never, uh, never been abroad actually. This is the first time. I guess this is like a holiday?"

Everyone chuckled, and Jennifer could *feel* the confidence radiating from the boy. *He's made people laugh. There isn't a rush quite like it.*

"I remember the first time I went abroad," Aarav said, nostalgia painting his words. "I was ten, and my two older brothers teased me mercilessly about flying. I was *terrified.*" Jennifer supposed this calm man sitting opposite her was his true self, not the guarded one who sent her glares every so often. "I am much better at flying now, but I do still get a little nervous."

Riya laughed and bumped shoulders with him. "A little?" Aarav shrugged and lifted his arms in a *she got me* gesture, causing everyone to chuckle again.

"I probably hate flying more than Sergeant Wright hates horses."

"Woah, I don't think so. My hatred of horses is astronomical. *Five hours.*"

"You didn't enjoy the helicopter ride?" James asked, his mouth twisting up on one side. Had she seen him smile before?

"I did not." Aarav laughed, but it sounded forced. "I am *not* getting on another plane or helicopter ever again. I don't care if I have to walk back to India. I'm not doing it."

Riya patted his arm reassuringly. "We won't get on any more aircraft, don't worry."

Jennifer couldn't recall noticing his fear, but they weren't best friends. She thought she understood—spiders were her worst fear, and if someone threw one at her, she would freak out.

"You can't deny that I'm a great pilot, though," Wright said with no hint of modesty.

Aarav gave her a tight-lipped smile. "I'm sure you're very good. Can we talk about something else?"

"My first serious boyfriend was on the swimming team at school," Victoria pitched in. Wright's story idea was working—everyone relaxed, and the stifling atmosphere from earlier evaporated. "He had an embarrassing accident and ended up quitting after a short while. We broke up with each other not long after, actually."

"What happened?" Curiosity pricked through Jennifer. She loved stories.

"Ooh, I bet this involves someone pulling his swimming trunks down," Wright laughed.

"It does, yeah," Victoria said. "A group were in the boys' changing rooms,and one of them pulled his shorts down as a joke. He was so surprised he pissed himself."

"He *didn't*." Wright grinned from ear to ear.

"He did," Victoria's smile faded as she tutted. "I feel really sorry for him, even now. He lost so much confidence because of it. Ever since becoming a teacher, I know how cruel kids can be, and how crucial those teenage years are for development. He went on to study law, so I hope he did all right for himself."

"My first boyfriend was a dick." Wright grimaced. "The less said about him the better." She turned to Jennifer, and her stomach sank like a stone to rest somewhere around her feet. She knew what came next. What always came next. How would they react to her bisexuality? Were they homophobic? Biphobic? She didn't want them to think she was greedy or unnatural or somehow *wrong*. Because she *wasn't*. Every sexual orientation was normal and natural.

"What about you, Immune? Was your first boyfriend a total dick, or a knight in shining armour?"

Take a deep breath and just say it. Like pulling off a plaster. "My first real relationship was with a girl, actually," Jennifer said. Pride filled her as her voice didn't waver. Everyone looked surprised. *Stupid heteronormativity. Straight people always assume everyone else is straight.*

"You're gay?" Dan asked. He looked confused. "What about Damien?"

"I'm bisexual," Jennifer replied firmly. She wasn't ashamed of her sexuality. She was more than willing to fight her corner if the others had an issue with it. Looking around, nobody seemed to care. Relief made her stomach swoop. Until she locked eyes with Aarav.

He didn't try to hide his judgement. His lip curled in contempt, and he looked at her with open abhorrence. He didn't say anything, though. Jennifer's hackles raised. She had to shield herself against homophobia before, and she probably would again in the future.

"I had no idea you swing both ways," Wright said as she had a sip of her water. "So, do you think I'm hot?" She flicked imaginary hair and batted her eyelashes.

Jennifer rolled her eyes at the pilot, secretly pleased they weren't bothered. "Just because I'm attracted to more than one gender doesn't mean I'm attracted to everyone."

"Is that a no then?" Wright pouted, throwing puppy dog eyes at her. She couldn't hold the look as a wide smile broke out, and Jennifer laughed along with her. "So, you've had boyfriends and girlfriends?"

"One of each. My first girlfriend's name was Robin," Jennifer said nostalgically. "We dated for five years, and I was devastated when she broke up with me. I thought I would never find anyone ever again." Jennifer chuckled. "Melodramatic, I know. My friend Evelyn helped me get over her."

"She sounds like a good friend," Victoria smiled.

"The best." It hurt to talk about Evelyn, but Jennifer knew it would hurt more not to. She would keep the memories of her friends alive.

Alexia entered the cafeteria, smiling her warm smile at everyone as she drew up a seat. Jennifer shuffled closer

202 - | Amy Marsden

to Dan to make room for her. A particular type of heat spread through her skin as Alexia sat close. She'd thought the soldier was pretty the moment she saw her. Alexia had gone out of her way to make them feel welcome, and a desire to get to know her better bloomed in her chest.

But what about Damien? *I know he was more a friend than boyfriend, but still. Am I that heartless it's taken me so little time to move on?* Well no, that wasn't quite right. She'd moved on from the relationship a while ago. They hadn't officially ended it, though. Did she feel guilty?

Jennifer turned to tell Alexia what they were talking about but became lost in her brown eyes before any words made it past her lips. The bright overhead light illuminated the different shades swirling around her irises, and Jennifer forgot to inhale for a few seconds. *Like coffee*, she thought. Deep, rich browns spinning around lighter ones, not unlike the different types of coffee she and her friends used to drink together. From the black coffee Rhys liked occasionally, to the cream coffee Amanda used to down like water, Jennifer found every shade spiralling around Alexia's pupils.

She decided coffee was her new favourite drink.

As she remembered herself and turned back to the group, she caught sight of Wright's smirk. *Oh no.* The pilot looked between Jennifer and Alexia and raised her eyebrows. Jennifer shot her a warning look and Wright made a small placating gesture with her hands. She went back to her food, her smirk widening. She had a feeling the pilot was going to have some fun.

"What is going on?" Alexia's soft voice coaxed the annoyance out of Jennifer.

"We were discussing our first relationships," Wright said, her smirk punching Jennifer in the face. *God, how many teeth does that damn woman have?* Wright turned to Alexia, Jennifer's warning look falling on blind eyes. "I am, sadly, straight, but Jennifer here is bisexual. Did you know that?"

Alexia looked confused. "I did not. Jennifer should be the one to tell people, yes?"

"Yes, thank you," Jennifer said angrily, glaring at Wright. "*I* get to out me, nobody else."

Jennifer had been out for years, but it was a continuous process. She had to do it all over and over whenever she met new people. It had gotten easier, but she still felt a little flutter of nerves beforehand. Some didn't bat an eye, while others looked taken aback before saying something horrible. Jennifer shook her head. *And why do I have to keep coming out at all? Straight people don't have to come out.* It was ridiculous—why did people care so much about other people's sexual orientation? *Live and let fucking live.*

To her credit, Wright seemed to realise her mistake. "Huh, you're right. Sorry, I didn't mean to out you. I assumed you're comfortable with it."

"I am comfortable, it's just—" *How to explain?* "—It's just something I have to do for myself."

"I respect that." Wright smiled, and the left-over anger Jennifer harboured faded away. *At least she understands now.*

James opened his mouth to say something when an explosion rocked the table.

Chapter Sixteen

James went for his weapon, which he belatedly remembered he didn't have. Wright and Trueman jumped to their feet with guns drawn, and James felt incredibly vulnerable in a sling with nothing to protect himself. His heart began to pound in his chest as the sound of distant gunshots reached him, and memories of firing at the enemy at the other base resurfaced, clouding his mind.

He was back lying against that rough tree, the cold eating away at him as he bled out, when Wright grabbed his good arm. "I need you focussed here, James," she hissed as she dragged him to his feet. "Can I rely on you?"

Her hand on his arm burned, and James thought he would let himself be consumed by the heat if it meant never feeling such all-encompassing cold again. Her eyes held an intensity he had never seen from her before, and all he could do was nod in the face of her fire. She maintained eye contact for another beat before she nodded once.

"Good," she said shortly. She let go of his arm and turned to the civilians, and James immediately missed the contact. His arm still tingled from her touch, and he took comfort in her closeness.

"We need to find out what the fuck is going on." Wright wasted no time trying to console the frightened civilians. "And we need more weapons. It looks like you're all getting thrown in the deep end of your training."

"*What?*" Martin exclaimed, his eyes widening with fear. "We're going to fight?"

"There's no time like the present," Wright grinned but ended up rolling her eyes at the panicked looks everyone shot her way. "Oh, relax, people. Based on the gunfire, we're under attack from non-infected people, so you don't have to worry about catching the virus. You'll help us carry more weapons and ammunition, that's all. Worst case scenario, we'll make you hold them, so it looks like there's more of us than there actually is." She paused and frowned at the civilians, taking in their fear-filled faces. "If that happens, at least *try* to look intimidating."

James had to bite back a snort at her disdain-filled tone. He, too, couldn't imagine them making an enemy shake in their boots.

"Let's go," Wright said, her stance relaxing as she became more vigilant. "Trueman, take the lead. Sunshine, you're in the middle with the civilians."

The look she gave him when he opened his mouth to protest was enough to curdle milk. He snapped his mouth shut and moved next to Dan, his jaw clenching painfully as he cursed his shoulder. He felt like a glass hammer—ready to strike at the enemy, but contact would cause him to shatter.

They didn't even make it half-way across the cafeteria before the doors burst open and a woman rushed through, her hair damp with sweat. *This must be Elise.* "Ah good, you are all here," she panted. "We counted fifteen attackers, all armed. The Commandant wants you to get weapons and help."

"That's what we're doing," Wright said as she shoved Jennifer to get her moving again. The other woman glowered at the pilot as everyone moved through the doors and out into the corridor.

"What's the situation?" James asked, feeling nervousness and excitement greet him like old friends. He welcomed the familiar emotions, falling into his pre-mission routine with ease. Except he didn't have any weapons or armour to check. *Fucking brilliant*, he thought as cracks formed in his newfound equilibrium.

"The explosion was from the North, but it was a diversion," Elise explained as they hurried down another corridor. The glaring walls were the same white as the room he'd woken up in, and they seemed never ending. James wanted to reach the armoury quickly, to feel his weapon in his hands again, feel the weight of it as he raised it up and settled it against his shoulder. Holding it would surely get rid of the *off* feeling he had ever since he regained consciousness, and he would feel like himself again.

"The only reason we are still alive is because they stopped advancing." Elise continued. "I think we surprised them by fighting back, and they are short on supplies. Perhaps that is why they are here."

"Looks like you might get your own weapons after all," Wright said as they stopped in front of a narrow door. What little colour Martin and Riya had in their faces drained away at Wright's words, while Aarav grinned eagerly.

Elise pushed open the door and rushed inside. The room beyond was dark until she turned the light on, and the blackness barely receded when faced with the dim glare of the bulbs.

James couldn't get a good look at the equipment before Wright shoved what looked like a PAMAS in his face. His fist curled around the small weapon as she turned away and reached for something else. It *was* a PAMAS. The civilians were being armed with FAMAS assault rifles, while he got a 9mm pistol. No fucking way.

Some of his fury must have bled onto his face. Wright scowled when she pushed a couple of magazines at him. "Don't even think about complaining, Sunshine. Do you seriously think you can handle anything else? Your arm's in a *sling*. You were *shot*, remember?"

Like he could forget. His shoulder began to throb again, the pain radiating up his neck and down his back. The painkillers he had been given were shite. He did feel stronger—food and moving around must have helped a bit.

He glared down at the PAMAS as he felt the weight of it, light in his palm compared to a FAMAS rifle. He supposed Wright was right—he wouldn't be able to hold and aim a rifle, but it didn't make him any less annoyed. Bitterness gnawed at him until he felt like he would burst. He contemplated throwing the pistol away and getting a rifle anyway, but he knew he was being irrational. Besides, Wright would notice, and he would end up as far away from the action as possible whilst still being in the hospital.

Instead of throwing a tantrum like a two-year-old, James kept his mouth shut and followed the others out and down another white-walled corridor. The pistol felt *too* light, and James knew he wouldn't have much to contribute to the fight. The bitterness swelled up anew, but he gritted his teeth and did his best to ignore it. His shoulder already screamed at him, and his blood rushed in his ears as he hurried to keep up with the rest of the group. He'd be lucky if he even reached their destination without collapsing.

Elise halted everyone. Sunlight streamed through the two small windows set high in a pair of double doors, illuminating the little flecks of dust floating on the air without a care in the world. Dust didn't understand there were enemies on the other side of the doors. It didn't understand the adrenaline flooding through James's veins, the anticipation jamming him up. It couldn't comprehend the way his heart raced, didn't know why he felt so cold, couldn't fathom how gunshots from another place and time were still ringing in his ears. James wondered if he would become dust if he made a mistake here. Blown away in the wind, unknowing and uncaring of the struggle humanity faced.

"Okay, people," Wright said. "These weapons are real, with real bullets, so try not to shoot each other, or, more importantly, me." She fixed them all with a pointed stare. "You hold it like this, okay, the butt of the weapon rests against your shoulder, and you hold the barrel like this—" The pilot gave a quick demonstration and grew frustrated when everyone wasn't perfect straight away. James would have thought it funny if they were in any other situation.

She emitted a sound like a growl and snapped at the civilians. "For fuck's sake, try to look like you know what you're doing. Don't rest your finger on the trigger, Aarav. This isn't a fucking film. Keep it outside the guard and keep the safety on. Let's go."

Wright pushed past Elise and through the doors, not waiting to see if anyone followed. There was a pause as the civilians momentarily froze, but as soon as James barked *"move,"* they all rushed forward at once, creating a brief bottleneck at the doors as they scrambled out into the cold sunlight.

James followed Trueman out into the bright day, blinking as his eyes slowly adjusted to the onslaught of light. He jogged across a car park over the entrance to the hospital grounds. A rounded building with a roof that looked like wings stood in between two white gates, both of which were closed. They didn't run all the way up to those barred gates—a line of sandbags about waist height split the car park in two, and everyone crouched down behind them.

James pushed his way in between Wright and a weedy-looking man with greasy hair and a ragged beard. The man threw him a sneer, his eyes lingering on the sling, and his face twisted as if he'd smelled something rotten. James gave him a grin that was more teeth than smile and turned back to face the enemy who dove for cover behind several cars. *That must be Dubois,* he thought with annoyance. James hadn't even said hello to the man and he already didn't like him.

They didn't have a good view of the enemy. The high walls around the grounds blocked sight, and James felt blind as he looked through the gates. He took comfort in the enemy being as restricted as they were. The street outside the hospital looked narrow. Everything felt claustrophobic.

A tall man who was built like a tank addressed the enemy. He spoke in rapid French, and James didn't have a clue what he said. *That must be Commandant Phillipe.* He had a look about him that demanded respect, and James in turn respected that. *You don't get that kind of aura without being competent at what you do.*

The Commandant's deep voice stopped, and the enemy leaders higher one started up. He didn't sound as confident, his head jerking left and right along the group. *Having the civilians pose as soldiers is paying off after all,* James thought with a grin.

The enemy's eyes found Dan, and his voice cut off. James watched as the man's brow furrowed, his eyes tracking back down the group, paying close attention to each person. A chill trickled down James's spine—the damn boy was too young. Why had no one thought of that? James met his gaze with a glare of his own and startled at the flash of recognition in the other man's eyes. James frowned. He didn't know him. Why did he seem to recognise him? He spoke again, and James knew it was directed at him.

"Shit," Wright muttered, adjusting her position so she aimed at the enemy leader instead of one of the other soldiers.

"What?" James whispered to her. "What did he say?"

"He said you're the one he shot back at the other base."

James felt something ignite inside him, searing away the cold buried in his veins. This bastard had shot him? Well, James was more than happy to return the favour. His body thrummed with pain at the memory of the bullet ripping into his shoulder and spinning him around, and his muscles tightened with expectation. His grip grew sweaty on the PAMAS, but it didn't matter. He could rest the gun on the wall as he took aim, not at the bastard's shoulder, but his chest instead—

"*James*," Wright's urgent whisper cut through his thoughts of revenge, and he turned to her angrily, ready to snap at her for breaking his concentration. Instead he noticed a change in the atmosphere, tension thick in the air as agitation twitched through everyone—soldiers and civilians alike. The negotiation had ended.

The enemy leader shouted something, and the Commandant's lips pressed together in a flat line. James knew it was past time to get the civilians out of there. Everything was about to go to shit, but he needed to make the bastard who shot him feel what he had gone through first. Ignoring Wright, James carefully took aim again and began to squeeze the trigger—

Chapter Seventeen

Jennifer understood the need to be trained how to use a gun, she really did, but as she held one and hid behind a wall of sand pretending to be something she wasn't, she wanted nothing more than to throw it away and run in the other direction as fast as she could. She held it the way Sergeant Wright demonstrated, resting it on the wall so it wouldn't grow too heavy. Her hands were slick with sweat, so much so she feared her grip would slip and she would be exposed as a fraud.

She aimed at a hollow-cheeked man crouched behind the wheel of a jeep, and her mind flashed back several days. She saw another narrow-faced man aiming down his sights, saw Evelyn's big brown eyes pleading with her. It seemed like she gripped that gun, pointed it at Evelyn, pulled the trigger.

Gunfire blazed loud and hot. Jennifer was so lost in her nightmare it took her a second to register the shouting and screaming all around her. The soldiers exchanged bullets, and a sharp, acrid scent clogged Jennifer's nostrils as she ducked lower behind the wall.

Panic sparked deep in her stomach, and she froze, clutching her gun tight to her chest. She flinched away as one of the bags above her blew open, sand raining down as she fell on her bad elbow. *Holy shit!* Pain shot up her arm as she caught Dan's wide-eyed look of horror. His fear spurred her into action. She didn't know where this need to protect him came from, but he was just a kid and she needed to get him to safety.

She reached for his arm as Alexia appeared and pulled him along after her while she fired over the wall. Jennifer scrambled after them, her panic flaring at the thought of being left behind.

The wall abruptly ended, and they dashed behind an abandoned white van in the middle of the road as Alexia continued firing. Jennifer could barely breathe. The smell of burnt metal wound its way down her airways until she felt sullied by it. Dan and Martin were next to her, but she couldn't see the others. Where were they? Worry bled into her system, adding to the toxic fear and panic already filling her up.

A grotesque stain across the side of the van made Jennifer flinch away from it. It looked like someone had dipped a massive brush in red paint and smeared it over the vehicle. Her stomach roiled, forcing her to look away.

She tried to remember what Sergeant Wright said about the gun, but she could *not* recall a word of it. Was she even holding it right? Pressing the end back into her shoulder, Jennifer tightened her fingers around the front and moved up next to Alexia. She had fired at people before—she *could* do it again.

But before she so much as thought about pulling the trigger, Alexia pushed her back. "What are you doing? You almost blocked me. Stay behind cover!"

Jennifer fell back next to Dan, his eyes meeting hers as he held his gun stiffly. She only wanted to help and had ended up almost ruining everything. God, she needed to calm herself down.

A loud burst of gunfire exploded from the other end of the van. Jennifer raised her gun without thinking, only to find Martin slowly lowering his, light wisps of smoke rising from the barrel.

He met her gaze, the hazel colour of his eyes shimmering with unshed tears. "He was—I—I reacted," he stuttered. He began to hyperventilate, and his skin took on a greyish colour as Jennifer watched. She moved her gaze past him and saw the body of a man lying still only a few strides away, a dark pool of blood stretching outward. A gun lay by his side, and Jennifer felt a chill creep through her. If Martin hadn't shot him first...

"You did good, for sure," Alexia said, trying to offer some encouragement as Martin spiralled down into shock. "We have to move now if they are flanking the side." She pushed Dan forward gently and gestured for Jennifer and Martin to follow him as she covered their backs. "Head for the doors to get back inside. Run now!"

Running from the van to the building was a blur to Jennifer. She heard her blood rush through her so loud it almost drowned out the sound of bullets. Sweat stung her eyes as she reached the door, pushing it open and pulling Dan inside. Martin and Alexia piled in after, and the soldier slammed the door shut behind her. The battle outside became muted, but Jennifer could still feel the reverberations of the bullets in her bones, shaking them until she felt weak and fragile, moments away from breaking.

Martin sank to the floor, his breathing short and shallow as he dropped his gun. Alexia crouched down next to him, concern shining from her beautiful dark eyes. "Hey, I know it is scary, yes? But we must keep going. You need to get back up, Martin. Can you do that?" Jennifer was struck by how patient Alexia was. If Jennifer had been in her shoes, she would have dragged Martin to his feet. Hell, she wouldn't have let him fall to the floor. She'd tried to be friendly toward him over the past couple of days, but he'd brushed off her every attempt. She'd eventually given up. Hopefully, he would come around.

After what seemed like an eternity, he nodded and pushed himself back to his feet, picking up his gun along the way. Alexia smiled at him, but he stared at the floor with vacant eyes and didn't notice.

"Follow me," Alexia said. She started down the corridor, keeping her gun up and alert for any danger. Jennifer quickly copied her, the gun heavy in her hands as they started forward.

The sound of gunfire faded as they moved further into the building until their uneven breaths were louder than the sharp cracks. They had been told to evacuate to a truck loaded up with emergency supplies like food and medicine if anything like this were to happen, and Jennifer knew Alexia was guiding them there. But what about the others? Would they already be there? Or were they lying dead, their blood spreading out around them like a crimson halo, soaking up the dust on the ground?

Jennifer pushed the troubling thought from her mind. Although she had only known everyone for a short time, they had quickly worked their way into her heart, and she didn't want to lose anyone else. She looked to

Dan, who had, in such a short time, become the little brother she never knew she wanted. They had to get to safety. Jennifer didn't think she would manage well if anyone died.

She slowed to a stop, a little jolt of alarm firing through her. Dan stopped a few paces ahead, turning back to her in confusion. "Jennifer? What are you doing? We have to follow Alexia," he said, his young face tight with fear as his breath came in short puffs. At the sound of Dan's voice, the other two also stopped and turned back, frowning at her as she stood motionless in the corridor, her gun hanging limply in her hands.

"We have to go back to our room," Jennifer spoke fast, agitated, hoping they would understand. "I left my camera there this morning, and we have to go back for it."

"Camera?" Alexia sounded confused. "Sorry, but we do not have time to—"

"*Please,*" Jennifer cut in. "I'm documenting what's happening. I *need* that camera." She had taken pictures of the hospital and French soldiers over the past few days. Everyone except Dubois, of course, who'd sneered and refused to let her get a shot of him. She thought about the pictures of her family and friends—she couldn't bear the thought of losing them so completely. Her desperation must have etched itself onto her face. Alexia's confusion melted into something more sympathetic, and her face softened. Those pictures were all Jennifer had left. She couldn't leave her camera behind.

Alexia stared at her for a few seconds, a small frown marring her brow. Jennifer implored the other woman to understand, to realise how important it was. If she said no, Jennifer knew she would go alone anyway. What she'd seen of Alexia over the past couple of days made her think she would help, though.

Alexia closed her eyes briefly and released an almost inaudible sigh. When she opened them again, Jennifer saw she had relented but wasn't happy about it. "Okay, we will get your camera. We must move quickly." The words were clipped. Jennifer didn't think she'd ever seen her so irritated.

She nodded and tightened her grip on her gun. Her hands weren't as sweaty as they had been outside, but her hold was still traitorously weak.

They moved through the corridors as quickly and as quietly as they could. White walls and white floors streaked past as they raced back to the room, and Jennifer half-expected enemy soldiers to be lurking behind every turn. They encountered no one, however, and she was more than happy to keep it that way. God, what a *mess*. She had no idea when she woke up her day would turn so shit. She had begun to settle in here, had participated in building the sand walls and barring the windows and some of the doors. She had let herself grow complacent. It wouldn't happen again.

They slowed to a stop outside the door to the room they had all been sleeping in since they arrived. Jennifer darted in and grabbed her camera, cradling it close to her chest with reverence, the treasure it contained burning through to her heart. She put the strap over her head and arm, so it fell securely down her side.

Jennifer thanked Alexia. The woman nodded, brushing aside an errant curl of hair. Jennifer thought her attractiveness had an effortless quality to it. Natural. Not the striking beauty of Victoria, but a quieter one, a softer one that wasn't apparent at first, but once noticed it couldn't be ignored.

"We have the camera. Now we *must* go."

Jennifer nodded. She clutched both her camera and her gun with fingers of steel as she jogged down the corridor after the others, hoping everyone would be waiting for them and they would all get away safely.

*

Victoria gingerly put more of her weight on her bad ankle. It hurt like hell, but it held. Louis had been surprised by her recovery, saying it was healing remarkably well. He crouched on her left, his eyes narrowed with concentration as he peered over the sandbags at the enemy soldiers.

They had been behind the stupid wall for several minutes, pretending to be soldiers, and Victoria's legs began to cramp. The wall wasn't big enough or long enough to offer much protection, and quite frankly Victoria hadn't seen the point of it. Dubois had suggested they build it. To slow down infected or enemies, he had said whilst looking straight at them. Victoria hadn't bother hiding her eye roll. The man hadn't quite mastered the art of subtlety.

He crouched on her right, scanning the soldiers through the gates. If things did go horribly wrong here, she hoped he was a better soldier than person.

What are we doing? This is a terrible idea. Why she had agreed to it, she did *not* know. She wanted to be trained in how to defend herself, but no matter what James said, she wasn't some raw recruit ready to ask, '*how high?*' when one of the soldiers barked, '*jump.*' They didn't even have helmets or armour, for crying out loud.

Her heart beat a mile a minute, and it was only a matter of time before one of the enemy soldiers saw straight through their little circus of lies.

A chill ran down her spine at a sudden thought. Why hadn't she realised earlier? Dan was a *child*. Surely, they would spot that. Victoria resisted the urge to look down the line at him. She didn't want to bring unwanted attention to the boy. Bloody hell, she half expected her heart to jump right out of her chest. The situation was already stressful enough without throwing a Dan-shaped wrench into the works.

The enemy soldier droned on in his monotonous voice, so Victoria allowed herself to hope this impossible situation would be resolved without bloodshed. She didn't want to find out what she was capable of if everyone started firing. No, she *did* know what she was capable of, and it scared her more than she could express.

The voice cut off, and Victoria's eyes darted away from the person she had been watching and over to the boss. *Oh, no, he noticed Dan.* Victoria's skin prickled as the hairs on her arms stood on end, and she watched the soldiers' eyes scan down their line, taking careful note of everyone. Victoria shuffled on her numb legs as the air became thick with tension. When the man's eyes landed on James, they narrowed, and he shouted something. Victoria had never wished she could understand French more than she did in that moment.

Dubois let out a low growl, but before Victoria could turn and ask what had prompted the noise, gunfire rang from all around. She sucked in a large gulp of air and sand from the stupid wall, which set off a coughing fit. Louis gave her a concerned look, but she waved him off as she ducked low.

Sergeant Wright's rushed instructions came back to her in startling clarity, and Victoria ignored her burning throat as she steadied her breathing. She moved the selector from safe to automatic fire and shifted so she could point the gun over the wall.

She had never fired a gun before, but it looked simple enough in the movies. *Point and shoot, right? How hard can it be?*

The gun seemed to come to life in her hands, an explosion of noise and force so shocking Victoria almost dropped it. She knew she pulled too hard on the trigger when the gun threw itself back into her shoulder and shoved its muzzle upward. She left a trail of bullet holes in a jeep, starting from near the wheel, up through the door, and over the roof.

Squeeze the trigger, you idiot. Her internal voice sounded suspiciously like Sergeant Wright. *Fire only in short bursts.*

She tried again, pressing down gently on the trigger this time. The difference was immediate—the gun still felt like a wild animal, but Victoria had more control. She spotted the man she had been firing at, still crouched behind the jeep, and took aim once more. Shooting the gun felt easier, and Victoria relaxed as she fell into a nice rhythm of aim, squeeze, release. Aim, squeeze, release.

She couldn't get the man. *Aim.* The stupid fool kept ducking behind cover. *Squeeze.* How could she get him? *Release.* Maybe if she moved slightly—

Victoria threw herself down as bullets tore through the space she had been, and the sandbags blew apart. Dust filled her vision and her lungs, setting off another coughing fit. She couldn't hear herself think over the ringing in her ears, and the gravity of the situation slammed into her like a physical force. She wasn't a soldier. Why was she doing this?

She had to get away. They all did. They couldn't win this. Victoria sluggishly pushed herself to her knees, making sure to stay below the wall. The chaos reminded her of that night months ago when her sister had come over—her mind drowning as panic filled the crevices in her brain. She needed to breathe, but the ubiquitous dust saturated the air so much she could only manage short inhales. They made her feel like she was suffocating.

She looked up and saw Louis and Anthony not too far away, still fighting. *Foolish idiots. We can't win.* Still, seeing them try stirred something in Victoria, and heat flooded through her. The panic choking her boiled away as something she had only felt once before reared up, and Victoria relinquished control.

She straightened her back and looked over the wall once more, spotting the man she had been shooting at immediately. The angle was difficult—he had moved behind a silver car, and the rounded building at the gates made it difficult to see him. Victoria moved down the wall until she had a clear view. *Aim.* She didn't rush. She felt the gun's weight, felt the coiled power it contained, the danger it represented. She respected it. *Squeeze.* Her finger rested lightly on the trigger, and she curled it back toward herself with precision. The wild animal jumped in her hands, spitting bullets out of its snarling mouth with a ferocity the monster in Victoria revelled in.

She got him this time.

Release.

*

The air filled with the sharp crack of gunfire, and James didn't know who had fired the first bullet. He kept squeezing the trigger, intent on killing the man who ruined his shoulder. Ignoring Wright's shouts, James moved around her and along the wall, planning to flank the enemy and reach the leader. A blue car rested flush against the wall to the right—James could climb it and hop over.

He didn't get far. He only moved a few paces before he bumped into the Commandant. It was like walking into a boulder.

"We must protect the civilians, Sergeant Mollino. Retreat back to the main building." He spoke with an unshakable calm, and James was halfway through forming a plan to get the civilians out of harm's way before he remembered his objective. *Kill the bastard who crippled me.*

James looked around and saw Jennifer, Dan, and Martin with Alexia, taking cover behind a van. He waved in their direction, so the Commandant thought he was going to help, and the giant of a man nodded once and turned away. James shuffled around him and continued his way along the wall, constantly checking on the status of the enemy leader. The man lurked behind a silver car, occasionally leaning out to fire.

James darted out to the van Alexia and the others had been behind. He couldn't see them anywhere. James briefly wondered if they were all right, the stirrings of guilt making his chest tighten. His job was to protect them. He squashed the sensation before it could grow and become a problem. He *needed* to get to that man. He *needed* to make him pay.

With the PAMAS heavy in his hand, sweat stinging his eyes, and his heart working tirelessly to keep him going, James half jogged, half stumbled around the van only to trip over a dead body. He landed awkwardly on his injured shoulder, and almost blacked out as pain lit every single nerve on fire.

He didn't know how long he lay there, his breath making the dust dance with every exhale. Even the slightest movement sent shockwaves of pain through him, and James felt tears burn his eyes. He blinked them away as hands gripped his good arm and pulled him up. He bit back a gasp as he settled back on his knees, Wright's dark face swimming into focus.

"There aren't words to describe how fucking stupid you are. I hope you're aware of that."

Hysterical laughter bubbled up, and he couldn't stop it from spilling out. What was wrong with him?

"Great, now you've snapped and gone insane." Wright's exasperated voice was like a light in the dark, chasing away the shadows and making everything bright again. The hysteria faded, and blood rushed to his face as embarrassment burned hot.

She helped him climb to his feet, and he leaned on her for a second before he clenched his jaw and pushed away. The need to reach the enemy leader overrode all else. "I have to do this. I *have* to find him." James begged Wright to understand, his green eyes boring into her brown ones. She gazed back impassively, and James had no idea what she thought.

She broke eye contact and shook her head. "This whole thing is crazy. We need to be protecting the others. Come on, James. We need to get back."

He couldn't believe she wasn't going to help him. Fine. He would do it on his own. He didn't need her. He became aware of the firefight again, of bullets deafening in their explosive flight, men and women shouting, falling, dying. He hoped they were all the enemy. He knew he would have trouble forgiving himself if some of the civilians died, but he *couldn't* let this go. That man needed to suffer like he had. James wasn't crazy. He felt calm, clarity shining around him like a soft light, warm and comforting.

Wright looked at him strangely, a small frown creasing her brow. "James?" He chose to ignore her as he picked up the PAMAS from where he'd dropped it and crouched at the back of the van, sucking in a large breath before he leaned out. No one seemed to have noticed him—they were all still firing on the wall.

A flash of blonde caught his eye as a couple of bags were blown apart. *Was that Victoria?* He didn't have time to check as an enemy soldier tried to open the gate and caught sight of James. He ducked back behind the van as bullets ricocheted where he had stood.

He waited until the soldier stopped to reload before he leaned out again. Raising his weapon, he managed to get three shots off before he had to take cover once more, the enemy's assault rifle superior to his shitty pistol. He shook his head at Wright—they were pinned. They had to go around another way. James eyed a little blue car flush against the wall. *So close.*

The bombardment cut off, and James stood still for a moment, frowning in confusion. The man couldn't have been halfway through his magazine, could he? Carefully,

James leaned back out from behind the truck and saw the man slumped against the gate at an odd angle, blood pooling beneath him.

James didn't spare him another thought. He rushed over to the blue car, ignoring Wright's call, his head pounding in tandem with his heart. He began to feel a little groggy, and his shoulder seemed to be burning. James pushed his growing worry aside as he moved to jump onto the bonnet.

He didn't get the chance to so much as bend his legs as a large hand tightened on his good shoulder and spun him around. He almost shot the man before he recognised him as Dubois. In a fit of anger, he shoved the Frenchman away and turned back to the car. James still had good chance to get over the wall before they spotted him.

Dubois spun him back around again, and this time pinned him to the car. "Listen to me, Englishman," he whispered in a rush, a vein pulsing in his forehead. James would have punched him for calling him English, but his left arm was trapped in the sling, and Dubois still had a tight hold of his right. *Fucking bastard!* James *definitely* didn't like him. "The Commandant has ordered us back to the truck. *Go.*" Dubois shoved him back, and James stumbled a few steps. Once he regained his balance, he spun on Dubois and pointed his gun at the man's face.

"*James.* What the fuck are you doing?" Wright's alarmed voice buzzed in his ear, but James swatted it aside like an annoying fly. He *had* to get to the leader. They weren't going to stop him.

"Listen to me—"

"Lower your weapon," Elise said in a hard voice.

James felt a hot barrel press into his side, and he couldn't stop the snarl that twisted his mouth as the heat soaked through his thin t-shirt and scorched his skin.

"Okay, okay, everyone needs to calm down," Wright said.

James saw her make a placating gesture out of the corner of his eye. Calm down? What fucking planet was she on? He needed to get to the bastard who shot him, and they were preventing him from reaching his goal. Besides, she should be defending him—the damn soldier had a gun shoved in his side. He needed her backing more than ever.

A shout came from somewhere, and bullets were falling all around them like hellish rain. James ducked back against the car, banging his shoulder as the ground where he had been standing erupted in an explosion of dust and tarmac. He didn't have time to register the pain as the four of them ran like hunted animals, the enemy chasing them with whips of steel that could tear through flesh with barely a pause.

They retreated behind the van. James noticed Dubois clutched his leg, bright red rivulets snaking around his knuckles and dripping fat and heavy to the ground. *Good,* James thought, not registering the callousness. *He can't stop me now.*

They were still pinned, and the element of surprise had been snatched away. James could have shot the French soldiers for that. If they hadn't interfered, he would have killed the bastard already.

"We have orders to retreat," the French woman shouted over the cracks of gunfire. "What do you think you are doing?"

Wright stepped in and started making excuses for him. "Elise, listen, he was doing his job, engaging the enemy—"

"Our orders are to retreat," Elise repeated, glaring between James and Wright.

"I don't give a fuck what your orders are," James snarled, shoving past Dubois, who had been covering them as the enemy managed to get through a smaller gate set in one of the larger ones. At least the man had basic training. The Frenchman stumbled on his bad leg, crying out as he put his weight on it. James felt warmth splatter his face, and Dubois fell to the ground, thick blood pulsing out of the wound below his neck with every rapid beat of his heart. James couldn't take his eyes away from him as he convulsed, more blood spilling from his mouth as he tried to speak.

"Merde."

Dubois moved, and it took James a moment to realise Wright and Elise were dragging him back behind the van. When he was behind cover, he wasn't moving anymore. The blood had stopped pulsing. It flowed lazily out of him, trapping the dust in its sticky grip. Did the dust care? Did it understand a man had died amongst it? James couldn't look away from his greasy hair and scraggly beard, his dark blue eyes staring accusingly up at him.

I did this.

"What the fuck, James?" Wright's shocked voice jarred him back to reality. "What the fuck is wrong with you?"

"I—I don't—" James couldn't finish the sentence.

"No time," Elise yelled, throwing James a glare that stabbed daggers into his chest. "Move."

He did as he was told. All thoughts of revenge bled out of him, like the blood surrounding Dubois. He felt cold again. Had Dubois felt cold in his last few moments? Had he longed for heat, for warmth, as James had?

What had happened to him? Ever since he'd woken up, he hadn't been himself. James followed Wright and Elise back to the building, firing at the enemy until his clip ran out.

Chapter Eighteen

They waited in a reception area as Alexia checked outside. The soldier had been gone for less than a minute—thirty-five seconds to be exact—and still Jennifer felt panic try to claw its way up her throat, felt her lungs struggle to draw in air as imaginary walls closed in.

She tried to focus on her surroundings. The way the sunlight filtered in through the dirty window, illuminating a small patch of the opposite wall. It revealed tiny imperfections, the smallest of cracks. *Is this how the world has fallen apart?* The virus had been the first fissure, spreading and weakening the foundations until it was too late, and everything came crashing down.

Jennifer herself felt fractured, like she was shattering in slow motion. Could she do nothing to stop it? *I need to feel safe again. Secure.* She couldn't live like this, in this state of constant stress. She couldn't even relax during sleep, not with the nightmares stealing any rest she hoped to gain.

At fifty-six seconds, Alexia returned. She beckoned them out, and together they all jogged across the open space to where the army truck idled. The chilly air stung as Jennifer breathed in, and it did little to relieve the constriction inside, like something had reached within her and coiled around her lungs, squeezing and suffocating.

They were almost at the large vehicle when she saw them. One shoved another around a red car, causing the man to stumble and lash back. Jennifer and the others skidded to a halt as insane eyes landed on them. *Eighteen*, Jennifer counted frantically. *Eighteen*. She sucked in a deep breath as her lungs burst free of their chains, the rush of oxygen blowing the panic aside. *Strange*, she thought. *Infected bring clarity*.

The stillness in the air smashed into fragments as the infected surged forward as one, screaming and yelling, murder in their twisted faces. Jennifer raised her gun as fast as she could, pulling hard on the trigger.

Nothing happened.

What the fuck? Jennifer tugged the trigger back again, and still nothing happened. What was wrong with it? *God, just my damn luck—*

She didn't get the chance to try a third time. She barely had a second to turn her body to protect her camera before a man barrelled into her, his disgusting breath all she could smell as she shoved the gun up between them. She didn't know how she managed to stay on her feet—the guy was over six foot and looked like he used to bench press cars for a living. Before Jennifer could worry about being overpowered, the man collapsed to the ground, writhing as blood gushed out of his side. She didn't have time to dwell on who shot him—Dan was in trouble.

Another tall man—albeit not as solidly built as the one Jennifer had faced—ripped the gun out of Dan's hands and tossed it away like it was a toy. Dan was super-imposed with Rachel in her mind's eye, and Jennifer felt herself speed up, determined not to fail this time. The rest of the world fell away as the man grabbed hold of the boy and punched him in the face. Jennifer watched blood and saliva spray from Dan's mouth as his head snapped side-ways, and something in Jennifer screamed, cried, com-pelled her forward. *No. I can't lose anyone else!*

The man was going to bite him. Infect him. Maybe even kill him. Jennifer couldn't let that happen.

She reached the pair, not slowing down as she shoved Dan out of the way and threw herself at the man. Sharp pain exploded, stabbing inward as if a hundred knives pierced her skin at once. Her world boiled down to the ag-ony in her arm, her vision dimming until all she saw was his teeth buried in her flesh. She tried to wrench her arm away, but he had too strong a grip. She didn't know where her gun was. What could she do?

Forgetting her fingers were broken, Jennifer curled her hand into a fist and slammed it into his face. She felt a crunch, and he reared back, yelling in pain. His shouts changed to gurgling as his throat tore open, blood spray-ing everywhere as he fell heavily to the ground.

Jennifer stood still for a moment, not registering the quiet. She couldn't stop her body from shaking. Blood poured out of her arm. It dripped down her face. Warm. Warmth was good. No, wait, blood was bad. Her thoughts were sluggish and hard to hold onto. Was this what shock felt like?

She cradled her bleeding arm close to her chest as sound returned, dragging lucidity along with it. She looked up to four guns pointed at her. Victoria and Sergeant Wright rushed to put themselves in between her and them.

"She's immune! Don't shoot her. She's immune." Sergeant Wright's strong voice carried clearly on the still air, and the guns wavered with uncertainty.

Jennifer met Alexia's eyes, saw the bewilderment there and nodded to reassure her. "I'm immune." She didn't say any more; the simple fact was enough. She had to check on Dan. Turning away from the guns, Jennifer squatted down next to the fourteen-year-old.

He was crying. Jennifer wanted nothing more than to pull him into a hug and tell him everything was going to be all right, but she didn't dare touch him. Not when so much blood covered her. God, was she getting used to having another person's blood on her? What a horrible thought. She moved her camera, lay down next to Dan on the cold concrete, and waited for him to open his eyes. When it became apparent he wasn't going to any time soon, Jennifer tried a different tactic.

"Hey, Dan," she said softly. He screwed his eyes shut tighter and gave a minute shake of his head. "Hey, it's all right. They're all gone now. You don't have to be afraid anymore."

He blinked open his eyes, and Jennifer smiled when she saw their deep blue colour. "You promise?" he whispered, blood dribbling out of his mouth. Jennifer's heart shattered for the broken boy.

"I promise," she whispered back, her chest constricting with something entirely other than panic.

She didn't move until he did. Once back on her feet, she found herself face to face with the Commandant. He did *not* look happy. A storm brewed behind his dark eyes, and Jennifer didn't want to be anywhere near that tempest.

"Explain."

He said the word with no inflection or force, and yet Jennifer felt like she'd committed mass murder and was being hauled before her judge, jury, and executioner. She tried to wet her lips but found her tongue to be too dry.

"There's not much to explain," she started, unsure of how much detail he wanted. "I was bitten back in the UK, and I didn't turn crazy. That's the gist of it. We're going to use my blood as a cure." She tried to smile but ended up wincing instead as she moved her arm and pain flared. Why was it always her left arm? It had barely healed, only to be torn open again.

The Commandant held her gaze for some of the most uncomfortable seconds of Jennifer's life. He didn't look away as he barked an order in French, and Louis jumped forward, pulling gloves from a military backpack he had acquired.

"I will bandage this for you in the truck," Louis said as he fished around in the backpack. "Here, before you get in." He poured water over the wound to wash away the blood, and Jennifer bit her lip to stop from crying out. He cleaned around the bite with an alcohol wipe, and the pain increased tenfold. Jennifer couldn't stop a whimper from escaping. Louis grimaced as if he were the one in pain. "I'm sorry, but I need to clean it."

She took the water canteen from him and washed the blood off her face as best she could with Louis directing her to the spots she missed. It was easy—the blood had yet to dry. She still felt unclean as she climbed into the back of the truck, but there was nothing more she could do about it.

Dan stuck by her like a second shadow, sitting so close he was practically on her lap. She wrapped her good arm around him while Louis cleaned and bandaged the left one, his sharp face filled with concentration. Jennifer turned her head away and focused on comforting Dan, who shivered more than the temperature called for. His tremors radiated through her and rattled her bones as well.

Was this it? Running from place to place, continuously fighting to survive? The thought had a brittleness to it, crumbling like the world around her. She longed for the way things were, for her parents, for her friends. She longed for the sense of security and warmth they used to bring her. She needed their strength to help her survive in this new world.

Clinging to Dan with one hand and her camera with the other, Jennifer felt herself shattering a little bit faster.

Chapter Nineteen

Her arm burned like a blowtorch seared through her skin to the bone. *Well,* Jennifer corrected, *maybe it's not that bad. Still hurts like hell.* It had been a day since they fled the hospital, and the pain in Jennifer's arm had steadily worsened. Pain had become a constant in her life. Why was it always her? *No, don't think like that. Better me than Dan.* The boy hadn't left her side the whole time, except when nature called. Even then, he was skittish, like a puppy kicked one too many times.

They parked the truck in the middle of a road with a good view of the surrounding area, including the small town to the south. When Jennifer complained about her arm not getting better, Louis had taken one look and declared it infected. An ordinary infection, he'd quickly clarified, as everyone tensed at his words. Thus, the small town they stopped outside of, boasting a small building with '*Pharmacie*' in big green letters above the door. Jennifer had seen it herself when Alexia passed her the scope. She hoped looters hadn't taken the medicine she needed.

They managed to avoid other people. An hour after leaving the hospital, they intercepted a radio message urging all who heard to head to some castle. Jennifer had almost fallen off her seat with relief. Could it be the safety she craved? A chance to pause for breath and figure out what to do next? She hoped it would turn out better than the hospital.

They had yet to arrive, though. Jennifer got the impression the soldiers were being extremely cautious, and even though they had been driving for a day, she didn't think they'd travelled far at all.

Commandant Phillipe left Sergeant Wright and James with them as he and the rest of the soldiers went into the town. Jennifer caught the quick parting words to Wright along with the doubtful look he gave James and knew he didn't trust the Scottish man. Jennifer didn't know what happened to the soldier—he hadn't spoken since they left the hospital, barring the occasional word to Wright. He seemed to be constantly on edge. Jennifer only saw him relax once when Wright passed him some water and sat next to him for the rest of the night.

Aarav also went with them into the town. The Commandant was fine with it, much to Jennifer's surprise. He handled himself well during the attack, impressing everyone who saw. Riya told her how he saved Anthony as they rushed through the hospital to the truck. She told her several times in fact, gushing with pride with each retelling. Jennifer started to get sick of hearing about it.

Sergeant Wright was in charge, and she and Victoria were the only ones with weapons. Jennifer had been confused when the Commandant told the two women they were the ones with the responsibility of protecting the group, and Victoria went pale. When Jennifer asked her about it, she refused to say anything. Jennifer had to ask Riya instead. Riya's expression sobered, and she said in hushed tones she never expected Victoria could be so cold-blooded. When Jennifer asked for clarification, Riya shook her head and changed the subject. Back to Aarav, of course.

"Hey, Miss Immune, pass the rations."

Jennifer sighed at Sergeant Wright's call, resigned to the stupid nickname, and picked up the bag next to her in the truck. The food wasn't bad, and she knew it was all they had, but it wasn't appetising at all. Jennifer had to swap her tuna and potatoes with Alexia's beef salad when it threatened to make a reappearance after a couple bites. The instant soup was surprisingly good, though.

The sergeant had a little fire dancing at the side of the road, water boiling in a can on a tripod over it. Jennifer dropped the bag next to her and she started pulling out packets to prepare them. The rabbit casserole went to Jennifer, which she didn't mind. It had looked nice yesterday when Dan ate it. She settled down on the hard mud next to Riya, and Dan joined them a moment later, folding his long legs under him as he dropped gracelessly to the ground.

Jennifer wrapped her big coat tighter around herself against the cold and dug into her meal. It was tasteless, but she welcomed any kind of warmth she could get—the chill snapped at her. She thought back to the last casserole she had, back at her parents' house after New Year. It had been chicken casserole, as her dad didn't like any other kind of meat. She missed the way he used to wrinkle his nose at a beef burger or steak and claim he didn't understand how she and her mother could stand the stuff. Her mum used to tell him to go vegetarian, but he argued he liked chicken too much.

Jennifer smiled around a mouthful of food and knew he would wrinkle his nose at her for her choice of meal. Her smile dimmed then, as the ever-present darkness surged forward like a treacherous wave in the night. Jennifer wondered why she still fought it, still pushed back, when it would be so much easier to give in. The thought had crossed her mind over the last few days, but it had been easier to disregard it back at the hospital when she felt like they had been building something, like she had a purpose. It was harder to find the resilience she needed on the empty road.

Jennifer realised she had been staring at her food and forced herself to take another bite. She knew these little meals wouldn't last and she needed all the strength she could get. Who knew what lay ahead?

She needed something to distract her from the bleakness of her future. Looking around, she noticed Riya staring toward the town, her own meal forgotten in her hands. Jennifer gave a mental sigh and steeled herself to hear about Aarav saving Anthony for the hundredth time.

"Hey, Riya," she said, trying to get the woman's attention. She had to say it again before Riya turned to her, a concerned look on her face.

"Ah, yes?" she asked, distracted.

Jennifer nodded in the direction the other woman had been looking. "He'll be fine. Try not to worry too much."

Riya gave a small, humourless laugh. "That is a difficult thing to do." She sighed and drank a mouthful of water before smiling tiredly at Jennifer. "Do you know what it is like to love someone so completely?"

Jennifer thought of Damien, and Robin before him, and knew she hadn't experienced what Riya and Aarav had. Sure, she *liked* Damien, but as a friend. She wouldn't have ended up married to him or anything. They would have broken up. She thought she had been in love with Robin, but the less she thought about her the better. Jennifer gave a slight shake of her head and shrugged one shoulder. She would like to have what the young couple had. Alexia pushed into her head, but she shook the thought away. She didn't even know if the soldier liked women that way. Maybe she would find love one day, if shit ever stopped hitting the fan.

"We have known each other since we were very small. We have experienced childhood and adolescence together, and we have started adulthood together. We have grown into the people we are today with each other. I love him," she said simply, and she smiled a beautiful smile. "I am going to worry about him."

"Well, when you put it like that," Jennifer laughed, and the two women shared a grin. "How did you meet?"

Riya seemed to visibly relax, and even took a bite to eat before speaking. "I was only five, and yet I can remember it as if it were last week. It was Holi and—" She paused at Jennifer's puzzled look and muttered something in her language.

"Holi is the festival of colours," Riya explained. "You have heard of it, yes?"

"Yeah. It's where you get covered in coloured powder, right?"

"That is part of it, yes." Riya relaxed even further as she began to describe Holi. "It is about saying goodbye to winter and welcoming spring. Friends laugh and love together while enemies put aside their differences and repair their broken relationships. I remember the morning after the Holika bonfire, I was so happy from all the singing and dancing the night before, and so excited for the day ahead that I thought I would burst," Riya chuckled.

"My family took me to a nearby park, and soon I and all the other children were covered in colours. I never wanted to be washed, lest the brightness disappear." She shook her head, the smile on her face said memories had taken her. "Aarav threw a water balloon at me, and it smashed on my shoulder, washing away some of the colour. I was *so* mad at him." Riya laughed, and the sound made Jennifer glad she managed to distract her from her worry.

"I chased him until I could run no longer, but he was a fast boy, and I did not catch him." Riya snorted, and Dan jumped at the harsh sound.

"But I take it you did eventually?"

"No." Riya grinned at Jennifer's confusion. "He came back to me and rubbed some colour on my shoulder. I remember he apologised, and for the rest of the day we were inseparable. It turned out we lived close to each other and, what is the phrase? The rest is history?"

Jennifer smiled. "Yes. The rest is history." *What an adorable story*. She turned back to her casserole, feeling lighter than she had in days. Riya ate her food as well, but Jennifer noticed her tense back up again, and she kept throwing concerned looks at the town. Jennifer had no idea what she was going through. "Hey," she said, and Riya turned back to her. "Do you have any other stories? Why don't you tell me about India? I've never been."

Riya gave her a look like she knew Jennifer was trying to distract her, but she appreciated the effort. "Fine. I will tell you about our wedding. Indian weddings are different from Western ones..."

Jennifer settled back on the hard mud and let the sound of Riya's lilting voice wash over her.

*

Victoria stood in the middle of the road not too far from the group, a light breeze tugging her hair into her eyes before it passed on, dancing through the short grass and over to the town. She shook the strands free as she tugged her coat closer around herself. The blonde had lost its shine, becoming limp and lifeless as grease took root. How she longed for a shower and indoor plumbing. Victoria shuddered, thinking of squatting behind trees instead of using a toilet. And who knew what she would have to do when she started her period. It didn't bear thinking about.

Her coat was warm and waterproof, but too big, and the sleeves kept getting in the way as she adjusted her grip on her gun. It was the same wild animal she had at the hospital. Victoria hated it. Holding it made her grit her teeth in disgust. It reminded her of things she didn't want to think about.

She sighed. *To thine own self be true.* Shakespeare had been a large part of her desire to study English. She'd lost count of how many times she'd read Hamlet. She clenched her jaw. She needed to acknowledge what she had done—she couldn't keep running from herself. It was stupid to even try.

She'd murdered people. At the hospital and... before. She'd never thought herself capable of such evil, but desperate times, right? It was all self-defence.

Even her sister.

Victoria's legs burst into action, like walking would somehow chase her demons away. She didn't get far before she stopped. She had resolved to *not* run from herself, and here she was, literally walking away. *Pull yourself together, woman,* Victoria chastised herself. Easier said than done.

The first time she became aware of the monster within was only about half a year ago. Summer had been relinquishing its hold to autumn, the leaves beginning to lose their bright green colour, beautiful reds and yellows and oranges becoming more prominent as the days shortened. Victoria remembered thinking about the chill in the air as she opened her front door and lamenting the loss of summer dresses. She looked good in summer dresses.

They hadn't heard her enter over their shouting. Mike's deep voice was quieter than Katherine's sharper one, but he was ill, and Victoria supposed he didn't have the energy to yell. He claimed to be fine, a little run down from working long hours maybe, but okay. Victoria knew he had lied to her. She was about to make herself known when one shrill sentence stopped her in her tracks.

"I should never have started sleeping with you!"

Victoria felt like someone kicked her in the stomach. All air left in a rush, and she deflated, sagging against the wall. She had misheard. She must have misheard. Mike and Katherine weren't... They couldn't be...

"Fine. Get out of my house." Mike's voice. Angry. Hard.

Short, sharp footsteps. Katherine's heels on the laminated floor. Victoria pushed herself upright as her sister stomped through the door between the living room and the hallway. She could never forget the look on her sister's face when she saw her, never forget the way she stopped in front of her, not breathing, mouth hanging open. Her bright blue eyes were glassy, almost like she was coming down with something as well. Victoria didn't know how long they stood there, not talking. Betrayal filled Victoria up, the pressure building to a breaking point as shame and guilt warred across Katherine's face.

In the end, her sister dragged her gaze away and brushed past Victoria, out into the chilly afternoon as autumn strengthened its grip around summer's throat. She let her go. She didn't know what else to do.

Victoria didn't remember much of the ensuing argument with Mike. She had been so *angry*, so *hurt*, and the monster reared its head for the first time. She'd wanted to hurt him, genuinely hurt him, worse than he'd hurt her. Instead, she'd managed to curb that urge and settled for throwing her engagement ring back at him and telling him to get out of *her* house.

It was the last conversation they ever had. His work had called her the next day, sprouting some nonsense about an accident in the labs. Victoria barely listened. She'd felt relief. *Relief.* Only for the briefest of seconds, but it had been there. If that didn't make her a monster, she didn't know what did. She was glad she wouldn't have to face him again and relive his lies and betrayal.

The reality of his death didn't sink in until she called Katherine and asked her to come over so she could tell her the news face to face. Her sister was visibly ill, sweating, pale, a crazed look in her once bright eyes. Victoria didn't register the symptoms at first, focusing instead on hurting her sister as much as possible. The confusion and paranoia eventually warned her something was off, but before she knew what was happening, Katherine had attacked her. It was all Victoria could do to defend herself.

Katherine was like a rabid beast. She grabbed Victoria and yanked her forward, opening her mouth to bite her as she fell into her sister's arms. Victoria still didn't know how she managed to push herself away, only that she had. For the second time in her life, the monster came alive. This time Victoria let it take control, welcoming the cold hatred as she fought for her life. By the time the police arrived, her living room was a complete mess—ornaments smashed, TV broken, the curtains ripped down.

Katherine dead.

The following months were a blur of cover-up after cover-up as they buried the disease and claimed she had been overcome with jealousy and killed her sister over the affair. An open and shut case. They were so convincing Victoria almost began to believe it herself. She gave up during the trial and accepted her fate. Her family, her friends, they all turned away from her until she was left with nothing.

And then the world ended. Thanks to the generosity of an unnamed guard who released her handcuffs as infected attacked them, she stood on an empty road in the middle of France, surrounded by people who were all but strangers, holding an assault rifle as she protected them from a different kind of monster.

The cold breeze was nothing compared to her heart.

Chapter Twenty

James accepted the meal Wright gave him wordlessly. His shoulder hurt, which was no less than he deserved. Dubois had been killed because of him. James hadn't known him, and by all accounts he had been an arsehole, but he hadn't deserved to die.

What was wrong with him? He kept reliving getting shot, his shoulder flaring with heat each time. Anger consumed him. Anger at the civilians, anger at the whole fucked up situation, anger at himself. He felt an absence of control over his own thoughts, his own feelings.

He remembered the haunted faces of some of the soldiers who returned from a tour of duty. The way they always seemed to see things that weren't there. They always seemed on edge, like a bomb ready to go off at the slightest pressure. Some recovered; others never quite found their way back to themselves. Was it happening to him? James desperately wanted to feel like himself again.

His neck prickled. Eyes were on him. Looking up, he met the dark gaze of Wright, who arched an eyebrow at his meal. James didn't have an appetite at all, but he shoved some food into his mouth to keep Wright off his back. It tasted of nothing, but she nodded to him and turned away. He swallowed with some difficulty and put the food on the ground, the smell making him nauseous.

He scrubbed a hand over his face, feeling the rough bristles scrape against his callused skin. When was the last time he had a shave? It felt like at least a week's growth. He'd been able to grow a decent beard since he'd turned sixteen, and he always had to shave at least every two days to avoid looking rough.

He needed to sort himself out. None of his army mates had gone through this, he was sure. Andy had been the exception, but he'd always had a screw loose. James suspected he had come out of the womb half-crazy.

What would Andy say to him? Probably something both stupid and profound at the same time. He would have offered him food. The man had always been eating. James didn't know how he'd been such a skinny bastard.

James hadn't liked Andy at first—he'd been disrespectful to his superiors, loud and obnoxious—but after all they went through together, he became like a brother to him.

What would Andy do? James realised he wouldn't say anything. He would sit next to him, and that would be it. And somehow it would be all James needed. Andy would say, without words, that it would be all right. He would be there no matter what. He would help him through this, and James would find himself once again.

James's eyes stung. Andy wasn't here. The stupid bastard had gotten himself killed long before the world fell to shite. How was he supposed to be himself again if he had no one to support him? He didn't think he could do it alone.

A shadow passed over him and he looked up, bracing himself against another of Wright's rants about eating. Except it wasn't the pilot this time.

Dan sat down next to him, a cup of steaming hot chocolate clutched in his hands. James waited for the boy to say something, but he continued to sit there in silence. James attributed it to his shyness and put him out of his mind.

He turned his gaze away and caught sight of Victoria, standing in the middle of the road with the wind blowing her hair behind her. He noticed the weapon she held and knew he would have to get a hold of himself soon. He couldn't expect the civilians to do his job for him. She stood like she knew how to use it. Was that a good thing or a bad thing? *Is this what the world has come to?* James thought. *Teachers standing guard with assault rifles and children with no childhoods?* He turned back to Dan and really *saw* him for the first time.

Saw his dirty blond hair sticking up in the wind. Saw the dark bruises on his cheek from the hospital. Saw eyes that should have been bright with laughter and happiness but were instead dull with pain and a heaviness no adult should have to endure, never mind a child. What happened to this kid? His mouth looked like it had forgotten how to smile, and he hunkered down in his big coat against the cold, taking a quick sip of his drink. The steam blew in his face, making him look faded and wraithlike.

He must have sensed James's gaze because he turned and caught his eye. The contact didn't last long. He swirled the hot chocolate in the cup for a few seconds before holding it out to James.

"Here," Dan mumbled, still not making eye contact. "It's warm."

James had to use his voice to decline as the boy didn't look up. He had to cough before any words formed.

"No, thanks," he muttered back. He wanted to say more but couldn't think of anything else.

Dan lowered the cup and spoke haltingly. "Erm, Sergeant Mollino, sir, please. I, uh, don't know what happened, but I think I can understand. Or, well, kind of, I guess. I've seen some... some horrible stuff as well." Was he tearing up? "You've got to keep going. That's what I'm doing. It seems to be working. So far, at least." Dan finally made eye contact. "Please be a soldier again."

He held Dan's gaze—the boy's worn eyes were older than his years. James reached out and took the cup from him, taking a large mouthful and letting the liquid sear its way down his throat. *Please be a soldier again.* Was it really that simple? James didn't think so. But looking at Dan, at the young kid whose childhood had been snatched away, James wanted to try.

Please be a soldier again.

*

Victoria's stomach rumbled for what felt like the hundredth time, and she finally gave in to its demands. She walked back to the group quickly even though she knew all the good meals would be taken. As long as she wasn't left with the tuna abomination Jennifer had yesterday. Just thinking about it made her stomach clench in disgust.

She passed by Martin, who sat a little apart from everyone else, as usual. His knees were drawn up to his chest and his arms were wrapped around them. Was he all right? Did he look pale? Sweaty? He kept moving his jaw and mouth like they were uncomfortable. He avoided her gaze as she slowed her half-jog, and a chill ran through her which had nothing to do with the wind.

Food forgotten, she made straight for Wright, who climbed to her feet as Victoria reached her. "I'll take over watch while you eat. You get the instant soup today—" She broke off when she caught sight of Victoria's expression. "Great. What shit do we have to deal with now?"

"Have you seen Martin?" Victoria cast a quick glance back at him over her shoulder. She pulled Wright to one side so nobody got alarmed. "Does he look sick to you?"

Wright frowned over at him for a long moment before she sighed. "You've got to be kidding me."

Victoria didn't answer—Wright had said that more to herself than anyone else. The pilot pinched her brow and shook her head, clearly having an internal debate with herself. "You think he's infected? How did we miss it? We checked everyone."

Victoria shrugged. "We need to check him again. If he is infected..." She left the sentence hanging and gave a meaningful look to Wright, who scowled at her.

"Yes, I know what will have to be done. You don't have to shepherd me to the right answer. I'm not one of your fucking students."

Victoria didn't respond to the anger. She knew this would be hard for the soldier—no amount of bravado would change the fact that she needed to kill someone she was supposed to protect. Victoria didn't envy her these next few decisions.

With a shake of her head, Wright stomped over to Martin. "Stand up."

Martin jumped at the harsh sound of the pilot's voice, and Victoria was sure he would have paled if he hadn't already been deathly white. He tripped over his own feet in his haste to do as Wright commanded. Everyone watched them, meals left abandoned as they trained their eyes on the unfolding drama.

"What's going on?" Martin squeaked, clearly terrified of Wright. *Well,* Victoria thought, *who wouldn't be?* The pilot stalked forward like a cat going in for the kill, her eyes ablaze with an anger that spilled out into the rest of her, coiling around and around until it was in danger of snapping.

"Are you infected?" Wright barked. She didn't mince words. Victoria liked that about her.

Jennifer stood up, Riya and Dan not far behind her. James was slower, climbing up like an old bear shaking off a winter spent in hibernation. The man needed a shave. He *looked* like a bloody bear.

Martin laughed nervously. "What? Of course not. Don't be daft." He smiled at them, probably in some misguided attempt to ease their fears. Victoria wasn't buying it.

"Don't lie to us," Victoria said, hefting the gun up so it rested more easily against her shoulder. Martin's eyes widened, and she noticed the rapid rise and fall of his chest. She hated this infection, and she hated liars. She made it plain as day as she glared at him.

Whatever he saw in her face made him gulp and he looked from person to person, trying to find an ally. "It's not even a bite—nothing to worry about—I'm fine—" He cut off when Wright took a step toward him. Victoria couldn't see the look on her face, but Martin held up his arms in a warding off gesture.

"It's not a bite I *swear*," Martin said imploringly.

"Then explain," Wright growled.

"I don't know." He looked seconds away from crying. "At the hospital, the fighting, I don't know. I bit my own cheek by accident." He let out a great rush of air, like a balloon deflating. "Then this man, infected man, he was bleeding and I don't know, it all happened so fast I don't—"

Wright cut him off. "His infected blood got in your mouth, where you had an open wound from biting yourself."

"Please," he cried. "Please don't kill me. I could be immune like Jennifer. Or, or she could give me some of her blood to cure it. *Please.*"

Victoria turned away. She had taken an instant dislike to the man back in London, and his pitiful display wasn't doing him any favours.

"I could give him some blood," Jennifer piped up. "That could work, right? As long as we're the same type."

"No."

The gravelly voice belonged to James. It was a shock to hear him speak after so long. He strode up to Wright with some of his earlier confidence, and Victoria saw a glimmer of the man she'd come to know. She didn't know what had caused him to become a shadow of his former self, but she was glad to see him finally over whatever it had been.

He studied Martin, and his shoulders drooped a little. "Open your mouth," he said.

Martin did as he was told. "Necrosis," James said to Wright.

She nodded. "Jennifer doesn't have it."

"Why can't I give him some blood?" Jennifer loudly cut into the soldier's quiet conversation.

Victoria knew. Mike had often talked about his work, and even though she hadn't understood most of it, some stuck. "Not only do we not have to equipment for that, it's not as simple as it looks on TV," she said. She racked her brain to remember what Mike had said. "Blood can't go straight from one person into another. You can have some kind of fatal reaction." She knew she was missing a lot of the information, but she was pretty sure she had the gist of it. Louis would be able to explain it better, probably.

Hope fell from Jennifer's face almost as fast as Martin crashed to his knees. The curly-haired man reached out to grab Sergeant Wright, but she stepped out of his reach. "*Please*. You have to try something. *Anything*." No one spoke. Victoria watched as he became more desperate, the paranoia creeping into his eyes reminding her of Katherine. "Of course, you won't help me. You all hate me. You probably can't wait for me to die. One less mouth to feed."

"That's not—" James began, but Martin rounded on him.

"Do you even know my name? You've never said two words to me since we met."

James looked taken aback before something akin to shame stole over his expression. He looked down at his feet and the returning confidence seemed to drain out of him like water down a plug hole.

"None of you care about me," Martin ground out. "You don't give a shit about what happens to me. Did you know I was a well-respected man before all this? You don't even make an effort to talk to me."

Victoria had enough. He sounded crazier with each word.

"Shut *up*, Martin," she said, sick of his nonsense. He recoiled away from her outburst. "We've tried to include you, but you made it so difficult we stopped bothering. When I first met you, I was the one who started the conversation, but you droned on and on about yourself, not giving me a second thought. You cut me off so many times I eventually left. I know for a fact Jennifer, Riya, Louis, and Alexia have tried to have a conversation with you. Dan tried to play that card game with you, but it's been like talking to a brick wall."

It felt good to let off some steam. Victoria drew in a deep breath, the muted smells of winter filling her nose as the cold air rushed in. She released the breath in a measured movement, and she watched it curl in front of her before it faded from view. Her frustration dwindled away with her breath.

"I'm *frightened*, okay? Everyone and everything I've ever known is gone." Martin broke down again, and Victoria felt a stirring of sympathy for him. "And now I'm going to die. Either by you or this virus—" His words cut off as he choked on his tears.

Victoria frowned. Had she been too hard on him? As she glazed down at him pity wormed its way past the dislike. She supposed people dealt with things in different ways—maybe his way was to retreat into himself.

Well, she thought, *it's too late to say sorry now.* Victoria watched as James pulled Martin to his feet and supported him as he fell against the soldier, obviously too distraught to stand on his own. James struggled for a moment with his injured shoulder, but he scowled at Wright as she stepped forward to help.

"You don't have to do this. Not alone," the pilot said, so softly Victoria had to strain to hear.

"Yes, I do," James replied, just as quietly. The two soldiers shared a look, and an entire conversation took place that Victoria wasn't privy to. Wright gave James a handgun, and the wounded soldier led Martin away. Victoria thought he wasn't even aware he was moving.

Silence descended on the group. *Is it me, or does it seem colder than before*? Dan moved first, picking up a steaming cup. He swirled the contents around, his eyes unfocused. With a sudden violence that shocked Victoria, he threw the cup as hard as he could, letting out a frustrated yell at the same time. Burning liquid splashed over the frozen ground as Jennifer moved to comfort him.

"Try to eat something. I'll stand guard." Sergeant Wright looked miserable, and the expression didn't suit her. The woman had taken it upon herself to smile for everyone when they couldn't. During their time at the hospital, Victoria had seen her with a grin on her face more often than without.

Victoria watched her walk a short way down the road, and she had never seen her look so small.

She turned away, determined to eat something to keep her strength up. Maybe the others would follow suit if she ate something. Looking at them as she picked up her soup, and seeing their misery, Victoria thought that unlikely.

She caught sight of the cup and the dark stain on the concrete. It still steamed. Victoria hoped the people here weren't going to burn up and spill over. They needed each other and—

They needed each other.

The realisation startled her, but Victoria knew it was true. They made it through the end of the world together. They needed the familiarity and comfort that went hand in hand with surviving something traumatic. People didn't turn their backs on those they travelled through hell with.

I was too hard on Martin. The truth was cold, and guilt hardened around it. He made a terrible first impression, and she never gave him the chance to improve upon it. She dismissed him as a spineless coward, not giving him a second thought beyond her distaste, and the man would die believing he was hated and weak.

Her soup tasted of ashes in her mouth.

Chapter Twenty-One

James's shoulder burned like fire, but he pushed on regardless. He gripped the gun weakly in his left hand, his right preoccupied with supporting Martin. His hand was so numb he almost dropped the weapon several times. His arm wasn't in a sling anymore due to it being dirty and covered in blood from the hospital, so he had a little more freedom of movement. Only with his lower arm though, and even that hurt.

The other man stopped crying and seemed to have gone into a state of shock. James was sure Martin would crash to the ground if he let go.

They continued staggering forward, James glancing at the other man every few seconds. He didn't look ready attack him, but better to be prepared for any eventuality, unlikely as it seemed. Martin's sweaty face was devoid of colour, and James had no idea what he thought. *If he's thinking anything at all. I'm walking him to his execution.* James had faced death several times, the most recent leaving him scarred in ways he was only beginning to understand, so he had an inkling of what Martin was going through. But everyone dealt with it differently. Death was a truly individual experience.

Please be a soldier again.

Dan's words rang in his ears, resounding deep within him. Was being a soldier all about murder? *No. I'm protecting the others. I have to believe that.* But looking at the broken man he carried, James couldn't see it.

This is not the time to have doubts. If he began to second guess himself, he wouldn't be able to go through with it. And it had to be done. For the protection of everyone else. What was one man's life against those of a group?

This shouldn't be so difficult, right? *If it wasn't hard, then that would mean there was something wrong with me,* he supposed. *Killing should never be easy.* It took a toll like nothing else. James remembered the first time he ever killed someone, way back when he was barely out of his teens. It hadn't registered until much later when he had made his way back to camp, but it had hit him with the weight of a tank. When he'd managed to get a minute to himself, he'd cried in his bunk.

Many years had passed since then, and he'd grown tougher, more calloused, with the passage of time. He hoped his skin was tough enough to do what had to be done. It didn't feel like it. He felt like the slightest scratch would tear him apart. The pressure weighted him down, the responsibility, the way people counted on him. *Please be a soldier again.* Could he?

He wasn't strong enough to continue carrying the other man, so they stumbled to a halt and James slowly lowered Martin to the ground. Sweat beaded on his forehead—the short walk had been more tiring than he expected. He moved the gun from his weak left hand to his stronger right, but it still weighed more than it should. Was that physical, or psychological?

Would the young man he used to be hate what he'd become? Private Mollino had stressed about cleaning his uniform, chemical, biological, radiological, and nuclear training, and how to stand out so his commanding officers noticed him. He'd worried about missing a beat on the drums during a performance; now, he worried about how to keep people alive during the end of the world. Now, he had to execute an innocent man.

James fought back a rush of sadness as he focused on Martin, who still kneeled on the road. "Hey, man," he rasped. Martin's eyes flicked up to meet his, and James saw the anger burning there. "I'm so sorry about this, Martin, really—"

"Are you? Do you care about anything? You haven't spoken for ages. You're a *mess*." Martin's voice increased in volume with every word, and James let him release his frustration. "You're supposed to kill me? You?" An hysterical laugh escaped his chapped lips, and tears soon took over once more.

James didn't know what to say. What was he supposed to say? Should he get it over with? No, he should hear the man's last words. He could give him that, at least.

Martin reached for him with hands like claws, and James flinched back before he could stop himself. "Listen, you could let me go. The others don't need to know." His voice took on a pleading tone, and James felt his heart break. "I could be immune as well—I could be fine. Just let me go, please."

"You know I can't do that, Martin," James said, sorrow lacing his words.

"Please, James. Please." Martin's eyes were red from crying, and when he saw James wasn't going to relent, his whole body sagged. He let his arm drop, the limb looking already lifeless as it banged into his leg.

James crouched down in front of Martin, passing the gun back to his left hand. He reached out and grasped him on his shoulder until he met his eye again. "What's your favourite memory?"

"What?"

"Your favourite memory? Or perhaps memories? Something from your childhood?" James wanted him to be in a good place when he pulled the trigger. Or as close to a good place as he was ever going to get.

Martin sniffed and wiped his eyes, gazing up at James with a mixture of confusion and suspicion. "One of my earliest memories is of my brother and I playing in the rain," he said, the words hesitant.

"Aye? Can you remember much about it?"

"I remember we had matching bright yellow wellies on. He was a year older than me, but we were the same height. I remember feeling smug about that." A flicker of a smile. "We were jumping in puddles outside our house pretending to be Batman and Robin. My brother got to be Batman because he was older." Martin sniffed. "I miss him."

"What was his name?"

"James, same as you." Martin seemed to relax a little, and James wanted to keep him talking about happier times. Simpler times.

"Can you see the puddles? Smell the rain? Close your eyes and picture it." James removed his hand from Martin's shoulder and took up the gun instead. From comfort to violence in one movement.

Martin smiled softly. "Mum had made cookies that day as well. I can see them, their smell mixing with the rain. We raced each other to the kitchen when she called. My brother won but I almost caught him." A tear escaped from his closed eyes, and James knew the time had come. He stood up and moved back, careful not to disturb the man. He levelled the gun at his head.

Still, he hesitated. Why couldn't he pull trigger? His finger wouldn't curl, and his arm shook. He needed to do this while Martin had some kind of peace. *Fucking hell, James, pull the fucking trigger.*

Martin opened his eyes, and James froze. "I was so afraid. I was responsible for my brother's death. Does that make me a bad person?" James didn't have an answer for him. Martin started rocking on his knees. "Maybe he'll forgive me." He closed his eyes again. "Maybe he'll forgive me." He started repeating the sentence over and over. *It's time now.* He'd seen this in other infected people—repetition holding them captive as they tried to cling to reality.

There was a beat, and James pulled the trigger before he could hesitate any further. His ears continued to ring long after the gunshot had faded.

*

Jennifer tried to follow Victoria's example and eat her food, but she couldn't. Her throat stung with unshed tears. How had they missed it? After all they had been through, they shouldn't have missed it. They should be more careful. They *had* to be more careful.

She hadn't liked the man, but she hardly knew him. It still hit close to home. They needed to be better prepared. This couldn't happen again. She adjusted her camera in her lap and wrapped her arm tighter around Dan, who cried into her shoulder. She suspected thoughts of his mother and sister crowded his head. He was too young to be going through so much trauma. Hell, *she* was too young to be going through so much trauma. At twenty-four she should still be learning about life, not coming to terms with death.

A single gunshot rang out. Dan flinched into her side. She didn't know what to say to him. Why could she never find the right words?

In the end, she didn't need to. Victoria cleared her throat, stirring her soup absently as she frowned at nothing. "Did Martin ever talk to any of you? A real conversation?"

Riya shook her head. "I tried—we all did—but he brushed off my every attempt. I think he was still processing everything. I assumed he would open up to us eventually, but..." Her voice drifted off, and she looked down at the ground, her own meal forgotten beside her.

"I first met him in the cafeteria at Knightsbridge," Victoria started. "He was a mess, and looking back now, I guess he was in shock. I was too caught up in my own panic to register anyone else's." She made a bitter sound. "I guess hindsight really is twenty-twenty.

"I arrived after him. He was the only person in the cafeteria, and I needed someone..." She paused, gripped by memories. "Not someone to talk to necessarily, but someone to be close to, you know? I sat next to him, but I don't think he even knew I was there until I spoke. I still don't know why I did. Like I said, I didn't feel any particular need to say anything." She sighed and put her half-eaten bowl of soup down. "I used to regret starting a conversation with him." Victoria's lips twitched in a poor attempt at a smile as she looked up at Jennifer.

"You said he wouldn't let you get a word in?" Jennifer asked. She knew about Victoria's dislike of the man, but not really what caused it.

"Yeah," Victoria sighed. "I introduced myself, and that was the only complete sentence I was able to say. I guess he was waiting for an excuse to unload his stress and fear. He went on and on about what had happened to him and, looking back, I can see he was getting more and more distressed. Maybe I sensed that because I ended up walking out.

"He told me he and his brother were dropping their mum back off at her nursing home when everything went bad. The building was on fire when they got to it, and they didn't know what was happening—nobody seemed to know what was happening. They decided to go back to his brother's house and try to find out what was going on. They never made it. He became a bit incoherent at this point, but I gather he watched his mother and brother die. I thought about my own mother then, and how she'd abandoned me when—" She cut off, her lips forming a thin line as she squeezed her eyes shut. Jennifer wondered what that was all about.

"Anyway," Victoria continued after she'd composed herself. "He went on about how his brother saved him and how he'd in turn had to leave his brother behind. I don't know what happened there—he didn't go into much detail—but I remember getting the impression he was a bit of a coward and maybe if he'd been braver, his brother would still be alive.

"I tried to comfort him and talk more about other things to distract him from his grief, but he would *not* shut up. He kept getting louder and louder and had started repeating himself. I didn't know if he was going to get violent or break down in tears, and I didn't stay to find out." Victoria looked guilty, but Jennifer didn't know what else the woman could have done. It had obviously been too soon to talk to him, and if she thought he could get violent she was right to leave.

"I didn't give him another chance. He was a cowardly idiot in my eyes, and now I'll never know if that's true or not."

A heavy silence blanketed the four of them as Victoria picked up her soup once more. She ate it mechanically and didn't look up at any of them.

Dan pulled away from Jennifer's shoulder, scrubbing his nose with the back of his hand and trying to look like he hadn't spent the last few minutes crying. He tried so hard to be brave. Jennifer was proud of him, but he needed to know it was all right to cry. She nudged him with her shoulder. "Hey, Dan, it's okay—"

"No, I, erm, I'm fine," he mumbled, his eyes red as he rubbed them.

"No, you're not, Dan," Jennifer said with more force than she intended, startling the boy into making eye contact. Riya and Victoria turned to her as well, so she raised her voice. "None of us are. We need to acknowledge that fact, accept it, and get past it." She made her voice softer. "It's okay to cry. It's not a sign of weakness—it's one of strength. It means you care. It means you grieve. It means you love. We'll all need that strength to move forward."

Dan dropped his gaze to his hands, but Jennifer knew

he considered her words. He looked up at her and gave a tiny nod. She would take it. A little tension drained out of her, and she felt like she'd accomplished something. She thought of her earlier promise to make them hope again. The renewed sense of purpose was enough to stave off the emptiness. For a while, at least.

*

James still sat on the side of the road next to Martin's body when the other soldiers ran into view. He knew they would have heard the gunshot, and they'd made it back in record time. He quickly wiped his eyes as he stood up.

Alexia and Aarav continued past while the others formed up around him. Trueman and Roux threw him concerned looks, but James shook his head at them. Trueman was a good man, and he was inclined to believe the doctor was as well. They'd both tried to talk to him, which he appreciated even though he'd wanted to be left alone. Elise's cold eyes held little expression as she scanned Martin's corpse. She didn't even look at him as she turned to cover the opposite side of the road.

"Explain."

The Commandant spoke softly, but James had to stop himself from grimacing. He knew the man didn't trust him. *With good reason.* He knew he would have to earn his trust, and it would be a long time coming, but James wouldn't give up. *Please be a soldier again.* He would start with the basics—following his commanding officers orders.

James stood up to attention. "He was infected, sir," he said. "We missed it. I had to..." He faltered, and the weight of what he'd done pressed down on his shoulders.

Commandant Phillipe held his gaze before giving him a small nod. James felt a knot in his stomach loosen, and he returned the nod. "Your weapon."

James tried not to be too disappointed as he handed over the handgun. *Baby steps. I'll earn your trust, Commandant.* He knew it would be an arduous undertaking, but he was more than willing to try.

"Capitaine, how did you miss this?" Commandant Phillipe continued to speak in English, no doubt for James's benefit.

Roux scrambled over to the body, crouching down and studying it thoroughly. James took pity on him as he searched and didn't find anything, his frown deepening.

"He has a cut on the inside of his mouth, and infected blood got in during the fighting at the hospital," James said.

The doctor's expression cleared, and he looked almost... relieved? *He must feel like he's been let off the hook.* A cut inside the mouth was easy to miss.

"I'm sorry, sir," Roux said, examining Martin's mouth. "I suggest we screen people more," he paused, searching for the right word, "*meticulously* from now on."

The Commandant gave a sharp nod. "Do it. Move back to the truck, now. We'll have to leave—there were infected people in the town who will have heard that gunshot."

"Sir—" James started.

"Leave the body, Sergeant Mollino. We don't have time to bury him."

James hurried to keep up with them as they jogged back up the road. The Commandant was right in that they didn't have the time, but James felt bad for leaving Martin out in the open.

They made it back to the truck a couple of minutes later. *I hadn't walked as far as I'd thought.* His heart sank as he thought about his shoulder and how weakness had set up shop in his body. Maybe he should take Roux and Wright up on their offer to help him with physical therapy.

The truck was a hive of activity as everyone packed everything back up. A yell echoed over the road, and everyone picked up the pace. They needed to be long gone before the infected showed up. Cups were emptied of their contents and thrown back into backpacks without being cleaned. People packaged food back up, and the fire became a smouldering pit as Wright destroyed it, first with water and then her boots. She caught his eye, questions filling her face. He nodded back. Yes, it was done. Yes, he would be all right. Yes, he knew she was there for him.

He didn't know when that happened. They had only known each other for a short amount of time. He supposed he shouldn't be surprised—you formed quick bonds with your squad, becoming a true band of brothers and sisters. You had to trust each other. He supposed the process was bound to be accelerated during the end of the world. He could count on Trueman as well, he knew.

Team Apocalypse, out to take on the world, he thought with no small amount of weariness as he observed the nervous bustle around him. Wright and Trueman were soldiers; they understood. But the civilians were well out of their comfort zone. The need to train them pressed down on him with an urgency that hadn't been present back at the hospital. *Please be a soldier again.* In helping the civilians, he would also be helping himself.

He felt something stir within him that had been absent ever since he was shot.

Purpose.

Chapter Twenty-Two

The truck juddered as it pulled away, Elise fighting the clutch before the vehicle settled down. Jennifer sat at the rear, leaning on the tailgate and watching the road disappear behind them. The sun idled high in the sky, but it offered little warmth, and her breath streamed out as they sped away from their impromptu camp.

Her renewed sense of purpose wasn't enough to stop her from feeling numb. Detached. Like she clung to the truck from the outside and watching everyone within. An observer to the melancholy swirling around as people came to terms with what happened. God, it wasn't even one in the afternoon yet. *Well, I don't suppose it can get any worse.* Jennifer looked up to see if it was going to randomly start raining, but her eyes were greeted by bright blue sky. *Not a cloud in sight. As good a day as any to die on.*

She wondered if Martin had looked to the sky. Had he cared? Had he even noticed? Would she notice the weather if she was about to die? *Probably not. Get a grip, Jennifer.* She sighed and watched her hot breath mist in the cold air, ruminating on the fleeting nature of life. Like her breath, there one second and gone the next.

Louis thumped down on the seat opposite her with all the grace of a house falling down and started rummaging through a backpack he dropped at his feet. A few seconds later, he pulled out a small tube of cream. He also had fresh bandages and what looked like alcohol wipes. Her arm began to sting at the thought of using them.

"Take your coat off, please," he said as he pulled on blue gloves.

Jennifer handed Dan her camera as she braced herself against the cold and shrugged out of her oversized coat. She was still in the clothes they had given her at the hospital, and she craved a shower and something new to wear. Only Wright appeared close to fresh—even Victoria looked a little grubby.

Louis gently peeled away the old bandage and exposed the red and inflamed and *painful* bite. *No necrosis though.* Jennifer supposed she really was immune. She averted her gaze as Louis wiped around it with another alcohol wipe, and she clenched her fists when the stinging started.

"All our preparation stocking the truck and we forgot antibiotics," Louis smiled. It still looked forced. Were all his smiles like that? "We're lucky there was some left in the pharmacy. I really thought it would have been picked dry," he said, mostly to himself. "Are you allergic to anything?" he continued as he threw the used wipe out the back of the truck. It swirled in the turbulent air from their passing before dropping to the ground and disappearing from sight.

"No," Jennifer said, wishing the stinging pain would fade already.

"All right, I have an antibiotic cream here. Rub it on your arm every morning and night." Louis jiggled the tube before he handed it to her.

At least it's not tablets, Jennifer thought. *I hate swallowing tablets.* Thinking about it made her throat dry. "Can I have some water?"

"Uh, sure." Louis rummaged around in the numerous bags for a moment before Victoria reached around Dan to pass her a canteen.

"Thanks." Jennifer smiled at the blonde woman and didn't miss the look Louis gave her. Like Riya's retelling of Aarav saving Anthony, Jennifer was sick of the *looks* Victoria and Louis kept shooting each other. She huffed. *They need to hurry up and do something about it and spare me the lovesick puppy eyes. We're in the middle of a global catastrophe, for crying out loud.*

She took a large gulp of water and rubbed some of the cream in. She turned back to watch the sky as Louis bandaged her arm again. He finished faster than she expected.

A light tap tickled her knee. She turned to Alexia, who sat next to Louis. The soldier gave her an expectant look. Jennifer stared at her. Had Alexia said something? *Shit.* "I'm sorry, what did you say?"

"I said I will put the water back in the bag. We must save as much as we can," Alexia smiled, holding her hand out for the canteen.

"Right, yes. Of course." Jennifer handed her the canteen and hoped she didn't think she was being weird.

She had been so lost in her thoughts she hadn't put her coat back on after Louis finished bandaging her arm. She was promptly reminded of her gross oversight when the truck turned a corner and a gust of icy wind blew in, leaving her shivering and scrambling for the huge jacket. She took her camera back from Dan and slung the strap over her head, making sure it hung secure against her.

She caught Alexia watching her as she settled the camera on her lap, and the soldier's grinning eyes made it seem like butterflies had taken up residence in her stomach. Jennifer smiled back but turned away before she was caught blushing. God, she was hopeless at this sort of thing. Besides, she needed to focus on herself, not on her love life, or lack thereof.

Jennifer sighed. She should nip this crush in the bud before it got out of hand and she ended up pining after a straight woman like a fool. A quick glace back up showed Alexia frowning down at her hands. *Why is she frowning? Because I turned away? What does that mean? Could she like me?* She sighed. *Get a grip, Jen, and stop projecting your feelings onto her.*

Unwilling to be alone with her confusing thoughts, Jennifer looked inward at everyone sitting in the truck, not talking. A morose cloud hung over everyone's head. Today had been awful, and she didn't want anyone feeling the same emptiness she did, so she thought she would start her self-appointed task of giving people hope.

"So, I was thinking," she started and stopped, trying to collect her thoughts. "Back at the hospital, you said you'd train us. We need to start soon. What do you think?" Jennifer directed the last question at James and Wright, who were next to the cab right at the back of the truck—*or front, depending on how you looked at it*—furthest away from Jennifer.

The two sergeants shared a look. Wright raised her eyebrows in a question and James nodded decisively in response. *When did they start having nonverbal conversations?*

James turned to face her. "Aye, your training should begin as soon as possible. We should go over some basics when we stop, if we can."

Jennifer turned to Louis. "Can you teach us first aid too?"

"Yes, of course," Louis said.

"I'd like that very much," Riya said eagerly. "I cannot raise my hand in violence, but I can certainly learn how to heal."

"Yeah, that's a good idea," Wright smirked. "Can't have you running to us every time you fall and scrape a knee like children. No offense, Dan," Wright winked at the boy, who shrugged in response. "Ah, there's that lovely teenage angst—"

"Martin was just killed, and you're joking around?" Dan cut her off vehemently, sitting forward to glare at the soldier. Under any other circumstances, Jennifer would have been proud he maintained eye contact. "What is wrong with you?"

Jennifer tried to pull him back, but he shrugged her off. "No, Jennifer. Martin's dead, and what? Nothing? Continue as normal? That's not right. Even if you didn't like him, he still deserves some kind of mourning. Right?"

Silence greeted his outburst. James's working shoulder drooped, and Sergeant Wright had the decency to look embarrassed. Jennifer took hold of Dan's hand and squeezed until he looked at her. "You're right. Martin's dead, and he does deserve to be mourned. But people deal

276 - | Amy Marsden

with grief in different ways, Dan. Your way might be being quiet and thinking about him. Sergeant Wright's way might be being loud and making jokes. Neither way is better, only different. We should respect each-others' process."

Dan had maintained eye contact as she talked, but he bowed his head when she finished. "Sorry," he muttered.

"You don't have to apologize. Certainly not for this."

"He was brave," James said, his voice quiet and gravelly. "Said he'd be with his brother again." He looked at Dan, who held his gaze. "He was brave. And I'll carry him with me for the rest of my life."

Man and boy shared a nod, and Dan leaned back again, reclaiming his hand from hers. He shut his eyes tight and balled his hands into fists. Jennifer sat back as well, mirroring him as she gave him some space. Was James lying about Martin to make Dan feel better? She couldn't imagine the broken man being brave. Although Victoria had mentioned a brother. And what was being brave, anyway? Being fearless? No, not quite. Maybe being brave was when you were terrified out of your mind but carried on regardless. Maybe Martin had been brave. Would she, if she was ever in a similar situation? Jennifer shied away from the thought, not wanting to dwell on her own mortality.

The truck continued shaking as they sped away. Jennifer leaned on the tailgate and watched the road disappear behind them. The sun sat high in the sky, and Jennifer hoped the soldiers would stop meandering around and drive straight to the castle. It was a beam of clarity in an increasingly insane world, and she couldn't wait to take shelter behind massive stone walls.

Chapter Twenty-Three

The truck entered a large clearing in the trees, circled around and rolled to a stop facing the way they drove in. Elise cut the engine and the soldiers quickly jumped out. Victoria followed, shouldering her gun and moving to guard the truck as they spread out.

It took several minutes for the soldiers to make sure the coast was clear. Victoria stood still, composed but ready to move if they came under attack. She resisted the urge to fidget. The gun felt alive in her hands, straining against her hold. Part of her wanted them to be in danger so she could release the wild animal, feel it roar as it cut down those in its path. Did that mean she was coming to terms with the violence within? She hoped not. She didn't want any part of the monster.

Yet, that side of her had saved her life on more than one occasion. She owed the monster. *I never wanted any of this.* She'd dreamed of a life with Mike, a promotion at work, maybe even a couple of kids of her own. Maybe she would like them if they were her own. They would move to a better house and—

No. There was no use dwelling on has-beens and what-ifs. *Focus on the here and now.* Even if the world continued as normal, she wouldn't have had any of it. The affair had stamped the brakes on her life.

Best come to terms with her situation. In a certain light, it was better than what her life could have been. She breathed in the chilly air, the smell of nature all around her. Winter's grip was steel—the trees bare and the mud hard under her feet, but it was infinitely better than rotting in some prison cell.

The soldiers returned, calm and collected. Victoria relaxed her stiff stance and moved further into the clearing to where Commandant Phillipe beckoned everyone.

"We are in the Parc naturel régional du Perche. It is a beautiful place, and we will stay here for the rest of the evening before we continue on to Château de Creully in the morning," the Commandant said. "Today has been difficult, and I don't want to travel by night." He moved off to Alexia, Elise, and Louis, talking in French and gesturing around them.

Wright stepped forward. "Right, people, lets help set up this camp. Pass the bags out and unfurl the tents..."

Victoria put the gun down and felt immediately better. She knew it was a tool, an inanimate object, but she couldn't shake the association of a vicious beast that thrived on tearing throats out. *It frightens me,* she realised. It wasn't the gun, but herself. She had control of the weapon. She pulled the trigger. It all led back to the part of herself that scared her. The monster. If she couldn't accept it, where did that leave her?

She threw herself into the work, desperate to tire her mind out so she wouldn't be so disturbed by a part of herself.

*

James followed Wright as she gestured him around the truck. He almost walked into the Commandant.

"Sir?"

"Sergeant. I know you've been through a traumatic experience. Please believe me when I say I understand." James had to turn away from the other man's gaze before the sympathy overwhelmed him. "Trauma affects us all differently. You became reckless and irresponsible, and your actions cost a man his life. Romain Dubois left a lot to be desired, but he was a good soldier. I don't blame you, sergeant. I truly don't. You were reacting to your trauma. But please don't take my words the wrong way. What you did was wrong and foolish, and it will *not* happen again." He fixed James with an intense stare, and all he could do was nod.

"Now, Capitaine Roux and Sergeant Wright will assist in both your physical and mental recovery. And I want you to know you can come to me with any problems, James, at any time. I want all the soldiers under my command to trust me and be able to talk to me." The taller man clasped James's good shoulder. "We need you fit and well, soldier. Work hard. Prove you have what it takes."

He stepped back, and James stood tall and saluted. Commandant Phillipe returned the gesture and nodded before turning smartly on his heel and going back to help the others set up camp. Gratitude rose within. He would redeem himself. Prove himself. *Please be a soldier again.*

"Okay, Sunshine. I know you wanted to help the little civvies out, but you've got to look after number one first, yeah?" Wright said, her eyebrow arching as she gave him one of her *looks*. Her eyebrows still looked like she plucked them regularly even though it had to have been over a week since she last done them. Right? James had no idea how often people styled their eyebrows. *Why the fuck am I even thinking about it?*

He glowered even as he gave her a reluctant nod. He received a beaming smile in return. The kind sappy poets claimed eclipsed the sun or chased away darkness or some shite. But he wasn't a poet, and he couldn't afford to let his developing feelings get in the way of his recovery and duty. In another life, he would ask her if she wanted to go for a drink, but there was no time for that. They needed to focus on survival.

Roux sighed, and James snapped back to the present. When had he showed up? "Like I've told you before, sergeant, I'm not a physiotherapist. I will still assist you to the best of my abilities."

"Thanks," James grunted.

The captain nodded. "The shoulder is the weakest joint in the body, very easy to damage and dislocate. The bullet tore through your muscles and stopped before your shoulder blade. Luckily, neither your shoulder blade nor collarbone were damaged. I was quite surprised. The bullet must have been slowed down by something, perhaps your armour? Otherwise, it should have gone straight through you. The muscles and tendons were the worst hit, particularly the pectoral muscle and deltoid muscle." He paused. "Those muscles are—"

"I know what pectoral and deltoid muscles are," James cut him off. The man was nice, but he seemed to think James didn't have basic anatomy knowledge. "You can call the shoulder blade and collarbone the scapula and clavicle as well. I'll try not to get too lost."

Wright snorted.

"Ah, sorry, I do not know how familiar you are with the, ah, terminology." Roux looked between him and Wright sheepishly before settling his gaze on James. Did he look apprehensive? James resisted the urge to fidget. "I'm afraid it is not good news. Your shoulder will have to be immobilised until it is fully healed, and only then can we start building your strength back up."

James wasn't surprised. Disappointed, yes, but not surprised. His only issue was the time it would take.

"How long?"

"Roughly about six weeks?" It sounded like a question.

Irritation pulled his brows down. "You're a *doctor*. How long?"

"About six weeks is the best I can give you. You need to rest it, allow it to heal, but I don't know what is going to happen now that..." Roux trailed off, but he didn't need words to say what they all knew. What *was* going to happen? Chaos reigned with infected and uninfected alike fighting everyone who crossed their path. James would probably die long before his shoulder got the chance to fully heal.

Wright pushed away from the truck and into Roux's personal space. The captain leaned back a little, perhaps unconsciously, and looked at the small woman with wary eyes. "What the fuck can you do for him now? Anything?" She looked angry, and James felt a small tug in his stomach. He had to supress a smile at her frown and the way the taller man leaned further away from her. He was in danger of falling over if he wasn't careful.

"I will change the dressing, and give him a new sling, and view the wound. I also got you some antibiotics from the pharmacy. You should not have stopped your course, but I suppose it was inevitable. You should have let me look at your shoulder before now, but, well, you retreated into yourself."

James looked away. He wasn't *ashamed* of his little breakdown, but he didn't want to be reminded of it. At least not this soon.

"Here." Roux reached around the side of the truck and picked up his backpack. He rummaged around inside and pulled out a box of tablets. "Take these once a day until there is none left. I don't want to have gone through all the trouble of saving you just for you to get an infection and die anyway." Roux smiled, and James felt obliged to return it with one of his own. It had been a poor attempt at humour, but he gave the man points for trying.

"Will do, Doc."

The captain nodded and pulled on blue gloves. "Good. Okay, let me have a look at your shoulder now."

James stepped close to Roux and tried to stay as still as possible as the doctor took his coat and top off and started undressing the wound. He shivered in the cold air. The constant dull ache flared at the man's poking around, and James had to grit his teeth to prevent any involuntary sounds escaping. The last thing he wanted to do was fuck-ing *whimper*—or something equally embarrassing—in front of Wright. Best to avoid looking at her.

He glared at the surrounding trees instead. The bare branches swayed gently in the cold light of the early evening. The shadows they cast stretched toward him as the sun inched ever closer to the horizon, and James wondered if they would see summer again—his favourite season. The vibrant colours shouted *life* to all who saw them. The green of the grass and trees, the blue of the warm sky, the cascade of colours that made up the multitude of flowers. He even missed the annoying insects.

He closed his eyes and lifted his head to face the sun, pretending its rays were warm and welcoming instead of cold and distant. He hated the cold. Good things happened when the sun burned hot. He learned to play the drums over a summer. He'd had his first kiss during summer, decided to join the army during summer. The three times he had been promoted had been during summer.

Bad things happened when the sun burned cold. Both of his parents had died during winter. Andy had died during winter. His first serious girlfriend had dumped him during winter. The fucking world had ended during winter.

Roux pulled hard on the bandage, and a shot like fire burst through his shoulder, yanking him out of his thoughts. He opened his eyes to meet the dark gaze of Wright.

"Where did you go?" she asked. He'd never seen her eyes look so soft.

"I got lost in sunshine." *Maybe some good things do happen during winter. I met her.*

They held each other's gaze until Roux awkwardly coughed. James hadn't even noticed the man had finished redoing his bandage and putting his arm in a new sling.

"That should be good for now," the captain said, helping James back into his top. James nodded his gratitude. "I'll be checking it regularly. Make sure to take your tablets."

James clapped Roux on his shoulder. "Thanks, I will."

The captain nodded. "We should help put up the camp." He nodded at them again, somewhat uncomfortably, and wandered over to the Commandant.

James cleared his throat and pulled on his coat. He glared at Wright when she stepped forward to help. She held her hands up in surrender and retreated to the truck, smirking all the way.

"We should help."

She raised a damn eyebrow at him. She needed to stop doing that. "*I* need to help. *You* have to rest your shoulder. You heard Roux. Go find firewood, or something easy."

He nodded and walked away without another word. He didn't know how to deal with the charged atmosphere around Wright, so he didn't linger. He hoped things weren't going to get awkward or anything—they were soldiers first, which superseded anything else. Navigating this new world was their top priority. They needed to keep the civilians alive and get Jennifer to scientists for a cure.

Surviving came first.

Chapter Twenty-Four

Jennifer finished hammering a peg into the ground and looked around the group. She let the bustle wash over her—everyone was busy doing a specific job—and a weary kind of hope soaked through her skin. A hope that they would be all right somehow. That against all the odds, they'd make it to the safety of this castle and figure out where to go from there.

What if we get separated? We'll probably get separated. The emptiness whispered to her, commanding and insidious. *I'll be alone then.*

No. She had to fight it. She would not give in to the temptation of apathy and she would not let the numbness overcome her. She would fight with everything she had, for herself, for her friends and family, for these strangers who meant so much after such a short span of time.

She hoped they wouldn't get separated. She hadn't known them long—the French soldiers even less—but she felt bonded to them in a way she couldn't fully describe, not even to herself.

Seized by a sudden desire to freeze this moment in time, Jennifer jumped up into the truck and retrieved her camera from its perch on the seat. Covered in scratches and scrapes, it had been through the wringer, but to Jennifer it was worth more than the most expensive camera. Nothing could replace it.

She switched it on and went to remove the lens cap before she realised she didn't have one. When had she lost it? She would have to take extra care not to scratch the lens.

Lifting the camera to her eye, the world became smaller, but also sharper, more focused. The late afternoon sun that streamed through the bare trees was a little bit brighter though the lens, giving the image a more positive vibe. Jennifer thought of changing the setting, but decided she liked the extra colour. It helped remind her that even though the world was a dark and scary place, it could still be beautiful, and could often be breath-taking. She had to remember that when the darkness threatened to overwhelm her.

She'd been about Dan's age when she first got a taste for photography. Her grandmother had bought her a cheap camera for her birthday, but she never used it until the summer when she took it on a trip to Wales. She remembered an overwhelming desire to capture an incredible sunset, to hold it in time so it never faded. The camera enabled her to stop time. Ever since, she captured anything and everything that made the world beautiful.

Looking through the camera, Jennifer felt something akin to peace settle over her. She was doing what she promised to do—document everything, the beautiful and the ugly. She settled on Dan and Anthony first, moving to a position where they were front and centre putting a tent up. She pressed down, and the moment froze, forever cradled in her hands. Satisfaction always curled around every picture taken—the little moments would live on even as times changed and people grew older.

She loved looking at old pictures from decades past. Even though people did age, their hair thinning and their skin fading as their journey wearied the body and made the bones brittle, they were once young and so full of life. It helped her live with more spontaneity. She'd always wanted to make the most of her life, and she was surprised to find she still felt that way. The despair loomed over her, but it didn't seem as dark somehow. What had changed? Her sense of purpose with a cure or her sense of peace with the camera? She didn't know, but she latched onto the feelings anyway, determined not to let go.

She took more pictures of Dan and Anthony, switching the settings to get the best shot. They were all still bright and colourful. The moment didn't need shadows. When she snapped a good enough picture, she moved over to Riya, Aarav and James, the soldier watching the couple with a critical eye as they put up their tent. Determination filled everyone's faces as they worked.

The camera floated in her hands as she lifted it to her face once more. She zoomed in a little for this shot, Aarav on the left and James on the right with Riya standing in between, framed by their raised arms. If only she could have a computer to fiddle with the images—make everything sharper and play with the colours and saturation. But she would take what she could get.

She moved around so it only Aarav and Riya remained in the shot, ignoring the raised eyebrow James shot at her as he moved out of her way. It looked like Wright's favoured expression. *Great, they're picking up each other's mannerisms,* Jennifer thought with a mental eye roll. *There's nothing going on between them, is there?* Surely not. James hadn't spoken to anyone for ages. Wright seemed to care about him, though. *God, it's the end of the known world and I'm surrounded by lovey-dovey straight people.* She half expected to turn around and see Victoria and Louis making out.

But no. Victoria walked past with a pile of wood, dumping it in the middle of the camp with the rest before moving to help Wright. She got more good shots of Aarav and Riya, and a particularly great one of them both breaking out into unreserved smiles when Aarav lost his balance and almost fell over. She loved candid shots.

Jennifer moved on to Victoria next, the blonde woman taking note of her but continuing to follow Wright's instructions. Jennifer only took one picture of Victoria, a great one of her mid-movement, and it hadn't blurred. Jennifer studied the photograph. She noticed a steel to Victoria, concealed beneath her delicate features and amazing hair. She thought she finally understood why Riya refused to talk about what she had done back at the hospital. Colour burst from the picture, and the dark blue of the sky matched the storm in Victoria's eyes.

Turning, she caught sight of Wright walking over to her, carrying a couple of sleeping bags. The pilot dumped them at her feet when she reached Jennifer and pulled a ridiculous pose, one hand on her hip and the other behind her head, throwing her arse out one way and her chest out the other.

"Don't I look gorgeous?" she said in a wispy voice. "Quick, my darling. Take the shot."

Jennifer laughed, lining up the camera to get the best angle. She took several, and Wright came around to see.

"Fuck me, I'm hot." The pilot grinned, her eyes laughing at the pictures. Jennifer hadn't really been close enough to properly see before, but Wright's eyes were like polished black stone, impossibly dark yet shining with their own light at the same time. "Never take life too seriously, Jennifer," she added in an abrupt change in tone. "Even now, try to keep a sense of humour."

Jennifer bobbed her head. What brought that on? "Now, get back to work," Wright commanded, kicking the sleeping bags over to her.

"Yes, ma'am." Jennifer put on a fake American accent and mock saluted. Wright grinned as she walked back toward the truck. "Hey, Sergeant," Jennifer called after her.

Wright turned at her shout and Jennifer snapped a quick picture. She gave the pilot a thumbs up and Wright laughed as she turned away.

Jennifer looked at the photo. It had to be one of the best candid shots she had ever taken. The soldier had half-turned toward her, looking over her shoulder with her big smile fixed in place. The fading sunlight streamed down around her in a soft glow, giving the pilot an almost otherworldly look, the dark of her skin and clothing contrasting with the light in a way that robbed breath. Jennifer nodded in satisfaction.

She switched the camera off. The battery had dropped down to one bar. She wondered if she would be able to find a suitable charger anywhere, and a rush of sadness accompanied the thought that she most likely wouldn't. She resolved to keep an eye out for one—she couldn't lose the peace the camera brought.

She returned it to its perch in the truck where it lay watching over them all, ready to record moments of history at the push of a button. That was a camera's power—

giving people a glimpse into a different time, a different place. Allowing them to see what otherwise would have been beyond their reach. Jennifer understood images and recordings could be tampered with, and often were, but it didn't diminish the brilliance of photography. At least, not in her eyes.

She turned to get to work and caught sight of Alexia across their makeshift camp. The soldier put up a tent with ease, and Jennifer stared at the smooth movements of her body. She really did need to put this crush out of her mind. They needed to focus on surviving.

Alexia, perhaps sensing her gaze, looked up and caught her eye. Jennifer's stomach started trying out for the gymnastics team as Alexia smiled at her, and she knew she wouldn't be getting over her infatuation any time soon. *I hope it doesn't deepen too much. God, I'm such an idiot.*

Jennifer ducked her head and gave a shy smile back. A warm feeling settled inside, spreading throughout her limbs and broadening her grin. She picked up the sleeping bags, distributing them around the tents to people who were fast becoming family.

Chapter Twenty-Five

"Our families will have tried to get into contact with us, there is no doubt," Riya said, loose strands of her black hair blowing in her face as the truck sped down the empty road. "Hopefully, we will be able to get a message to them at this Châteaux."

James leaned his elbow on the tailgate, his fist propping his head up. Fatigue made his limbs heavy—his shoulder prevented him from getting any decent sleep last night. The ever-present ache gnawed away at him until he felt like screaming from frustration. The painkillers he had were so ineffective he might as well have not been taking them.

He rubbed his beard as Riya talked about getting home. *I need to shave.* The thing *itched.* The other men in the group must have all shaved at the hospital—they had a day or two worth of growth. Trueman had the most after James—his goatee had started to look unkempt.

"We lost everything at the hotel," Aarav said. "I hope we haven't lost them too."

"I'm sure your families are all right," Trueman reassured the young couple.

"They'll know the situation in India, won't they? We'll be able to get Jennifer's cure to them?" Riya asked, concern lacing her voice.

Trueman looked torn, like he wanted to put them at ease but didn't want to give them false hope. "We'll certainly ask. They should have more information than we do. We'll find out soon."

Riya and Aarav didn't look happy at the non-answer, but they accepted it and started talking about Aarav's brothers.

His shoulder was beginning to look more and more like a lost cause, so he put it out of his mind and focused on this castle they were going to. What would it be like? Ordered? Chaotic? Would the French and UK forces be fighting amongst themselves, or would they be united against the madness? James hoped for the latter. He hoped everyone understood they needed to be unified and able to mount a cohesive counterattack together.

They would likely be separated and reassigned. The civilians might be kept together. He hoped so, for Dan's sake if nothing else. The boy had grown attached to Jennifer and splitting the two up would be hard on the traumatised kid. He hoped he would be able to stay with Wright and Trueman, but he had to be realistic. He would be taken to some hastily built infirmary and left there to rot in all likelihood. *Fat chance of that happening.* He wouldn't let it. Even if he disobeyed orders, he wasn't sitting on the side-lines. Not for the end of the world as they knew it.

Please be a soldier again. Following orders was part of that. Go back to basics. *Can I? Can it ever be that simple again?*

He simply didn't know. He knew he couldn't stand by and let others do the fighting, though. What was he supposed to do?

His mind ran around in circles for a while before he got sick of thinking about it. He would decide when they arrived at the castle. He knew he'd keep worrying, so he turned to Wright to help take his mind off it.

She was asleep. James took a moment to study her. Not too long, though. She'd probably sense his gaze and spring awake, saying something that would make him look like a creep. Wait, was he a creep for watching her? He turned away, but not before the sight of her eyelashes curled on her cheek burned into his brain. Or the sight of her plump lips and slightly open mouth, relaxed instead of smirking or grinning. *You've only known her for a short while, man. You don't even know her, really.*

Only one way to change that. He reached over and gave her a nudge. She came awake like he'd tried to shove her off her seat, and with the reflexes of a cat, she *twisted* and punched him square in the mouth with a fist too fast to follow.

Pain erupted, and James reared back with a grunt, his hand coming up to hold his jaw. *What the fuck?* Perhaps he'd nudged her a wee bit too hard.

"What the fuck, James?" Wright cursed, her jaw clenching and unclenching. She sat up straight on the bench, her eyebrows pulled down in a fierce frown. James vowed to never wake her up in such close confines ever again.

"I'm sorry. I wasn't thinking—" he started, but she cut him off.

"That's right, you prick, you weren't thinking." She jabbed an angry finger at him. "Don't ever do that again, arsehole. I thought I was under attack. What possessed you to do that?"

Shite, an attack hadn't even crossed his mind. "I was thinking about getting to know you better. I'm sorry. I should've let you sleep."

She held his gaze for a couple of painful seconds before she tore her eyes away to glare at everyone watching them. "Show's over, people," she said dismissively as she regained her composure. "You want to get to know me better," she deadpanned in a quieter voice as the other conversations bubbled up again. "Seriously? You almost gave me a fucking heart attack, James."

"I know, and I'm sorry," he apologised again. He rubbed his mouth—all his teeth were still in place. Pushing the pain down, a thought occurred to him. "What's your name? I can't believe I don't know your name." *Fucking hell, James, how can you like a woman and not know her name?*

She frowned at him for so long he thought he would never get an answer. "You think you get to know my name after the dick stunt you pulled?"

"Wright, I'm sorry. I really am."

She held her glare for a few more seconds before she sighed and shook her head. "Teona," she muttered after a while, glancing around suspiciously. No one paid them any attention after facing the pilot's earlier glower.

"Teona," he murmured. A soft name for such a fierce woman. "It's nice." She narrowed her eyes at him. "It is. Why don't you want anybody to know it?"

She smirked, and the Wright he knew came crashing back. He hadn't realised how much he must have unbalanced her. "I have to maintain my air of mystery somehow, Sunshine." And there was her signature eyebrow raise.

He snorted. "Of course, you do."

"Watch your tone," she warned. "Even though I believe your apology, you're still in the shit."

He tilted his head in acknowledgment and smiled. It was nice to talk and not have to worry about infected or getting killed in some horrible way.

She took a deep breath. "The truth? To be honest, I didn't expect to be with any of you long enough to begin to view you as friends, but I guess that's what's happened."

"Friends?" She saw him as something more than a fellow soldier. Warmth spread through his chest.

"Yeah," she laughed. "Friends. I guess now we need a secret handshake."

James was unable to stop a smile from spreading.

"Okay, you need to stop doing that," Wright—*Teona*—complained. "It's freaking me out. Where have all the glares and growls gone?"

"I'm not a miserable bastard, you know," James grunted. "We met under difficult circumstances; forgive me if I wasn't all smiles and rainbows."

She snorted. "Okay so, you want to know more about me. I'm an only child. Clearly, when my parents had me, they saw how divine I was and didn't bother having any more kids."

"Divine?" James raised an eyebrow of his own.

"Deal with it, Sunshine." Teona flipped imaginary hair over her shoulder and smirked. "I ended up in the army because when I was in school the local army cadets came did a presentation, and I joined them because it looked cool. As soon as I was old enough, I left the cadets and joined the real thing. Didn't expect my whole career to be forged because I was bored one afternoon and thought the white water rafting the cadets did looked fun." She laughed, and the sound brought a sense of calm to James, washing over him and cleansing away most of his worry. "I was only thirteen, I think. What about you?"

"I decided to join when I was sixteen," James said. "My dad was a soldier, and I'd always looked up to him. Both of my parents said they were happy for me. Looking back, though, I don't think my mother liked it, which I guess was normal. She worried about me."

Both of his parents died a decade ago, and sometimes he had difficulties remembering them as healthy and happy, particularly his father. His mother died of a stroke when he'd been on his first tour of duty, and he hadn't been able to say goodbye to her. His father wasted away as the cancer crept through him, insidious in its destruction. He had been able to say goodbye to him. James didn't know which was worse—his mother's sudden death or his father's drawn out one.

He hoped they were proud of what he'd achieved.

"My mum was terrified for me. She told me to get the safest job in the army, whatever the fuck that's supposed to be." Teona shook her head. "I decided to become a helicopter pilot. She wasn't happy." She tutted. "But you can't please everyone, can you, Sunshine?"

James shook his head at the rhetorical question. He leaned his elbow back on the tailgate, his fist once again propping his head up.

"I hope you don't intend to keep that awful thing on your face," Teona said, eyeing his beard with distaste.

"You don't like it? It's growing on me."

She gave him a delighted smile. "What a good pun, Sunshine. I didn't know you had it in you."

"I told you, I'm not as miserable as you seem to think I am."

She hummed. "Maybe you're not."

He frowned at her for not believing him.

"See?" Teona laughed. "Then you go and pull that face."

He rolled his eyes at her. "Don't worry. As soon as I find a razor, it's coming off." He rubbed his knuckles along his jaw. "It's really itchy. I don't know how people with beards cope."

Teona rolled her eyes at him. Silence settled around them, but James wanted to keep talking.

Looking around, his eyes landed on Victoria, who chatted to Roux in a low voice. It was such a shame she had to learn the instruments of violence and death, but rather that than leave her defenceless.

"What do you think about Victoria?" James asked Teona. "She holds her weapon naturally."

Teona gave her an appraising look. "Yeah. Her and Aarav are the only ones who remembered my instructions."

"To be fair to the others, they were pretty rushed instructions."

"Don't mother them, Sunshine," the pilot scolded. "They have to learn, and they're going to have to learn it in highly stressful situations more likely than not."

James didn't argue. She was right, anyway.

Teona gestured to Jennifer and Dan at the far end of the truck. Jennifer and Alexia spoke quietly to one another while Dan dozed on Jennifer's shoulder. "Take Jennifer, for example. She seems to be able to handle herself, but it seems to be more instinct and luck than actual skill. She's got to be the most important person we know right now, and we need to make damn sure she's safe so they can find a cure."

"Aye," James said. "When we get to the castle, we'll take her straight to the person in charge. There could be more people who are immune, but we have to assume she's the only one alive that we know of. She'll be able to give people hope again. I think a lot will love her for it."

"Okay, so we'll have to protect her from superfans. And on the flip side, there'll be nutcases who will want to kill her. People who think the world is being cleansed or some shit. Religious nutjobs probably," Teona said with a twist of her mouth.

"You don't like religion, do you?" James asked. He didn't care either way. No one he knew had been particularly religious, but James never had a reason to dislike religion, either. *Each to their own, I guess.*

"Religion is at the heart of a lot of the world's problems, past and present. They preach love whilst spreading hate. It's ridiculous. Just look at the Crusades, the witch burnings, religious hate groups, terrorism. The list goes on."

James opened his mouth to respond, but the pilot cut him off. "Now, shut up. I'm going back to sleep. And don't wake me like that ever again." Teona glared, and James held his hand up in mock surrender.

Maybe he should try to get some sleep as well. He would need his wits about him if he was going to be able to stay with the group and avoid being shipped off to some cold infirmary. He needed to make up for his failure to protect the civilians, and they needed to make sure Jennifer's immunity got recognition.

*

Dan's head lay heavy on her shoulder, but Jennifer didn't dare move. Exhaustion had overcome the poor kid, and she didn't want to wake him. Jennifer had slept straight through the night, but one look at Dan's red rimmed eyes had told her he'd been up crying for a long time. *At least he's finally sleeping now*, she thought as she glanced at him. His mouth hung open, and little snores escaped with every exhale. His breath was awful, but Jennifer ignored it as best she could. Nobody's breath was good right now— they hadn't brushed their teeth for three days.

Alexia also slept opposite her. She supposed soldiers were used to snatching some shut eye whenever they could. They'd been driving for about an hour, and Jennifer only had her own thoughts for company. The way said thoughts constantly whipped from anxious to numbness to determination was frustrating to say the least. She decided to focus on the French soldier to try to bring the tempest under control.

What was this thing she felt for Alexia? If left unchecked, it had the potential to develop into something more. Yet she barely knew her. They'd spoken a handful of times, always about trivial things. Something tugged low in her gut whenever they locked gazes though, and it demanded her attention. *Everything I've ever known has come crashing down around me, and I get a crush? Talk about bad timing.*

Confused by her own thoughts and feelings, Jennifer looked down and away from Alexia. She caught sight of her arm and pushed her coat sleeve up—the scratches from her fall back in London were mostly healed, and it looked like they would fade like they had never been there in the first place. The teeth marks from her first bite were now visible, red imperfections stretching down her arm, almost running into her second bite. The deep gorges in her forearm near her elbow were red and angry, and pain pulsed through her. It would all scar, without a doubt.

She dug around in her coat pocket and pulled out her cream, having forgotten to put it on earlier. She delicately rubbed it in, trying not to be too rough lest she hurt herself. She dropped the tube back into her pocket and examined the bite as the sting faded. There was still no sign of necrosis, and it did seem to be getting better with the antibiotic cream.

Jennifer looked at Alexia again to find her gazing back. Her rummaging around must have woken the soldier. Dan remained flat out. "Oh, I'm sorry –"

"It is okay. It is about time I woke anyway." Alexia's accent was thick as she smiled sleepily, and those damn butterflies started up in her stomach again. "How are you feeling?"

Jennifer broke eye contact to look back down at her arm. "I'm fine, really." She smiled at Alexia and tried not to get too lost in her chocolate eyes. "I mean it hurts, sure, but I've felt worse."

Alexia smiled with her. "I am glad you are not in too much pain."

"How do you say thank you in French?" She already knew—it was one of the few phrases she did know, along with hello and goodbye—but she wanted to talk.

The soldier's smiled broadened. "Merci."

"Mercy?" Jennifer replied.

Alexia's laugh was melodic. "It is not your word mercy, but merci. You need to say it in a more French way. Copy me. Merci."

"Merci?"

"Good, again. Merci"

"Merci. Merci." Jennifer thought she had it.

"There you go." Alexia continued to grin at her. "You will be fluent in no time."

"Merci," Jennifer laughed. It was pathetic really, how she'd never been able to properly grasp another language. Especially when she'd wanted to travel the world for her photography.

Alexia nodded at her and pulled her ponytail out before redoing it more neatly. Jennifer felt the urge to run her fingers through the dark brown locks so similar to her own but squashed the thought before she could make a complete fool of herself.

She opened her mouth to ask the soldier more about herself when sudden movement down the other end of the truck distracted her, and Wright abruptly punched James in the face. *What's going on?* Adrenaline seeped into her system, but she wasn't overly alarmed. Dan didn't stir at all. *He must really be worn out.*

Everyone watched as Wright loudly berated James for something before the pilot caught herself and told them all the mind their own business. Jennifer shook her head and turned back to Alexia. Who knew what the two sergeants were doing? Jennifer tuned them out.

Alexia relaxed back into her seat. She looked wide awake, the remnants of sleep completely gone from her sharp eyes. Said sharpness dulled to something soft and welcoming as she looked back to Jennifer.

"Tell me a random fact about yourself," Jennifer said, kickstarting the conversation again.

"My mother taught me the piano at a very young age," Alexia said in her smooth voice. "I think I must have been four or five. Can you play?"

Jennifer shook her head. "I tried the guitar when I was about ten, but I didn't take to it. I'll leave that to more talented people such as yourself." Jennifer grinned and tilted her head in Alexia's direction.

The soldier smiled and looked away. Was she blushing? *She is!* A rush of heat flooded Jennifer, and she had to stop her grin from growing too wide. *Am I blushing at her blushing? Why am I so bad at flirting?* Robin and Damien had both found it endearing, but Jennifer always felt awkward.

"You are kind to say that." Alexia finally looked back up. Her smile still curled her lips but there was no trace of a blush. Had she imagined it? No. No, Jennifer chose to believe the other woman had been momentarily knocked off balance. She'd recovered quickly was all.

"Did you ever want to become a famous musician?" Jennifer launched straight into another question in the hope the soldier wouldn't comment on her red face. Jennifer could practically feel the heat radiating out, but she pushed on through her inelegance. She hoped Alexia found it endearing as well.

Thankfully, the soldier turned her gaze to somewhere over Jennifer's shoulder, clearly thinking of her answer. Jennifer felt like she could breathe again once Alexia's eye moved away.

"Music is something I have always done for fun in my spare time," Alexia said. "I wanted a realistic career, and I had been interested in the army for years."

"Well, I'm glad you joined, and I'm glad you're here," Jennifer said sincerely. Not only because she liked Alexia, but because the soldier had protected her, Dan, and Martin, and Jennifer would forever be grateful.

Alexia couldn't hide the blush that spread swiftly across her face this time. "Merci," she said quietly. She blinked, and Jennifer noticed a shine to her eyes.

"Are you all right?" Jennifer asked, concerned. *What did I say?*

"Oui." She took a deep breath and smiled a smile that buckled under the weight of the world. A change twisted the air, and Jennifer unconsciously leaned forward, careful not to dislodge Dan. Gone was the casual conversation, something heavier taking its place.

"I abandoned my post. Most of us did. I did not reach my family in time and I—" She stopped and took another deep breath, frowning as she gathered herself, her eyes unfocused. "I went back, and no one cared I had left. They were just glad I had returned. They are all gone now as well." Alexia pinned Jennifer with an intense gaze.

"I was not there for my family, but I can be here for you now."

Something swelled in her chest, constricting her throat. She managed to bob her head.

"Elise's story is similar except she didn't abandon her post. She wishes she did. She didn't make it to her family in time. All we have left is our duty, and that duty is to keep you all alive." The soldier smiled then, and this one was filled with resolve instead of broken regrets.

We may be able to rebuild the world, but can we rebuild ourselves? If everyone battled the same emptiness she did, the world would be populated by people who were shells of their former selves. *I have to keep fighting it.* It's what her family would want. *Think of the good things still left. Think of Dan's smile and Alexia's eyes and the safety around the corner. Evelyn would want you to be positive. Everything will get better soon.* She had to believe it. She *had* to.

Alexia nodded at her, and an understanding passed between them. She closed her eyes again, but Jennifer didn't think she'd go back to sleep soon. Jennifer relaxed back and leaned her head on Dan's. The boy still didn't stir. She hoped he was all right. Despite everything—Dan's pain, Alexia's shame—Jennifer felt better now compared to when they first climbed into the truck. Alexia trusted her with her story. She maybe even liked her. Dan would get the help he needed when they got to the castle, and Jennifer would feel safe again.

Today was shaping up to be a good day.

Chapter Twenty-Six

The sun burned cold as midday edged closer. Victoria held herself rigid on her seat in the truck—every bump and imperfection in the road reverberated up her spine. *It's like this vehicle was designed to be as uncomfortable as possible,* she thought with annoyance.

She chatted a bit with Louis to try to take her mind off everything. She'd discovered the captain and Commandant Phillipe were cousins; their mothers had been sisters and had married, giving rise to their differing surnames. Louis's father had been a white man, explaining the differing skin tones as well. He'd been a doctor for three years before deciding to join the army, following in the footsteps of the older cousin he idolised.

He talked about France and the long route they were taking to the castle, but he hardly said anything about himself. Victoria knew he held more back. He talked about his job and a little of his childhood, and mainly of Commandant Phillipe, but it was all artificial. *Clinical, almost,* Victoria thought. *He is a doctor, after all.* She learned almost nothing of him as a person, or of any friends or family he must have had.

Well, she couldn't judge. She hadn't mentioned Mike at all, or Katherine. *In fact,* she thought, surprised, *none of them know I used to have a sister. Or that I was engaged.* They'd been through so much together, yet there was still more to learn.

Victoria's hands clenched around the wild animal she held to her chest before she forced them to relax. The weapon dragged her arms down, but she told herself not to put it down until she accepted the violence it represented. The violence in herself. She had to come to terms with it if she was to continue to survive in this new world.

A loud bang reverberated around the truck as something struck the side, and the vehicle swerved to the right. Victoria slipped straight off her narrow perch and onto the floor as Elise fought to regain control. She hit her back on the bench and let out a low hiss as pain raced across her shoulders.

She was glad she clutched her animal so tightly. Aarav dropped his in the chaos, and Victoria watched as he scrambled to pick it up again. The soldiers were already up and jumping out of the stationary truck. Victoria rushed to copy them, compelling her tired muscles into action.

She didn't glance at the others as she leaped down and rounded the truck, but she did notice Jennifer placing herself in front of Dan and Riya. *Good, if it's infected and they get past us, she can protect them.* Victoria briefly entertained the idea *she* was also immune but decided she didn't ever want to find out.

They were stopped in the middle of the road surrounded by flat fields. Victoria spotted a prone body in the grass—it must have been what hit the truck. She looked up.

Infected.

Lots of infected.

Bloody brilliant. Adrenaline poured into her veins and surged around her body. Her tired muscles weren't tired anymore, and the dull ache in her ankle fled in the face of a wonderful waterfall of energy. She felt so *alive.*

The monster purred to life, and although a part of Victoria shied away from that side of herself, she knew it would keep her alive.

She didn't hold back.

Victoria flicked the safety off and raised the gun, anticipating the roar of the beast as she unleashed it. *Aim.* A thin woman. Greasy blonde hair. A snarling mouth. She ran straight for Victoria. *Squeeze.* Victoria's blood sang in harmony with the thunder of the beast as it spat bullets at the infected, cutting her down as she ran. She couldn't face the combined might of monster and animal, working in tandem to destroy her. *Release.* She didn't give the dead woman another thought as she moved onto her next target.

Another woman. *Aim.* She wasn't quite as skinny as the first woman. Greasy red hair. Wide, bloodshot eyes. She clambered over the skinny woman's body. *Squeeze.* She fell to the animal's unstoppable teeth, which tore through her as if she were made of smoke. *Release.* She didn't give the dead woman another thought as she moved onto her next target.

A man this time. *Aim.* Average height and build, perhaps leaning more on the overweight side. Tangled black hair. He snarled at someone to Victoria's right. *Squeeze.* He fell heavily, tripping another infected on his way down. *Release.* She didn't give the dead man another thought as she moved onto her next target.

Minutes, hours, seconds, Victoria lost all sense of time. She was one with the animal, the monster, and together they ripped into the infected, tearing them to shreds as they attacked. She was calm yet wild, collected yet crazed, in control yet so far out of it she couldn't remember what control was. Her world boiled down to *aim, squeeze, release,* and she revelled in the simplicity of it all.

The blood bursting from the bodies set her own blood on fire. The screaming, the shouting, the breaking bones sounded like music—the echoes of death dancing in her ears. Why would she ever want to repress this part of herself? The smell of blood and urine and faeces didn't bother her. It meant she was winning. It meant the threat was being eliminated.

The monster hummed in appreciation of a job well done.

*

The world constricted along with her lungs, and Jennifer stamped down her panic. Shouts and screams stuffed her ears as she shoved a man away from the truck. She stumbled into the path of James's knife—Jennifer's mind flashed back to London and Rhys and the night this all started. She turned away, unable to watch the man die.

They were surrounded. Every way Jennifer looked, infected were running toward them. *We're close to the castle, right? Why are there so many this close to the castle? Are people even at the castle?* Jennifer's panicked thoughts ceased to exist as a man jumped up at her, and she became a woman of instinct.

Cold air spun hot as Jennifer fought, desperate, frantic, her limbs becoming heavier as the fighting went on. How much time passed? All she knew was the burning in her lungs, the sweat stinging her eyes, the struggle to keep going.

A woman barrelled up to her, teeth bared in a silent scream. James was preoccupied with his own fight, so Jennifer braced herself against the truck and prepared to kick her away.

It didn't work.

The woman was bigger than her, and she managed to grab Jennifer's leg and pull her clean off the truck. Her surprised shout cut off as she slammed into the ground, the impact knocking the wind out of her. She bit her tongue and hot blood spilled into her mouth. She spit it at the woman, who reared back in disgust, a stabbing yell clawing from her throat as she wiped her face.

Another infected knocked into the woman, granting Jennifer precious seconds to regain her footing. She spat out more blood as she planted her feet, determined not to let any infected get to Dan and Riya.

With thoughts of her old friends and new family swirling around her head, Jennifer swung a fist at a snarling man.

*

James stabbed another infected man and shoved the corpse into two others. He turned in time to block a screaming woman, her hands scrambling for his face. Jennifer kicked her leg, and he sank his knife into her neck as she stumbled. The blood scorched his clammy skin, and James welcomed the icy breeze that ruffled his sweat-damp hair. His heart raced, so much so he felt it beat in his skin, felt the wild way it fought with him as infected surrounded them.

This wasn't good. They needed to get out, or they were going to be overrun. James ignored the panic scraping its way up his throat and threw himself into the fight, his shoulder on fire as he kicked and punched and stabbed.

His mind kept trying to dump him in another part of France, cold night air swirling around his burning shoulder. Gunfire blazed from every direction. Sweat trickled down his face. He caught flashes of Teona, cutting down infected after infected as they scrambled over each other, their madness stripping them of all sense of self preservation. She was all right. She was a good soldier. Was *he*?

A man grabbed his t-shirt and yanked him around to face him, but James anticipated the move. He let his momentum from the pull dig the knife deeper into the man's gut. He shoved him into the path of a man who dove for Jennifer, and they both fell victim to Alexia's weapon. Jennifer nodded her thanks before turning to ward off yet another infected woman.

He heard his blood rushing around his head. He needed to focus, *focus*. Teona was alive, the civilians were alive, and so was he. He was on a road, surrounded by friends, and he wasn't going to have another *incident*. He would help protect everyone.

He braced himself as two infected charged at him at the same time.

Please be a soldier again.

*

Jennifer ducked out of the way of a wild fist and grabbed the back of the man's shirt as he lurched past her. She used her depleting strength to haul him away from the truck and turned to face an infected woman as Alexia tore through the man.

The woman could have been her grandmother. Jennifer clenched her jaw against an unexpected wave of emotion and brought her fists to her face in a way she had seen James do. She couldn't punch an old lady, could she? *Who am I kidding? I have to keep her from getting into the truck.*

Feeling like the world had reached a new low, Jennifer swung a fist at the snarling woman. She connected solidly, bone crunching under her knuckles. The old lady reared back, straight into the path of Victoria, with her cold eyes and smoking weapon.

Jennifer's stomach clenched as she spun away. She kicked a much younger man's leg out from under him as he focused on James and concentrated all her energy on staying alive.

*

James couldn't feel his shoulder. He didn't know if that was better than the burning pain or not, and he didn't dwell on the matter as he shoved aside two infected people. They were gunned down by Trueman.

This is madness. We need to get out of here.

He slammed his knife into the eye of a middle-aged man and cursed his stupidity as it jammed against the bone and slipped from his fingers. The metal glinted at him as the man fell to the ground, mocked him as he elbowed another man in the face and broke his nose. The infected stumbled back, and Elise made sure he didn't come forward for a second round.

James wished he had a gun. He'd never felt so exposed in his life. Gritting his teeth against a rush of fury—fury at the bastard who shot him, fury at the crumbling world, fury at himself—he channelled it into his fist and feet, kicking and punching up a storm.

Infected fell all around him with stunned expressions and broken bones, easy pickings for the guns, but his ferocity was short-lived. Exhaustion hit him like a wall, and he stumbled, gasping for air. His knuckles were bloodied and bruised, his legs barely supported him, and the numbness on his left side began to give way to white-hot agony.

Roux was right—he needed to rest. And James was right—he didn't have time.

With a wordless growl, he threw himself into the fray, weakness notwithstanding. He trusted his fellow soldiers to protect him. He had a job to do. He needed to make up for his failure at the hospital, and he refused to be held back by frailty.

*

Jennifer was winded. She wasn't a fighter. God, she'd never fought with anyone in her life. A woman managed to strike her in the stomach, and Jennifer had been gasping for elusive air ever since. How long ago had that been?

At least she hadn't been bitten again. Yet. She collapsed back against the truck as James scrambled past, tripping an infected woman and pushing her into another infected man.

No matter how hard she breathed, she couldn't get enough air. She took a moment to gather her bearings and saw nothing but the mass of infected on all sides. *Fuck, how many are there?* She spotted Alexia not far off, downing infected after infected. Were they going to run out of bullets soon?

Insanity saturated the air. The little Jennifer managed to pull into her lungs felt tainted, like she every breath was poison.

A yell drew her back to reality, and she jumped as a man fell at her feet. Victoria breezed past, her icy gaze already scanning beyond Jennifer. She shivered, despite the sweat running down her back.

With another desperate draw of desperation-soaked air, Jennifer pushed herself upright and switched her mind off.

*

Victoria released the trigger and paused, searching for another target. She didn't have to look far. Infected were everywhere, and the calm she felt within the warm embrace of the monster rippled like the surface of a pond disturbed by a stone. They couldn't take on this many.

She selected a man. *Aim.* Tall, solid, arms pumping as he sprinted for the truck. *Squeeze.* She clipped his side and he twisted as he fell, the anger on his face giving way to pain. *Release.* Victoria turned away, not giving the man a second thought as she picked her next target.

Another man. Boy, really. *Aim.* He could have been a student in her classroom. Acne-covered skin, split lip.

Squeeze. His chest ripped open as her animal shredded into him without mercy. *Release*. She turned away, not giving the boy a second thought as she picked her next target.

A woman limped toward her. *Aim*. Blood dripped into her crazed eyes, and Victoria winced with each step she took on her clearly broken leg. *Squeeze*. Nothing happened. Another ripple disturbed Victoria's calm, larger this time. Her animal had lost its teeth.

She shouted it out, and Wright took care of the limping woman. "Get back to the truck," she gasped as she dashed by Victoria. "Retreat!"

Victoria wasted no time running back, Elise beating her there and jumping into the driving seat. She ignored James's blood-drenched hand and climbed up herself, dropping onto the hard bench as Aarav scrambled up behind her. Gunfire still cracked through the air like lightning, and Victoria felt it reverberate in her blood as the monster drained away.

Nausea rose, and she took several deep breaths as turned to the others, hoping everyone was okay.

They were all still alive, and Anthony fired into the mass of infected as Elise managed to get the truck going again. Victoria peered around him into the seething mass of bodies.

The sight that greeted her was one of carnage. *Butchery*, Victoria thought. Bloody hell, she felt like vomiting everywhere.

Blood and gore tainted the countryside, marking the place they almost lost everything. *Again*. A black stain that blazing in the harsh daylight, a mindless massacre dwindling as they drove away. Victoria had been part of the slaughter. She looked until it faded from view, the truck picking up pace. She had done that. *Her*, not some monster. She needed to stop referring to a part of herself as something *other*. She needed to take responsibility for her actions.

Yes, she thought decisively. *This is the way it is now. There is no time for appearing weak. The monster it is.*

"We're not far from the castle, right?" Victoria said, making sure none of her revulsion showed in her voice or face. "How are this many infected so close? I thought we were going to be safe."

There was a pause as no one responded. "Maybe the radio message is out of date," Wright said, scrubbing her hands on a cloth. "Maybe we were in the wrong place at the wrong time, and the infected won't go in the direction of the castle."

Victoria sat back and closed her eyes, letting herself feel a light breeze caress her face, soft as a lover's touch. She imagined she was back home with Mike before anything with Katherine had happened, back when they were happy. She tried to cling to the moment, but the breeze passed on as soon as it brushed her. *Fleeting, like most things in life.* She sat for a few more seconds as people shuffled around her but couldn't regain any sense of peace. Serenity had eluded her for a long time.

She opened her eyes and stared out at the road falling away behind them, not truly seeing it. She wondered what Mike would think of her. Murderer. Butcher. Sure, it was them or her, but that didn't change the fact she had become a killer. *My life has taken an extremely unexpected turn. As a little girl dreaming of my future, I could never have imagined this.*

Murderer. The word wasn't new to her. Her own mother had thrown it in her face during the trial, screaming she had lost two daughters that night. They hadn't believed her story of self-defence. Something changed in Victoria then. Was she broken? No. She would do it all again. *Self-defence.*

The nausea faded. This was life now. Kill or be killed. Victoria wasn't going to apologise for the monster. She was going to accept it.

Chapter Twenty-Seven

Jennifer was shaking.

The heat of the fight fled the further they sped away, leaving cold unimpeded as it stole under her skin. London, the helicopter, the hospital, this. Safety seemed like a pipe dream.

She stuttered like Dan as she thanked everyone, still under the influence of adrenaline. They'd protected them, and she didn't think she'd thanked anyone for everything they'd done so far. Jennifer noted their gratitude behind the modesty they projected.

She sent herself far way, with the hope the ever-present anxiety would ease. She spent the next little while in another place and time, laughing with her friends. If only it was real.

After a time, Jennifer began to feel restless. Was the castle still the haven it proclaimed to be? Would the infected follow them and overwhelm it? How close were they? *We have put some distance between us and the infected,* she rationalised. *It'll be okay. Maybe they'll fight each other and won't follow the truck.* She hoped she wasn't lying to herself.

Unable to remain still, she stood and leaned back against the wall of the cab. The world seemed small from her vantage point, like she gazed up at a painting on a wall. A cold, washed-out painting that smelled of rain arriving. A field full of hay bales disappeared on her right, and an old stone wall fell away to her left. The field gave way to thin trees the same time rickety branches reached over the wall, and she felt the world become even more enclosed, the tunnel of trees making it hard for her to breathe.

When she thought she couldn't take anymore, the sky burst through, and her lungs expanded upon seeing the roiling clouds tumble over each other. Buildings rose up, startling in their suddenness. They had the look of a farm, but where Jennifer expected to see animals or people, she found abandonment and neglect. She hoped the animals were all right. The poor things wouldn't know what was going on.

She grabbed her camera to snap a picture of everyone pressed in the truck against the grey background. She switched it on and raised it and—

The camera died.

Jennifer's breath stilled in her chest. She lowered it in disbelief. *Breathe In.* All her photographs, her friends and family, once immortalised, gone. *Out.* She cradled the lifeless camera close to her chest. *In.* Would she ever see her friends' faces again? She knew how fickle memories were, how faded they became. *Out.* Jennifer hoped beyond hope she would find a charger at the castle. She didn't know what she would do if the camera died forever.

The brakes squealed as they trundled to a halt, and Jennifer's muscles tensed. Everyone shifted on their seats. The soldiers readied their weapons again. Sergeant Wright handed Victoria another magazine, which she slammed home as she shouldered her gun.

The soldiers jumped out of the truck, and Jennifer grabbed a hold of Dan's arm and tugged him behind her. He wouldn't get hurt again, not if she could prevent it. A small amount of tension drained from her body when Anthony waved everyone down. *It's safe. Or as safe as it was ever going to get now.*

A tingle ran through her, like she'd been sprinkled with cold water. They were still outside. Still out in the open. She took a deep, steadying breath as everyone jumped out of the truck and forced herself to follow. The road felt solid under her boots, grounding her. Anxiety wouldn't control her. Deep breath in. Deep breath out. She was immune. She didn't have to fear the virus. She had to show the others she was okay, especially Dan, and they would feel better themselves, right? She knew that if she saw someone who was immune panicking all the time, she would be shitting herself. Better to project an air of confidence. She was all right, they were at the castle, and they would find a cure soon.

Jennifer tried to ignore how hollow those words sounded in her head.

The sign grabbed her attention. Creully stood out in big black letters, but the red border snared her gaze, a splash of colour in an otherwise dreary landscape. Her eyes rose up to the castle above. Sitting on a hill, it looked secure and impregnable, looming over the small town surrounding it. The thick stone walls made Jennifer's chest expand, and she yearned to be behind them. She felt sick out in the open. Why were they standing around?

Soldiers blocked the gate. They didn't have their guns pointed at them, which was good, but they did have a mean look. Jennifer counted six.

The Commandant stepped forward and spoke in French. Jennifer tried to follow their facial expressions, but all six remained stoic. When the Commandant finished speaking, one of the soldiers, a bulky man with a large nose, said something back to the Commandant and waved up to the castle.

Jennifer sensed a shift in the air around her. The wall loomed right in front of them, the thick stone close enough to touch, yet from the looks the castle guards were throwing her, it seemed an eternity away. *God, they aren't going to kill me, are they?* The thought left her feeling still, like what was happening wasn't quite real.

"I've told them you are immune," Commandant Phillipe said. "Not only did I have to anyway as they were always going to check us for bites, but I think it is the best way to proceed. No secrets. Keeping the virus a secret in the first place is why this global outbreak is so bad. In my opinion, that is."

Jennifer nodded. The logic was sound, but it didn't stop the suspicious stares from burrowing under her skin and laying doubts.

They were directed into a line by a woman, who then re-joined the soldiers guarding the entrance. *Aren't they going to check us?* Jennifer was confused. They stood in a line facing the soldiers, who stood in a line facing them. *What's happening? We don't have time for this.*

Jennifer thought she was going to burst from the stress building inside her. The infected from earlier could arrive at any minute. *Why are we standing around doing nothing?*

"Are we going to stand here all day? What are they waiting for? We need to get inside," Victoria said, voicing her concerns.

Elise answered. "They have radioed soldiers already out to check for the infected. A virus specialist is here, and he is coming down to check us." She glanced at Jennifer. "You in particular."

Did that sound ominous? Jennifer thought it sounded ominous. *No. Don't get stuck in such a negative way of thinking. He's a virus specialist, which is exactly what you want. He could find a cure.*

They didn't wait long, but the icy wind on top of the hill made it seem like hours, and everyone hunkered down in their coats to wait for the specialist to arrive.

He did so with little fanfare.

Jennifer put him in his mid to late forties, but she'd never been good at guessing people's ages. His dark hair was winged by silver, and he had his fair share of laughter lines and crow's feet. He walked with the sprightly step of a man much younger than he looked. *Him being clean-shaven helps*, she thought, glancing at James. His beard added years to him.

The specialist wore thick boots and a thick fleece, and Jennifer eyed his white scarf with envy. The man looked like he'd never heard the word cold before in his life. He eyed each of them in turn, his gaze lingering the longest on herself and Victoria.

"Which one of you claims to be immune?" he asked. "I was only told it was a young woman." Shock widened

Jennifer's eyes—he was Welsh. His accent didn't hide the condescending tone, and she took an instant dislike to him. The impression of a kindly uncle evaporated quickly.

Frowning, Jennifer shifted her weight from one foot to the other. "I don't *claim* anything. It's fact," she said. She didn't try to hide the annoyance in her voice.

His piercing eyes landed on her, and he didn't blink as he studied her. It was unnerving. Strange that such cold eyes could gaze out of such a warm face. "I'll be the judge of that," he said with such finality Jennifer felt like rolling her eyes at him. Who did he think he was?

"I've been bitten twice now, and I like to think I'm smart enough to deduce what that means." She gave him her best impression of Wright raising her eyebrow. "I like to think that *all* of us—" she gestured at everyone "—are smart enough to deduce what that means."

As soon as she said she had been bitten, the specialist and the other soldiers tensed. Jennifer would have missed it if she hadn't been looking for it. She rolled up her sleeve, carefully unfurled the bandages, and thrust her arm at him. He would have to be blind to miss the angry bite marks, and his eyes widened as he took in the red flesh, the way it was healing, the absence of necrosis. In fact, his whole countenance changed. He became *softer*. It was the only word Jennifer could think of. His mouth fell open, and his cold grey eyes held a spark that hadn't been there a moment before. He reached out, a question in his slow approach. Jennifer nodded, and he took her arm, studying the bites closely.

Had his arrogant attitude been a defence against disappointment? But no, he still had the bearing of an egotistical man. Maybe shock had knocked him so far off balance. How rare was her immunity?

"I've got cream for the normal infection," Jennifer said. He nodded absently, not paying her much attention.

He examined her arm thoroughly, turning it every which way, poking and prodding the tender flesh with no concern for the pain he caused. He didn't touch the wounds themselves, not without gloves, but the surrounding area felt raw and painful as well. Jennifer gritted her teeth and endured it. He was the expert, and she had to trust he knew what he was doing. She had to trust he could find a cure.

With a last lingering look, he let go of her arm and stepped back. Jennifer pulled her arm close to her chest and tried to massage away some of the soreness, but she only made it worse. She clenched her fist against the pain and lowered her arm to her side. The large coat sleeve fell and rubbed against the bites. Jennifer locked her jaw against the pain trying to escape past her lips. She set about ignoring it until it went away. She had gotten good at ignoring things she didn't want to think about.

The specialist spoke. "This is remarkable. I've heard tales of people with immunity, but you're the first I've come across. Stories from Canada and the little we've managed to get out of China. But you're *here*, standing in front of me." He nodded to himself. "Yes, I need to study this. Remarkable. I'm Dr. David Evans—" he said it like they should all recognise him— "and I'm a virologist and immunologist. I've been studying this virus almost since it was discovered, certainly since it became a problem—" *talk about understatement,* Jennifer thought sarcastically— "so I'm very familiar with it. Very familiar indeed.

You're lucky to find me—I'm probably the most qualified person around right now."

He took a breath to no doubt continue his tirade of self-importance, but Wright jumped in first. From the look of barely veiled contempt on her face, she didn't like his arrogance either. "Yes, yes, we get it," she rolled her eyes. "You're an amazing scientist. But I'm freezing my tits off, and infected were hot on our heels not half an hour ago, so why don't we take this lovely conversation inside?" It was phrased like a question, but anyone who took one look at the pilot could see it wasn't. Without waiting for a reply, she strode forward.

The soldiers guarding the gate raised their weapons, and Wright stopped short. "Not so fast," Dr. Evans said. "I need to check the rest of you for bites." He waved a hand as Wright scowled and fell back in line. "Our soldiers will take care of the *infected,* as you call them." His dismissive tone set Jennifer's teeth on edge. She still remembered the heat of the fight, the fear, the desperation. How dare he diminish their struggles?

What followed made Jennifer glad she'd been bitten. The specialist made everyone except her strip to their underwear in the freezing wind, and he checked everyone *thoroughly.* He combed through everyone's hair and mouth and every inch of their skin. They stood outside for a good half hour, waiting in line as he looked at everyone in turn. Jennifer felt sorry for all of them. Even Aarav, who looked outraged, standing there in his boxers with his arms around Riya, shielding her from the wind.

Jennifer didn't even look in Alexia's direction in case her face burned off. Victoria scowled at the wall the entire time. Dan stared down at his feet, his face bright red. *Not from the wind I'll bet, bless him.* Wright looked casual and unconcerned, if a bit cold, but James glared hard at anyone who so much as glanced at the pilot. Jennifer was surprised he didn't start fighting them, consequences be damned. She didn't think he meant for his attraction to be so obvious, but he had been about as subtle as a brick to the face.

Dr. Evans spent longer examining him, due to his heavily bandaged shoulder. It took a lot of convincing by Captain Roux to stop Dr. Evans from removing said bandages, and the Welshman did not look happy.

Eventually, he finished and allowed them all through. Wright wasted no time in throwing her clothes back on and marching to the gate, and the soldiers guarding it parted like the Red Sea in the face of the small woman's anger. Everyone else followed in a flood as soon as their clothes were back on. Jennifer brushed past the doctor, already looking forward to warmth. And nice food. And a bath. God, a *bath.* She could already feel the soft water caressing away the past few days. She almost cried at the thought of a bath. *Get a grip,* she thought with a roll of her eyes. She clearly wasn't made for the great outdoors.

As soon as she walked through the gates, the tension leached out of her muscles. A sense of security hung over the castle, with its high walls and military presence. She was sure Riya and Aarav felt it too—the young couple released a collective breath as they walked in front of her.

Winter still had the grounds firmly in its hands, with the trees bare and the land brown. She couldn't see any green anywhere—or much colour of any kind at all—giving everything a drab look. The gravel road crunched underfoot as they walked toward the castle proper, and the grass was little more than churned-up mud. A few men and women in uniform bustled about looking busy. Not many. Maybe they were all inside? Jennifer noticed the French flag on some of the uniforms and the Union Jack on others.

Turning away from the grounds, Jennifer looked up at the castle. It wasn't as big as she expected, but it didn't matter. The large stone more than made up for its lack of size. *Thank God castles are still standing. Medieval people certainly knew how to build things to last.*

The castle was the same dull colour as the rest of the grounds, but Jennifer put that down to winter. Its icy grip didn't seem to be letting go any time soon. She caught sight of some birds wheeling away from the crenelations, a sudden burst of black against the overcast sky, but she didn't turn to watch their flight. High above, two flags waved lazily in the wind. First, the French flag stood straight against the clouds, then the Union Jack, always shifting positions.

Jennifer returned to her study of the castle. They were closer, almost to the doors. A rounded part stood out from the rest of the flat building, and Wright marched straight to it. People walked in and out of the entrance, barely pausing to look at the dirty newcomers. Over to the right was a large ramp leading up to a walkway overlooking the town below, and a smaller building with a pointed roof lay off to the left. It was partially blocked by trucks like the one they had arrived in.

Jennifer noticed the large radio antennae. Were they in contact with other bases like this? Were they in contact with the UK? Hope bloomed in her chest like a flower in spring. Maybe her parents were still alive somewhere, maybe she could get in touch with them. She tempered the optimism flaring within. She didn't think she could handle convincing herself they were alive only to be proved wrong.

Jennifer took comfort in the shadow the castle cast. This was the safety she'd been looking for. *This.* The emptiness pushed to the back of her mind by the force of her relief, and when she smiled at Dan, she got a genuine one in return. Laughing, she pulled him into a one-armed hug, and together they walked into the warmth of the castle, thoughts of the infected fading into the recesses of her mind.

Chapter Twenty-Eight

They didn't get far before they were stopped. A young British soldier halted them as they walked through the doors, and Jennifer did a double take—he looked like Rhys. Well, if Rhys had blue eyes and was a touch shorter.

"I don't recognise any of you. Are you the ones Dr. Evans was called to?" He even sounded similar to Rhys.

"We are," Commandant Phillipe said. The young soldier's eyes widened. "Can you take us to whomever is in charge, please?"

"Is it true? Is one of you immune?" His eyes darted from person to person, trying to take them all in at once.

"Yes," was all the Commandant said. The soldier's mouth dropped open, and he looked ready to start babbling, but the Commandant cut him off. "Take us to those in charge." Steel wrapped around the command.

The soldier heard it. "Yes, sir. This way." With one last look at them, he turned on his heel and started off down the corridor.

Their boots rang on the stone floor, and Jennifer tried to take in as much in as she could. It was well lit with lamps placed everywhere, for which she was grateful. As much as she had grown to dislike the open outdoors, she liked cramped, dimly lit places even less.

The young soldier spoke quickly. "Did you know this place is classed as a monument historique? Which is what France call their national heritage sites. It was used in World War Two as a radio station for BBC war correspondents, and later it served as tactical headquarters for Field Marshal Montgomery." His sentences ran into each other as he barely paused for breath. "I like history. When we moved here, I found out as much as I could about it. Castles and stuff are cool. It was made into a fortress during the Hundred Years' War. Now it's used for weddings and exhibitions, stuff like that."

The soldier stopped outside a large hall. People rushed about inside carrying papers and clipboards, talking in groups or sitting at collapsible tables monitoring computers and other equipment. There were less people than Jennifer thought there would be, which was still more than she hoped for. It struck her that she hadn't seen anyone out of a military uniform. Where were the civilians? Were there any? Were they dressed in military clothing as well? She looked around the room again to see if she could spot anyone who looked out of place, but everyone seemed to fit in, going about their business like a well-oiled machine.

The room itself was big, with a low, domed ceiling that made it seem more intimate. Like the rest of the castle she'd seen, it was well lit with lights placed all around, which more than made up for the lack of windows. The walls made her feel safe and secure rather than closed in, and she was able to breathe with more ease despite the heavy weight of the stone surrounding her.

"There, sir." The young soldier pointed.

Stone steps at the far end of the room lead up to a raised dais. A long table took up much of the platform. Standing or sitting at it were several people with still others coming or going rapidly. Jennifer hoped they weren't like the arrogant doctor.

Commandant Phillipe thanked the soldier and strode toward the dais. The other soldiers followed, but before Jennifer or the other civilians could, the young soldier spoke again.

"So, um, to whoever is immune," he paused, trying to find the right words. "Thank you so much." Real emotion clogged in his voice. "We've heard rumours about immunity, but you are the first real person we've seen. With the doctors working with you, I'm sure a cure will be found soon, and this whole nightmare can end."

His earnest expression made Jennifer's chest ache. Could she be the answer everyone searched for? The weight of it all threatened to buckle her knees.

"Dr. Evans can take as much of my blood as he needs, for as long as he needs," she said. She wasn't a fan of needles, but the need outweighed her fear. "This nightmare *will* end, I promise you." Perhaps she shouldn't have promised anything, but the light in his eyes was worth it.

The young soldier looked at her with reverence. His second thank you was drowned out by Wright's loud voice, telling them all to hurry up.

"What's your name?" Jennifer asked before she moved past him.

He looked surprised. "Oh, call me Danny."

Jennifer smiled and continued on. He was a bit like how she imagined an older, more confident Dan. Funny they had the same name.

When she reached the dais, Commandant Phillipe spoke in perfect English to a captive audience. Dr. Evans arrived from somewhere, sitting at the table between a weedy-looking man and a plump, middle-aged woman. If Jennifer had to guess, she would say they were scientists as well. Two other men were also at the table, one young and one middle-aged. These people were in charge? They did seem old enough.

"—She is immune. Dr. Evans can confirm it," the Commandant said. "She's been bitten twice and has failed to show symptoms of the disease." He turned to Jennifer. "Here she is now. As you can see, she is healthy and in control of her faculties."

Jennifer didn't know what to do, so she gave an awkward wave. Needless to say, no one waved back. The younger of the two men leaned forward, his small eyes boring into her own and making the hairs on the back of her neck stand up. She pushed the memory of Johnson shooting Evelyn out of her head. They weren't going to shoot her. *They need me*, she told herself over and over as his suspicious eyes held her in place as firmly as shackles.

"You show the bite." His accent was thick, and it took Jennifer a moment to decipher what he said. When she did, she shrugged out of her coat—it was warm in the cavernous room—folded it at her feet and stepped up to the table. The raw bite marks were impossible to miss in the ubiquitous light, and everyone at the table leaned in for a closer look.

The plump scientist breathed out an *ooh,* her eyes darting over Jennifer as if she expected to find signs of insanity scribbled across her face. She stepped back as they finished their inspection, and the scientist spoke in a broad Mancunian accent.

"This is *marvellous.* Oh, the possibilities. We can finally begin to make some headway into the fight against Lyssa 15."

"Lyssa 15?" Wright asked.

"It's the official name of the virus. The other, far more popular name, is Morte Insano, which is Portuguese for insane death."

"Cheery," Wright snorted.

The older soldier spoke for the first time. Although Jennifer thought of him as older, he couldn't have been more than mid-thirties. "You are a Commandant, yes?" He gestured at the Commandant's uniform. His English was good, and his words took on a desperate edge. "Would you be willing to take over here? I am only a Lieutenant, and sir, I don't know what to do. We've been here for little over a week, but we've been steadily losing people. The radios are full of chatter we can't make sense of, and we're struggling, sir. Everyone is scared."

Silence fell after the man's rushed outburst. The words reached down Jennifer's throat and constricted her airway, and the heavy stone didn't seem as safe as it had not a minute before. They didn't know what they were doing. It wasn't safe.

The Commandant nodded slowly. "Tell me everything you know, Lieutenant. Spare no details."

The Lieutenant seemed to sag, like a weight had been lifted from him. "This town was abandoned before we moved here. We killed all the infected we found, but more keep coming. Although London fell not long ago, this place seems to have been empty long before that. I guess all the small towns and villages around the world that were being torn apart weren't reported on, with the media blackout and everything."

James spoke up for the first time. "Can you tell us anything about the UK? And the rest of the world?" he added with a glance at Riya and Aarav.

"It was a catastrophe. Still is. Most of the quarantine zones were breached, and many of the safe zones never got the chance to become fully operational. There were simply too many zombies."

The weedy looking scientist tutted. "They aren't zombies, Lieutenant." He was Welsh too, although his accent lacked Dr. Evans's haughtiness. "At least not in the traditional sense. They aren't dead for a start, and they don't go around eating people either. A shot to the head will kill them, as it will anyone, and so will a shot to the stomach or wherever."

The Lieutenant shrugged self-consciously and continued. "We don't know much about the rest of the world, but we are getting more information every day. Paris fell within an hour of London. The American, Russian, and Chinese Presidents are all alive the last we heard, buried in bunkers somewhere. We know nothing about Australia, South America, Africa, and the Middle East. Europe is in turmoil, as is Asia. There have been reports of immunity in China as well, but we can't confirm it."

"Please, what can you tell us of India?" Riya asked, her voice filled with both hope and trepidation.

The Lieutenant turned to her, his eyes soft with sympathy. "Not much, I'm afraid. Since the initial outbreak, we've had no reliable information from anywhere, not just India. I don't think it will be good. It's very densely populated—the infection will have spread quickly."

Aarav put his arm around Riya as she tried to hold back tears. He wasn't doing much better. "Is there any way we can get in touch with our family?" he asked, his voice shaking. "We left our phones in our hotel in the panic, but surely you have some?"

"We can't spare any resources," the Lieutenant said. "But we'll keep an ear out for information."

Aarav thanked him and hugged Riya. James clapped him on the shoulder in a show of solidarity.

"Thank you, Lieutenant," the Commandant said. "I expect a full debrief once we're settled here."

Was that it? They had been given a lot less information than Jennifer hoped. "You must know more. What about social media? People will have been posting about the chaos." An earlier thought returned to her. "And how was this virus kept a secret in the first place?"

If the Lieutenant was annoyed by her outburst, he didn't show it. The strain under his eyes told her all she needed to know. "We know emergency broadcasts were triggered, so hopefully people followed them. We know the World Health Organisation declared a global medical emergency. We know there are still some areas that have some kind of control, Iceland for example. New Zealand, Japan. You don't seem to understand the magnitude of this, though. There are seven billion people on this planet, yes? It is estimated three billion people across the world were infected before the breaches. It'll be more now." Jennifer tried and failed to comprehend how massive this disaster truly was. "It's chaos. Civilisation's infrastructure has collapsed in little more than a week. It's a miracle we know as much as we do."

The other Welsh scientist spoke up, his voice heavy. "It got in the food supply. Sugar cane at first, we think, before spreading to others. Went global. Before we isolated the origin, it was too late."

"The food recall," Victoria said faintly.

"The food recall," the man echoed. "Too little too late. The virus isn't as infectious as say, a respiratory disease. I mean, biting isn't a particularly effective way to transmit a disease around the world. It's the fact that it got into the global food supply. That's what elevated this disaster." He sighed, and it seemed to originate from his bones. "As for social media, you must have seen some of it. The governments tried, and mostly succeeded, but odd bits and pieces still slipped through." He thought for a moment. "What about the fight at a hospital in Germany a while ago? Or the attack in an American shopping mall? Or those kids filming that homeless man who was ranting and raving when he suddenly ran at them and the film cut off?"

Jennifer shook her head, and she wasn't the only one. She'd seen the riots and the protests, and she had felt the general unease permeating the internet in the months leading up to the outbreak, but she hadn't seen any of the videos he mentioned.

"Well, the point is, they didn't manage to censor it all," the scientist said. "I don't really understand why they collectively suppressed the whole thing to begin with," he continued. "I mean, sure, I get they didn't want a panic, and one on this scale would have been almost as bad as this outbreak, but to keep the public completely in the dark?" He mulled over his own question. "I guess they chose to believe there wouldn't be an outbreak, and they hoped to save people from a panic. They put a lot of pressure on us to find a cure. I practically lived at work."

"We three worked in the same lab," the plump scientist said. "Like Owain said, the work was non-stop. Our efforts weren't in vain though." She smiled. "We discovered it infects both plants and animals alike, although infect isn't the correct word when it comes to plants. It's very rare for a virus to be able to infect both plants and animals. Not that it doesn't happen, though," she chortled. Jennifer got the impression she rambled a lot. "It doesn't *infect* them per say—it uses them as a vector to replicate in."

The weedy scientist—Owain—leaned forward when the woman paused for breath. "Did you have any symptoms? What did you experience?"

Jennifer thought back to that horrible night she lost everything. Her mind tried to shy away, but she forced herself to look at the memories, to let herself *feel* them again. She needed to stop ignoring things she needed to pay attention to.

"From what I remember I was tired, I had a headache and no appetite." She stopped to think, pushing herself to remember, when Wright jumped in.

"She threw up when we were getting helicopter fuel. It was gross, no offense." She sounded like she couldn't care less if Jennifer got offended or not. Not that Jennifer did. Sick *was* gross.

"You were getting confused as well," James said. "Do you remember?"

Jennifer did. "I was trying to protect you all from the infected man following me," she said. "I remember everything boiling down to that. It was all very fuzzy."

"What happened afterward?" Owain asked.

"I knocked her out with the butt of my weapon," James said in a matter-of-fact tone. Jennifer's head twinged in memory, but she didn't hold it against him.

"Oh," the scientist said.

"I don't think I had any other symptoms. I can't remember any if I did."

Owain spoke again, his voice pondering. "Maybe immune people experience all the symptoms up until confusion, then sleep it off?"

Before the plump woman could answer, the younger man broke his silence. "Oui, this all very good. But you said something." He pointed a finger at Wright that looked like it had been fractured and not properly set. "Helicopter?"

Wright nodded. "I'm a pilot."

He smiled. "Good. We have helicopter—" He cut himself off and narrowed his eyes at the civilians. "You go with doctors now. Soldiers will show you to rooms."

They were being dismissed. Jennifer didn't like the thought of being split up, but she hoped it wouldn't be for long. A soldier appeared out of the bustle and gestured for them to follow him. Jennifer picked her coat up off the floor and grabbed Dan's hand, squeezing it as they were led further into the bowels of the castle.

It felt like the start of something new.

*

James stood as still as he could. The pain in his shoulder had been increasing as everyone talked, ramping up to an explosion of agony like a firework finale. Moving only made it worse. *The fight didn't help but stripping in the cold wind has made it worse.* He shot a sour look at the doctor. He hadn't gone out of his way to make himself popular.

He watched the civilians as they were led away, glad they were being kept together.

"Sergeant Wright," the Commandant said. "Can you familiarise yourself with the helicopter? We will use it to gather information."

"I can do that," Teona said with a firm nod of her head. "It'll be good to be back in the air again."

"Are there any safe zones in this country?" James piped up. The safe zones nagged him since they had been mentioned—they were designed to be self-sustaining, protected and to house lots of people for long periods of time. They were made for this eventuality, yet none of them seemed to have worked.

"There are a few, but the disaster struck so fast they weren't able to get them running, as mentioned before," the Lieutenant said. "We know one near Lyon almost succeeded, but too many people weren't screened properly, or they lied, and it fell into chaos quickly."

"Let's get cleaned up and rest," the Commandant said. "Lieutenant, if you'll walk with me..."

James wanted to talk more about the safe zones, but he was glad they could go. His shoulder was killing him. He needed to see Roux about better painkillers.

Teona frowned as they were led down more corridors by a French soldier. Trueman and Alexia murmured to each other behind them, and Elise was a silent figure bringing up the rear.

"Hey," he muttered to Teona. "What do you think of this place?"

She sighed. "It's shit that they don't have a clue, but at least the Commandant is in charge now, and he's someone I trust."

James nodded in agreement. "At least it isn't likely we'll get reassigned."

"Yeah," she smiled. "Scared you'd miss me, Sunshine?"

James scoffed, but the thought had crossed his mind. He would miss her if they didn't see each other as regularly. *Get a fucking grip, man. If Andy were still here, hell, if Mitch or Euan or Fin were here, they'd all rip the shite out of you.*

"Let's find our beds, get washed, and get you seen to," Teona continued, oblivious to his internal beratement. "We'll talk to Louis soon about your shoulder and recovery."

James nodded again. He let himself be swept along in her wake, glad for the strength she gave him. He would dedicate himself to his recovery. In this mad world he needed all his skill and ability—insanity wouldn't wait for him to feel better.

Purpose beat through him like a drumroll increasing in tempo. Jennifer would help find a cure, Dan could regain some of his childhood, and they would all have a moment of stillness in the storm. This castle could shelter them for a long time. The walls were strong.

They were going to be all right.

Weren't they?

Acknowledgements

This book wouldn't have been possible without an amazing group of people behind the scenes.

To my beta readers, who helped me mould this into shape.

To Ashley from NineStar Press, who believed in my query enough to offer me a contract.

To Liz, my editor, who made this the best it can be.

To Rae and NineStar Press as a whole, thank you for championing queer books!

To my friends and family, who kept badgering me for a release date. Here you go!

And to Fay, who has read this story more than I have, and who believed in me when I didn't. Thank you.

About Amy Marsden

As a child Amy loved reading and writing, so naturally she graduated with a degree in biomedical science and has worked in a microbiology laboratory ever since. Her passion is writing however, and she started her first novel while still at university. When she is not writing about surviving apocalypses, exploring space, and conquering magic—all featuring LGBTQ characters—she can be found reading or playing games about those very things. She lives by the sea with her wife and fifteen-year-old cat who still runs around like a kitten.

Email
amy.m309@hotmail.co.uk

Also from NineStar Press

I, Volcano by Eule Grey

According to ancient rhymes, the islanders of Ansar and Skarle are children of the volcano, born of fire and destined to be lovers. After the eruption, the prophecies are forgotten as all are forced to flee. Nobody cares about silly nursery rhymes now, certainly not Jalob.

When shy medic Jalob Baleine heads to war, it isn't for romance. She only wants to help refugees who have no home or allies. Because they are kin. Jalob was born under the same glowering volcano, on an idyllic island surrounded by dolphins. Like the refugees, she fled the lava and secretly cherishes the old ways.

She falls asleep, ignoring the pull of tides, and dreams of a loving touch. Who doesn't? And sure, maybe Jalob hasn't felt whole for years, but war isn't the time for fantasies. She keeps to herself and hopes someone else will sort the war out. One woman can't heal the world. After all, she has enough to do, what with tending the sick and her supervisor, Susan, always on her back.

Then Jalob meets stroppy violinist, Corail Esplash. After an explosive introduction, they're forced to spend time together. Stress makes them long for a reprise, and a fragile line dances between love and hate. Inevitably, the young women exchange island stories. Corail is head-strong and rude, a typical Ansar who loves to tease and be chased. And Jalob—strong, loyal, from Skarle—has such fast legs... Could the old rhymes about destiny be right? Ah, fate.

Death and war are relentless enemies, and difficult choices lie ahead. Can a shy girl rekindle the power of a dead volcano and harness the ocean? One woman can't heal the world, but maybe Jalob is the only one who can save Corail.

Foxfire in the Snow by J.S. Fields

Born the heir of a master woodcutter in a queendom defined by guilds and matrilineal inheritance, nonbinary Sorin can't quite seem to find their place. At seventeen, an opportunity to attend an alchemical guild fair and secure an apprenticeship with the queen's alchemist is just within reach. But on the day of the fair, Sorin's mother goes missing, along with the Queen and hundreds of guild masters, forcing Sorin into a woodcutting inheritance they never wanted.

With guild legacy at stake, Sorin puts apprentice dreams on hold to embark on a journey with the royal daughter to find their mothers and stop the hemorrhaging of guild masters. Princess Magda, an estranged childhood friend, tests Sorin's patience—and boundaries. But it's not just a princess that stands between Sorin and their goals. To save the country of Sorpsi, Sorin must define their place between magic and alchemy or risk losing Sorpsi to rising industrialization and a dark magic that will destroy Sorin's chance to choose their own future.

Connect with NineStar Press

www.ninestarpress.com

www.facebook.com/ninestarpress

www.facebook.com/groups/NineStarNiche

www.twitter.com/ninestarpress

www.instagram.com/ninestarpress

www.ingramcontent.com/pod-product-compliance
Lightning Source LLC
Chambersburg PA
CBHW050510110726
47899CB00005B/1404